MW00910585

Kingsway 37

A Novel About the Law

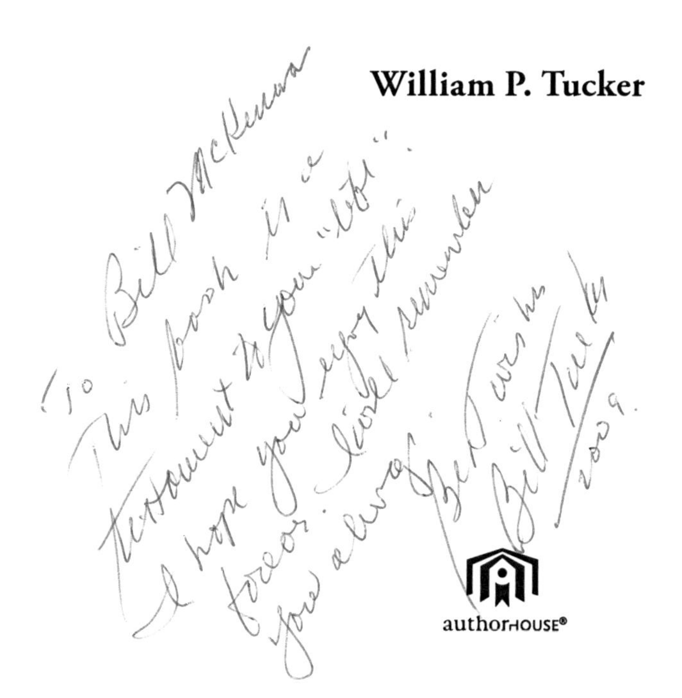

William P. Tucker

authorHOUSE®

AuthorHouse™
1663 Liberty Drive, Suite 200
Bloomington, IN 47403
www.authorhouse.com
Phone: 1-800-839-8640

First published by AuthorHouse 11/11/2008

ISBN: 978-1-4389-0367-5 (sc)

Library of Congress Control Number: 2008906644

Printed in the United States of America
Bloomington, Indiana

This book is printed on acid-free paper.

Cover design by Laura E. Stenger

OTHER BOOKS BY WILLIAM P. TUCKER

<u>Non-fiction: (Hard cover)</u>

Books about minor league baseball franchise purchase, operation, moving, and new stadium construction:

DP—OR BILLY AND JERRY

IN THE PROMISED LAND

And

MOVING HOME PLATE—

THE MIRACLE ON I-5

<u>Fiction: (soft cover)</u>

EXCALIBUR

A novel about an extremely unusual civil case and its solution

...WITH JUSTICE FOR ALL

The sequel to EXCALIBUR, continuing the characters, the story and developments

DEDICATION

If an author writes more than one book, say several, he has difficulty with the dedication as he goes on because he's probably used up all the accolades and special things he could write. However, a dedication is a major sort of treatise in itself, the embodiment of the things the author believes helped him significantly in life, in having the position and time and ability to write a novel, no matter how many he writes.

Writing a novel takes plenty of dedication itself, mixed with considerable discipline and a toughness that compels you to stay with the task until it is completed. You want to write something that is readable, enjoyable, and worthy of putting into publication. It takes all that, too, to write a bad or lousy book, as to write a good one. You never really know which it will be until the end.

For that reason, the author has to give particular credit to the person or persons who stuck with him through the long, agonizing and sometimes boring times a writer goes through. They have to endure with him the periods of writers block, when nothing the author puts in print seems to advance the project in any worthwhile way. There can be long days and nights of emptiness, while the writer sits in front of the word processor, trying to create the prose that will endear the book to its readers and the author to history. Sometimes the sitting is silent, both from the author and from the word processor. They are trying times.

As the writer matures, or gets older, the credit to others becomes easier to assess. There are many who cheer you on as they hear you're writing 'another book'. That's said sometimes in fear that they will be put upon to purchase yet another book they won't necessarily read or like if they do read it. (I buy and read every book someone I know has written and will continue to do so.) Everyone seems to recognize the effort and persistence a project like a book takes to write. They proclaim admiration, and even sometimes, indicate they can't wait to read it, and in many cases they well mean it.

Yet there are a few who do more than act as cheerleaders, who encourage you and endure with you the tougher times along the way. These people are mostly your own family, if you do not have an agent or a publisher who will set up the entire marketing process for you. My family has been great in that, constantly giving encouragement and as much help as possible. I am fortunate to have three wonderful children, seven grandchildren and a wonderful wife of now 47 years, Dolores. They are all my cheerleaders, good, loud and loyal.

Dolores, of course, is the best of all of them. She hangs with me no matter how good or rough the times are going. She knows when to encourage, push and just let things lie as they are, quietly. She is great and caring, a wonderful partner in everything I do and has catapulted my life into the greatest of things, far beyond what I could possibly have achieved without her. This book is therefore dedicated to Dolores and my family, one and all.

IN APPRECIATION

Many people help you along the way in writing every book. Besides those to whom this book is dedicated, the person to whom I owe the greatest debt of gratitude is my former secretary, Fran Manfredi Longo. For years while I was in active law practice with my former firm, Fran was my right arm. She was undoubtedly the best secretary ever created and certainly by far the best one I ever had.

Fran was so intelligent, and hard working, that you could not help but admire her. She helped out in so many ways during my active practice and led all the many secretaries in the office by her dedication, loyalty and work ethic. She set a high example for them and they all came to admire her as well. She knew much more law than many of the attorneys in the firm after just a short while, and exhibited an unlimited amount of initiative. She never left for home before all we did that day had been finished and put on my desk. She left me to have her children and raise them, which she also did well.

Fran did great work on this book, proofreading it and correcting errors that she found in the text, the syntax and the punctuation. She approached this task as a volunteer, and through her dedication and persistence, I was able to finish it. Her help and effort has been invaluable. I could not have done it without her. I owe her a huge debt.

The characters in the book are mostly named after people I know. Not one of them has been included without giving me permission to use their name and to assign them a role in the story according to what I wanted to do. One of the main characters, Tony Monteverdi, wanted a character role very much. He kept after me whenever we would meet up and make sure he was on track for a starring role in the book. He knew very well the character I had in store for him and how that character fit into the story and played out to the end. He liked that role. Unfortunately, Tony passed away before the book was finalized. We all miss him. He was a great friend.

All the others asked to be included and were accommodated. Only one character in the book is not named after a friend of mine. Most of them knew the role to which their name would be assigned, although they might not have known the role that character played. There is no resemblance between them and the character in the book other than their name, unless accidental. Because using the name of someone you know makes it easier for the author to keep track of the characters and how they fit in, I owe those persons a debt of gratitude as well and thank them for participating.

1

Everybody loved Margaret Barnes. She was a pert, vivacious girl who always seemed to be beaming and smiling. She had those twinkling Irish eyes, flowing black hair and genuine laughter that made her the hit of any group in which she found herself. She was the only child and much beloved daughter of Frank and Arlene Barnes, a couple that found each other at a Brooklyn Dodger baseball game in Ebbets Field one Sunday afternoon during a college outing. From there it was a swift courtship and ended in marriage at St. Ephrem's Church in Bay Ridge, Brooklyn.

Then the war came along and Frank, being married with no children yet, was drafted into the U.S. Army. He survived an intensive and arduous infantry basic training at Fort Dix, New Jersey, and moved on to be commissioned a ninety-day- wonder Second Lieutenant on graduation from Officers Candidate School in Fort Benning, Georgia.

On one of those rare occasions when the Army administration correctly recognized personal talents, it sent newly commissioned Second Lieutenant Barnes out to the Aberdeen Proving Grounds in Maryland to become involved in and to study tank warfare. It was late 1943 now and, with his tank group, Frank was shipped to England to join the Third Army Group which, at the time, was 'a paper army', or non-existent. Its sole purpose up until then was as a decoy to have German intelligence believe the US Army was stronger than it actually was, or that the expected cross channel landing would come at the Pas de Calais, and not Normandy.

Shortly after D-Day, on June 6, 1944, he was shipped to France as part of the now-activated Third Army Group under General George

S. Patton. There began a hotly contested, but very successful, rapid ride across France to the Rhine River. They took time out for a short detour to relieve an army group unexpectedly besieged in Bastogne. That was the unfortunate consequence of a strong German counterattack assembled and launched in total surprise without having been detected by Allied intelligence.

General Patton was an unusual personality and as tough a driver of personnel as he was of higher-ups and the enemy, with little regard for safety or dangers his troopers and his tanks encountered. "Move fast and win, then on to the next" was his battle cry. Almost nothing would stop him. They fought spirited battles almost every day, for farms, for bridges, for airfields, for cities, even nondescript crossroads, inflicting considerable carnage on the enemy, but sustaining heavy casualties in equipment and personnel themselves.

Frank Barnes received a battlefield promotion to Captain and Tank Commander and distinguished himself in almost every battle, certainly all the major ones. He was regularly decorated for valor. He particularly distinguished himself in France in a battle for a much-needed, bridge at an obscure village named Remagen. He was badly wounded but kept his tank in action, holding on to a very strategic position while subjected to a withering enemy artillery and small arms fire. He was awarded the Silver Star for bravery, and was recommended for the Congressional Medal of Honor. Then one day, they ran out of gas for the tanks, and the advance stalled. The tanks sat on roads and in fields as sitting ducks, awaiting an onslaught that never came. Truth be told, it was really already over for the Third Reich and only President Roosevelt's insistence on unconditional surrender kept the fighting going.

Once more refueled, but only after a showdown between General Patton and the British commanders, the race across the European terrain resumed at breakneck speed. Finally, driving almost to Berlin, the Allied armies surprisingly were ordered to turn to the south and to stop at Lubeck. The Russian armies came on to meet them after overrunning Berlin, and peace finally reigned. Patton's troops, by now legendary warfare heroes all over the free world, awaited reassignment to the Pacific Theatre but the orders never came.

Mustered out of the army, Frank secured a job with the New York State Banking Department with the aid of the veterans point bonus on the civil service examination. He started out as an apprentice bank examiner, serving on teams of examiners that regularly audited the safety and soundness of savings banks.

Life was good now. Frank and Arlene bought one of those spanking new cookie-cutter houses in Levittown, Long Island using a mortgage loan Frank was entitled to under the GI bill. They settled in and Frank actually enjoyed the commute from Levittown to lower Manhattan or to the other locations his job sent him regularly. The social life among the home-owning former veterans was pretty good, too. As this idyllic life continued, Arlene announced one day she was pregnant and months later, their daughter was born. They named her 'Margaret' after Arlene's mother, who was almost as proud as Frank and Arlene of the child's coming.

Then tragedy struck. Invited to a christening party of a neighbor one hot July afternoon, Frank and Arlene went and enjoyed the festivities. During the hot afternoon, Frank kept nodding off to sleep occasionally. That change in character made Arlene nervous, but he assured her he was only tired from a tough week at work. They left the party a little early and put Margaret to bed. Frank relaxed in an easy chair and promptly fell asleep. He began to sweat profusely and decided he would go to bed to be able to relax more and probably defeat what he thought was an oncoming cold.

The evening didn't go well and Frank tossed and turned in bed, sleeping fitfully. In the morning, he was still not well and had a temperature in the low one hundreds, terrifying Arlene. There was no pain, but she could see his obvious discomfort. She called a doctor who arrived not long thereafter. After examining Frank, he quietly informed Arlene out of Frank's hearing that he wasn't sure, but believed Frank had come down with a case of poliomyelitis, infantile paralysis, the crippling disease more commonly known as polio. The doctor said an epidemic of polio was going around and Frank might have contracted the disease from one of the children at the party, so little was known of the disease at that time.

In a few days, the fever abated, but Frank found he had little movement in his legs and could not walk without considerable help, and then only haltingly. This man who had endured the rigors of growing up largely without luxuries, who had come through the hell of World War II and survived severe battle conditions, who had recovered from bullet and shrapnel wounds with praise and decorations from his grateful country, now found himself leveled by a tiny germ that usually limited itself to infecting children, not grownups. The world of Frank Barnes had abruptly changed.

No longer able to get around well, he went to clinics that used the then trendy Sister Kenney method and tried through assisted exercise and manipulation of his legs to restore some movement. After a few months of concentrated effort both at the clinics and by Arlene at home, it became clear the painful therapy was useless and would have to be abandoned. Frank would have to content himself with a life of getting around on crutches to make himself ambulatory.

The Banking Department understood, having employed some service-disabled veterans who were wounded in the war. Frank was given a supervisory position that tied him to a desk but freed him from the need to travel to the various banks being examined by the staff. He became very knowledgeable on banking matters and regulations, helping the various politically-appointed Superintendents formulate new regulations to meet the needs of the changing banking society as it expanded.

But the trip back and forth to Levittown was difficult and he had to shorten that journey. Frank and Arlene sold their house, their life's dream, and moved to an apartment in the brand new Vanderveer Apartments built in Flatbush in Brooklyn. It was right near the Newkirk Avenue stop on the Flatbush Avenue subway line. It was an easier trip to work for Frank, but it was difficult for the family adjusting to life in a four room apartment and raising little Margaret in that atmosphere.

Frank and Arlene were faithful Catholics and became members of the St. Vincent Ferrer Parish on Glenwood Road. Frank became active in the Holy Name Society and Arlene in the Rosary Society. Frank had learned to live with his disability and his basic good humor returned, making him one of the more affable members of the parish. His health situation didn't improve, though, and his immobile legs atrophied. As he added pounds to his stature, the crutches became more and more difficult to tolerate, and he soon slipped into a wheelchair status.

Frank and Arlene were admired by their fellow parishioners for their courage and determination. Their pride and joy was their daughter Margaret and they centered all their love, attention and devotion on her. She became the center of their entire life and they were very proud of her. They recognized early on that there would likely be no more children, so all their hopes and expectations of family life revolved around her, her activities in the school band, her achievements in school activities and the girl scouts. They enjoyed her popularity with her friends and teachers and, as she grew older, they became prouder still. Everybody in the parish knew that.

Growing up in Flatbush, Margaret went through elementary school at St. Vincent Ferrer Parish School run by the Sisters of St. Joseph. After graduation, she continued her Catholic school education by attending Catherine Mc Auley High School on Brooklyn Avenue, not far from her home in the Vanderveer Apartments on Avenue D.

The nuns at Catherine Mc Auley loved her too. She was the center of attention wherever she went and in whatever she did. At times, the Sisters of Mercy who ran the school would have to cool her

down a bit, but they always smirked to themselves when they had to do so. Even her transgressions seemed amusing. Margaret was very popular with her classmates. Not wanting to be class president, she ran for and was elected class vice president every one of her four years at the high school.

Margaret had evaluated her skills and attributes correctly. Knowing she was short, and inclined to be a little chubby, although not much overweight, she reasoned that she would have to rely considerably on personality to make her way in life. She knew her popularity depended on her being a good friend and the outspoken good-humored one in her group. Her classmates just naturally flocked to her. The boys she met at school dances and generally 'around' seemed attracted to her too, but not entirely in the way she wanted.

She decided she would not aim for college and, instead, wanted to learn secretarial skills so she could get a good position in a large company after graduation. There, she hoped she would meet a life partner, get married, settle down with children and be happy. Margaret used to say she was aiming for an M-R-S. and not an M-B-A.

Catherine Mc Auley High School was the perfect place for her. Her father was a civil service worker who did not have a high income. The wearing of plaid pinafore school uniforms freed her from the expensive fashion competitions so prevalent in public high schools. It was a school for girls only and they taught the corporate secretarial skills so prized by the business establishment back then. The Sisters of Mercy prided themselves on their graduates being placed into good companies with very good paying jobs. The education the Mc Auley girls got was excellent for that vocational avenue and the nuns made certain the students paid attention to their courses to sustain the school's reputation. Margaret was no exception.

Despite having a good time while in school, playing pranks on classmates and teachers, Margaret, or "Peggy" as she was known to her friends, nevertheless applied herself when push came to shove and did well in grades. The good sisters were amused by

her shenanigans and did not look forward to the day when those hallowed halls would be without her. But that day came anyway.

On graduation, she interviewed for and got a position with the Metropolitan Life Insurance Company. The building on Twenty-Third Street was over thirty stories high and just loaded with men, many of whom were eligible bachelors. The commute by subway was not bad and she reveled in the corporate atmosphere, although her duties did not bring her in contact with the high levels of management executives she seemed to want. Nevertheless, she paid attention to the important things, ingratiated herself with her immediate supervisors, just as she had done with the nuns at Mc Auley, and again enjoyed popularity.

As the months flew by, Margaret began to feel that she needed greener pastures to search for her life's love, that Metropolitan Life wasn't going to provide her with that opportunity. One day, one of the young women in the steno pool she worked in, Joan Menino, suggested that Margaret accompany her to a parish dance that Saturday at Our Lady of Perpetual Help Church on Fifty-Ninth Street in Brooklyn. It was a type of mixer several parishes ran regularly to help the young people find enjoyment in a somewhat protected atmosphere and, hopefully, mates.

Margaret enjoyed the dance. There she met several young men who seemed to have more than a passing interest in her. She generally liked them but recognized that several of them were just happy to have jobs, and were not interested in pursuing higher education to improve their career prospects. Fearing a lifetime with a mate with no ambition in a dead end job, where prospects for improved lifestyle would always elude them, she shied away from that type of boy. She wanted to aim higher, and told Joan so.

Joan suggested she might be happier at college dances but warned that many of the boys available there would not be Catholic. Joan had a brother attending Brooklyn College and he was in a fraternity that had a frat house on Ocean Avenue. They had parties every Saturday night, almost without fail, and Joan had often been invited by her brother. She was reluctant to go, she said, because she would be more or less alone and on her own, and may have nobody to talk to and thus not enjoy herself. She would try it out, though, if Margaret went with her. Margaret agreed.

The two girls met at the Flatbush Junction, where Flatbush and Nostrand Avenues crossed, and walked over to the fraternity house on Ocean Avenue. The house was an older whitish gray frame house, built in the Queen Anne style so prevalent in that area of Brooklyn, generally referred to as Ditmas Park. They could hear the noise of the music coming from the house as they got closer and were a little intimidated by what they anticipated the party would be like.

However, once inside and introduced around to a few of the young men, they relaxed a little. There was a lot of beer drinking going on and they joined in but Margaret hung out on the periphery. The atmosphere was friendly and somehow Margaret and Joan got separated from each other, and then Margaret noticed Joan was no longer in sight.

A young man of obvious Spanish descent, Jaimie Gonzalez, came and sat down next to Margaret. He was pleasant and inquired whether she was having a good time. Margaret answered somewhat ambiguously and the young man seemed surprised. He wanted her to enjoy herself, he said.

"You know," he said, "there's something that will help,--- help you find the party more enjoyable."

She was surprised and communicated that surprise with a look. "What do you mean?" she asked.

"Some speed," he replied quickly. "It's something you take to relax you. I've got some here. You should try it." Saying so he reached into his pocket and pulled out a small plastic vial. "Here," he said, "you take this and it'll relax you and you'll enjoy the party more.

We all take it, some more than others, but we really like it a lot. You'll like it, you'll see."

"What is it?" she asked.

"It's called 'speed', it's a relaxer. It's very good. You'll see."

Inquisitive, but extremely naïve, she pursued the matter further. "What exactly does it do?" she asked. "How do you take it, just swallow it?"

"Oh, no" he laughed. "You have to put it into your arm, your veins. It's easy. You can use this," he said, brandishing a small case with a hypodermic needle inside.

Margaret recoiled. "I don't think I want to do that. I don't think I need that to make me enjoy the party."

"Don't be scared," he said. "Everybody takes this stuff and they have a good time. It wears off and then you get regular again. No harm done. All it does is make you a little warm and gives you a glow all over and you relax. Try it. You'll see, it's really OK."

"I don't think so," Margaret said uneasily.

"Come on," Gonzalez pushed. "Don't be a party pooper. Come on with me. We'll go into the next room where it's private and I'll help you do it. It's easy."

He took Margaret by the hand, almost pulling her from the sofa. She resisted but got up reluctantly and went with him, still being held by the hand. She followed him into a small room and he closed the door. There was a small bed in the room and he beckoned her to sit down on the edge. He sat next to her and took out the needle.

Holding her arm, he said, "This won't even hurt. You won't even feel it."

Margaret winced at the thought of the needle going into her arm and looked away, but she held still. She could feel the needle poking in the fold of her elbow, searching for a vein, and then the tiny prick of the needle as it entered. She felt the warm sensation of something being pushed into her vein. Within an instant, it was done.

"There," Gonzalez said. "I bet you'll like it. You'll feel good and enjoy everything around you. You'll see."

But Margaret didn't feel that good about it. She began to feel a little queasy and said she wanted to stay behind and not go out into the main party room right away because she was feeling a little dizzy now. Gonzalez left her and she lay back down on the bed and pulled her feet up. She relaxed and suddenly was in a deep sleep.

Margaret knew she had been sleeping for quite a while when she awakened. She felt cold and realized that she was naked; someone had removed all her clothing during her sleep. She was embarrassed and wanted to get dressed and get out of there as soon as she could. She struggled to get her legs to move, but she realized she was sore and felt the pain in moving. Then she reached down and felt that her vaginal area was covered with some sort of slime. Then she knew what had happened and she panicked and began to sob.

Sobbing loudly now, she spied her clothing over in the corner on a chair and got up and dressed. Still crying, the tears running down her cheeks, she peeked out into the other room to see who was there, and saw nobody. She did see that it was daylight out now and realized she had been there overnight. She wondered exactly what had happened. She knew she had been taken advantage of by the fraternity boys, but just didn't know how many. She became even more terrified when she thought she might have been made pregnant. "That would be awful," she thought. "I don't know how I can tell my parents what happened, or what I would tell them if I'm pregnant." Now she felt sick. As she staggered through the front door, she heard someone call, "Thanks. Come again."

2

Out on the street, Margaret walked rapidly, and sometimes ran, toward Flatbush Avenue. She wanted to get away from that horrible memory she had now left behind her. Still sobbing uncontrollably, she turned north on to Flatbush Avenue and headed toward home. She was sobbing and cursing now intermittently, feeling ashamed and dirty for what had happened to her. She felt like a leper trying to hide her tear-stained face as she staggered along Flatbush Avenue.

She tried to keep looking into store windows to hide her face from passersby. She did not want to run into anybody who knew her or her parents, not at that time. Her appearance had nothing apparently wrong, but she felt there was. She did look a little out of place dressed in a cocktail dress during the morning hours. Her crying and sobbing and cursing to herself, and occasionally punching the air, did little to conceal her presence or the fact that something was terribly wrong with her.

She finally reached the Vanderveer Apartments. Now all the more, she wanted to be as invisible as possible, didn't want to meet anyone from the building. The lobby was empty. Mercifully, the elevator came quickly and she got on, unnoticed, and rode to the fourth floor where the family apartment was.

Once inside, Margaret closed the door quickly behind her. She leaned against the door and tried to catch her breath, between the sobs. The apartment was silent and she was certain her father had gone to work and her mother was out somewhere. Fortunately, nobody was home. There was an eerie silence in the apartment and she was glad about that.

Margaret made her way into her bedroom. She undressed, and couldn't help but look in the mirror at her nude frame. She was disgusted by what she saw, and cursed herself for being so stupid to get into a position where that could happen to her. Margaret was hard on herself.

Putting on pajamas, she hopped into bed. She had already made up the story to tell her mother when she came home that she had felt sick on the subway ride to the office and decided to come back home. She would say nothing about being out for the entire evening.

She hoped and prayed she was not pregnant. She could get over this experience, but pregnancy would be the most awful predicament. In those days, abortions were illegal and done only surreptitiously by inexperienced persons in less than sanitary conditions. Things often went awry. She wasn't worried about something like that happening to her for herself; she worried about her parents who she loved dearly and who loved her so much.

After a few hours of fitful sleep, Margaret heard the door to the apartment open and knew her mother was home. Almost instinctively, as mothers do, she sensed that not everything was right at home. Margaret's mother peeked in the bedroom door and saw that Margaret was there, but awake.

"Hi, Margaret, dear. Is everything all right with you?" her mother asked.

"Yeah," Margaret answered, trying to sound sleepy. "It's OK. I just felt a little squeamish on the subway ride to work and I decided I should come home. I really didn't feel too good, but I'm feeling somewhat better now."

"All right," her mother replied. "You just rest now and feel better. Can I get you anything?"

"No," Margaret said. "I think I'll just rest for a little while more. Then I'll be OK."

Margaret wasn't sure, but she felt that her mother had bought the story. She didn't feel great telling her mother such a lie, but it was better and easier than describing her true feelings and going into the entire story about what had happened. A little lie was easier than the full-blown truth, and served the purpose better just now.

Surprisingly, the next day, Margaret felt her old self again. She spryly got up for work and dressed and left for the office without any question from either of her parents. She was happy that there was no mention of anything, especially the evening away from home. She was fearful of there being some questioning, especially by her father, and her blurting out some of the events of that awful night. She didn't want to get into a full blown inquisition in search for the real truth, and then try to do something about it. As far as the home front was concerned, she felt the incident had ended.

At work, she confronted her friend Joan as soon as the opportunity arose. She didn't want to tell Joan everything either, so she inquired gently about what happened to Joan and where she had disappeared to during the party. Joan professed total ignorance of anything unusual happening and merely inquired about where Margaret had gone. Joan had been told that Margaret had left early. Margaret left it at that.

Around noontime, though, she began to feel hungry, very hungry, much hungrier than usual. Margaret dismissed it as being just anxious to have lunch and said so to Joan. They ate in the company cafeteria and Margaret ate a lot. She couldn't seem to get enough.

Back at her desk, her hunger returned quickly. Close to the end of the workday, she again felt terribly hungry. On the ride home, she felt as if she were going to faint, but held on and toughed it out, got a seat, and made it to her stop.

Once inside the apartment, her parents almost instinctively knew not all was right. Margaret intemperately shrugged them off and did not respond at length to any of their inquiries. They had no idea of what was wrong, but just knew it was something.

During the evening, Margaret was impatient watching TV and got up frequently for water or a snack. She felt as if her parents were watching her every move. They were watching her, but not with any suspicion, just normal parental concern.

That night, she tossed and turned, getting little real sleep. She couldn't tell what bothered her so much, but knew in her heart it wasn't the fraternity house episode itself because she hardly thought back to it. She had a tightening knot in her stomach that pained a little, but made its presence felt all the time.

In the morning, she felt no better. Her stomach was still painful but she decided to go to work and left for the subway. As she approached the Junction, she saw Gonzalez standing on the corner in a doorway, a cigarette hanging from his lips. More angry now than ill, she anxiously crossed the intersection and walked up to him. She stood there, hands on hips, looking at him quizzically.

"What can I do for you?" he asked, the cigarette still dangling from his mouth.

"Don't you recognize me?" she demanded angrily.

"Not really," he said, but she knew it was a lie.

"Well, you should, you dirty bastard. You took advantage of me at the fraternity house on Saturday night. You and your 'friends'," she blurted out sarcastically.

"Don't know nothin' about it," he said, turning to evade her and walk away, but she confronted him again.

"What was that stuff you gave me?"

"Don't know what you're talkin' about," he said, almost embarrassed.

She would not let him off the hook that easily. "You and your so-called friends took advantage of me. You know what I mean. That stuff you gave me to enjoy the party knocked me out and you guys gave it to me, but good."

"Look, honey. I didn't do anything to you that you didn't want done. You didn't object. You even helped me give it to you. Don't complain now. It's too late for that. It's over. Let it go at that."

" I can't," she said. "I've been terrified since that I may be pregnant--that you guys made me pregnant. I have this hole in my stomach that won't go away. I don't know why, but it pains me. I have to do something to get even with you."

"Oh, that," he replied flippantly. "You might just have a craving for some of the stuff again. You might have liked it more than you thought you would. I can get more of it for you, if you want. Just come see me. I'm almost always around here."

Angry, she slammed her hands down at her side and started to walk away. "I'll get you. I'll get even, someway, somehow. You'll see."

The subway ride to Manhattan was noisy, but, in her anger, she hardly heard the noise of the riders or the angry screech of the trains on the rails. She couldn't get that confrontation out of her mind, and she knew her stomach still hurt badly. She began to wonder if Gonzalez had been right. Was she hooked?

During the day, she purposely bumped into one of the young men from the mailroom, one she suspected was on drugs. She asked him point blank if his stomach ever hurt him. "Yeah," he said. "All the

time. I know it's when I need a fix. Then I have to get the stuff. I need it a lot."

Now she thought she knew. She *was* hooked. She didn't want to get in any further, but she had to get this stomach pain to go away. She could control it, she thought. A fatal mistake.

Margaret got through the day somehow. She almost raced for the subway to go home and got off at the Junction after an anxious ride, cursing the delays under her breath. Climbing the stairs to street level, she began to survey the scene for Gonzalez. She thought she would ask him for just one more, to help her control it so she could have time to lick the urge.

She found him quickly. He was very sympathetic this time, almost too nice. "Sure, I can help you out," he said. "But this stuff costs money. I have to pay for it. I can't always give it out free. I'll give it to you now for only ten bucks. What's ten bucks? I'll even help you do it to make it easier for you."

She looked at him with disdain. She knew he wasn't a friend, but she needed what he had and by now, needed it badly. She reached into her pocketbook and took out a ten dollar bill and offered it to him.

"Not here," he gushed, almost under his breath. "Not in public view. Someone might be looking. Come around here."

Gonzalez now walked hurriedly and led her around the corner where there were not many people passing by. As they stood in the doorway, he reached down and took her hand in his, expecting to find the money there. She had put it back in her pocketbook.

"The hell with you," he blurted out. "I don't need anybody like you. You're trouble. Get lost!" He started to walk away.

"Please. Don't go. Don't do this to me. I won't make that mistake again. I promise you." She took out the same ten dollar bill and gave it to him. He handed her a small cellophane envelope with a tiny amount of white powder in it. She studied it, not seeming to comprehend its unusual powers, its hold on people.

"Come in here and sit on the steps," he said, opening the door. "I'll help you with it in here. It's easy to do, you'll see."

Once inside, he produced a hypodermic needle and some liquid. He mixed the powder from her envelope in the liquid and siphoned it into the syringe. Looking up, he saw that she had already extended her bare arm to have the needle inserted. "Will I be all right here if I pass out from this again?"

"Don't worry, you won't pass out this time. This dose isn't as big as the other one. You can handle it. But I'll stay here with you anyway, for a while." He began rubbing her back and caressing her shoulders and buttocks. She was alarmed at this overfriendliness and backed away but he pulled her close. This time she stayed close.

Gonzalez was right. She did not pass out from the dosage. She did get a warm glow and her pain in the stomach left her. She wanted to go home and walked out of the doorway, wobbling a little. She made the walk home fairly well but her parents noticed something strange about her when she walked in. Through dinner she hardly spoke and seemed far away.

The next day went normally, but a few days later, she began to have that longing again, and the pain in her stomach returned. She knew what the problem was now and decided she would give in to it again this one more time. This visit to Gonzalez found him friendlier than ever and he took her upstairs to his apartment for the dose administration, rather than just standing down in the hallway. Now his caresses became more personal and she felt unable to fight him off, although she wanted to. She felt his hand go up under her dress. She resisted at first but then gave in and he had his way.

The Gonzalez visits became more and more frequent. After a while, they were three times a week, then four, then almost every day. She was meeting him now at his apartment and every meeting involved a sexual encounter as well.

He raised the price, claiming the stuff was costing him more, so naturally, he had to pass the increased cost along, even to her although, he claimed, she was his favorite. Soon the price had reached fifty dollars a dose and the doses seemed smaller. She paid willingly, being in dire need of the fix to help her along.

She was a regular junkie now. She was hooked into the drug and to Gonzalez, her only source of supply. Her personality began to change, becoming more aggressive and sharp in her exchanges with her friends, her co-workers and supervisors and, worst of all, her parents.

Her work began to fall off. She was inattentive and didn't produce as much work as before, and definitely of lower quality. She began to take whole days off or to disappear from the job early in the afternoon without telling anybody. Friends and supervisors took her aside to see what was wrong, but she resisted telling them anything and declined their offers to help her out of whatever was bothering her.

Finally, the situation at work became so bad, the supervisors who truly had loved her, had to let her go. Now she had no money with which to buy the stuff she needed so badly. She couldn't find another job, partly due to her appearance and partly to a very neutral reference from her former employers. She was desperate.

Gonzalez said he was sorry, but he couldn't give her the stuff for free. She would have to get the money somehow. He suggested she try to get it from her parents, but she knew that could not be done without difficulty. Gonzalez suggested then that she take the money from her parents without them knowing about it. Stealing it. The thought revulsed her, but there seemed to be no other way. All the time he was turning her away without the drug for lack of money, Gonzalez was still extracting sexual favors from her on every visit. She gave in, thinking he would appreciate her favors and give her the drug without money, but he wouldn't.

Margaret's mother began to miss money from her pocketbook once the stealing started. Her mother then knew what was going on and tried to persuade Margaret to get help for the problem, to register at a drug-free house where she could gain control over her senses again. Margaret just couldn't face it.

Her mother hid the money so Margaret began stealing things to pawn. She was desperate one day and stole her father's twenty-five year jeweled watch, inscribed with his name and appreciation for his loyalty to the Banking Department. She was stunned to find the pawnbroker would only pay twenty dollars for the watch she and her father thought was so valuable. Worse yet, her father missed the watch terribly and kept looking through the apartment trying to find it. Seeing him do that, hoping against hope his daughter had not stolen it, made her miserable. There had to be another way.

Gonzalez had a suggestion; she could sell her sexual favors for money. She was disgusted by the idea. He just shrugged and appeared to dismiss her, saying no money, no 'sweet stuff.' Knowing she had to do something, she began to ask what that would involve, how it would be done, and what would happen to her if she did it?

He said he liked her a lot and would help her. He would set her up in an apartment and would send the guys to her and she would treat them sexually. He wouldn't want her out on the street trying to get guys like any common prostitute, no sir, not her. She was his girl and her best sexual favors were to be saved for him. Margaret was swayed by that kind of talk, wanting to think she was special to him, and she agreed. She would try it, she said.

Margaret walked with Gonzalez a few blocks to an apartment building. It was one of the Vanderveer buildings, the one in which she and her parents lived. She started to turn away, terrified at the thought of her parents finding out what she was doing. She saw no way to hide it in the same building where they lived.

When she tried to turn away, Gonzalez tugged at her arm and pulled her along. Once inside, they went down the stairs to the super's apartment. Margaret kept looking around, all the way down, to make sure nobody saw her or where she was going.

The super's apartment had a plywood door with the words "super man" written on it in crayon. Inside, the apartment was shabby. It was small and dinghy, smelled of a mixture of sweat and stale beer, and had a small bed with an orange chenille cover spread over it. There were only a few pictures on the wall, and a television and a small table with an aluminum kitchen chair.

"This is it?" she asked in a terror stricken voice.

"It's only for today, or a day or two," he said. "This came up suddenly. You know that. I need some time to get you something more fancy."

"I don't know," she said, still in great fear of the unknown. "I don't know about this. Who lives here, do you know?"

"Sure I know. What do you think, I go busting into other people's apartments whenever I want? I'm not like that. My brother Enrique lives here. He's working now so you don't have to worry about him."

"But what if he comes home early, or something, what about that?"

"He's hip to this. He knows I do this once in a while. He knows it's only for a day or two."

Margaret looked around wincingly. She didn't like it—not one bit. She started to stammer out her unwillingness to go any further but he interrupted her. He moved over next to her and hugged her. "Don't worry. It'll be OK. You'll see. I'll send you the guys and you just help them out, you know what I mean?"

She stared at him, thinking that she couldn't be very important to him if he wanted her to do this. Margaret was still trembling when he handed her a pink negligee. "Here, put this on. You should be wearing this when the guys come in. That way, they'll be tempted and know what you look like—all over."

Margaret fumbled with the negligee, it was so sheer and thin. She started to cry, saying,"No, I can't do this. Please don't make me do this. Please."

Gonzalez stepped forward and stood next to her. "Do it," he said commandingly. "Put that on. Don't give me any crap. I expect you to do this and do it well. Get it on! Now!"

Margaret was startled by his sudden and unexpected anger. She didn't know what to do. Gonzalez moved closer and slapped her across the face. Then, he pinched the nipple on her breast,--hard. She was hurt and the pinched nipple and slap hurt her terribly. Tears were streaming down her face now and she mumbled some unintelligible words that he didn't understand. She was a pitiful sight standing there, in that shabby apartment with the skimpy negligee draped over her arm, rubbing her slapped face.

"Get it on!" Gonzalez shouted. "Get it on now! Do you want some more? There's a lot more where that came from. Do you want some more? Tell me!"

"No," she mumbled through the tears and an aching face. She was sobbing and staring at the floor. Gonzalez grabbed her by the hair and pulled her face up towards him. "Get it on now," he said slowly and menacingly. "Do you want me to pull your clothes off?"

"Uh-uh," she cried, pushing her hands outstretched to keep him away. "No. I'll do it myself," she said angrily. Hurting and ashamed, she began to take her dress and other clothing off. Soon she stood there naked in front of him and noticed him staring at her. "You look good," he said. "You'll do a great job. You'll like it. You'll see." He started to leave. "Remember ," he said, turning back toward her, "do a great job for these guys. I want repeat customers. It's better for both of us. I don't want to have to come back here to persuade you again. Understand?"

Alone in the apartment, she started to cry more vigorously now. Sobbing away, she saw a mirror over in the corner of the room. She went over and looked at her image staring back at her. She hated it. She looked awful, and anybody could see clear through the negligee. It was as if she was naked. She cleaned her face a little.

Soon, there was a knock on the door. Without waiting to be invited, the person who knocked pushed the door open. She could see him clearly in the doorway. He was a huge black man, obese, sweating profusely and breathing heavily. She could hear him breathing as if he had just run a long way. His stomach hung out in front and his t-shirt didn't fully cover it, leaving the bottom rung of fat, shiny and streaked with sweat, exposed. This event was as much of a strain to him as it would be to her.

He mopped his brow with a white cloth. "Jaimie sent me down here. He told me to tell you I paid him. He said you'd know what I was here for."

Margaret looked at him. She was aghast. How could Gonzalez, how could anyone, do this to her? She rebelled. "No," she shouted. Sobbing, she kept saying "No, no, I won't do it. I can't." She backed away.

"Now, honey, don't be like that," he said. "You don't want me to have to go tell Jaimie I want my money back, that you wouldn't take care of me. Do you?"

She knew what that meant. She knew Gonzalez would be down on her in a flash and slap her around some more. She would have to take it. She couldn't do this. She was appalled at the sight of that huge sweating black man standing there. She couldn't do it. Not for him, not for anybody. "Get out!" she shouted, sobbing uncontrollably. "Get out!"

"OK," he said, backing away. "But, honey, you know what this means, don't you? You know Jaimie'll be down here to beat the crap outta you for sure. He won't like giving me back my money. Are you sure? I'd rather not do that. I'd sure like to make it with you."

"Get out!" she screamed again, still sobbing loudly.

The door closed. Margaret walked over to the mirror again. Staring at the mirror, she sobbed again. She didn't like what she saw. She was disgusted. She didn't like what she had become. She hated herself, and what she had become.

She was ashamed as she stood there looking in the mirror through teary eyes. She knew her parents would be ashamed too. She hated to realize how low she had sunk and how bad she would look in their eyes. She had let them down, terribly. Tears were streaming down her face. She took off the negligee and put her clothes back on.

Dressed now, Margaret walked to the elevator and pushed the 'up' button. Getting in, she rode to the fourteenth floor. From there, she went up a short stairway to the roof.

Outside on the roof, the air was fresh and clean. Margaret breathed it in and seemed to relax. She knew her situation was hopeless. She had to continue tumbling down the path of drugs and unwanted sex-for-hire or get beaten up by Gonzalez, and who knows what else. There was no future in sight. She couldn't take it. She wouldn't. Walking to the edge of the roof, she looked down. Then she bent down, took off her shoes, and stepped on to the top of the low wall. Within a second, she had jumped.

3

Monsignor Gately Auditorium was bathed in light on the hot evening of July 6, 1964. Passersby could tell by the activity around St. Vincent Ferrer Parish Church across the street that big things were going on. People stood outside both the Church and the Auditorium talking in groups of varying size, some smoking, and the discussions appeared to be animated. Both men and women hung together, although the meeting that night was of a men's organization, the Holy Name Society.

The Society met the first Monday of each month. Usually, the gathering for the meetings drew only about fifteen or so men, mostly attending out of a sense of duty to support a church-sponsored activity, just because their children attended the church school. Tonight was different. The Holy Name Society had invited both men and women of the parish to attend and meet with the police captain from the precinct that served the area. The notice of the meeting was enthusiastically received and carefully noted on family calendars. Most would not want to miss the meeting.

St. Vincent Ferrer Parish was under siege by drug dealers who preyed on the youth of the area. It had become an enormous problem, many kids being hooked on the drugs that were now readily available for purchase, without difficulty. Those that were hooked or became 'druggies' seemed to drop out of social activities of any kind and dropped out of school. They robbed and stole to support their habit. They became slaves to the drug influence and parents could see their lives being wasted. Some even went to jail for drug-fostered crimes, and others, less fortunate, died. What should have been the prime of their lives was now seen as lost.

The parents wanted to do something about it, but were confused. They did not know what to do. They had never experienced such problems before, drugs being almost unheard of in the forties and fifties, and earlier. Most had studied in school that drug problems were limited to the Orient, and the smoking of opium. This was different, and now it was close to home.

They were trying to find answers that would cut off the availability of drugs in their neighborhood, thinking that would save their children. Almost every house had some connection to the drug problem, either through their own children being affected, or their neighbor's, or just knowing people in the virtually all-Catholic neighborhood. The problem, never small even in the beginning, had become enormous now. People were desperate to regain a hold on their lives and the futures of their children. Something had to be done, and this meeting just might provide the entre to turning this problem around. At least, they would hear the official governmental position on what could be done and what could be expected from the police. It could be a start.

Captain John Nicholson came as the representative of the Police Department. Tall, and almost razor thin, he was the Public Relations Officer of the Department and trained in mass psychology techniques. He could charm an audience. He made an impressive appearance with his shocking white hair and in his dark blue dress uniform and gold epaulets. His tunic displayed a massive amount of medals and citations on the right chest side, making it clear to one and all that he was an accomplished police officer, not just any cop.

Chairs had been set up on the auditorium floor. Even Monsignor Bates attended, although he was not the actual moderator of the Society. However, he sensed, and correctly so, this would be an important event in the parish, especially when he became aware such an important representative of the Police Department was being sent. He reasoned that the police must have realized it too.

The auditorium also served as a basketball court for parishioners, so the basketball backboards and hoops were folded up towards the ceiling to allow for more air space. As the chairs began to fill up with still more people waiting outside, it was clear more chairs were needed. The Holy Name Society members began hurriedly to set them up.

The meeting started late, but the listeners were enthusiastic. That enthusiasm soon turned to disappointment as Captain Nicholson outlined the details of the precinct operations and precisely what the police were doing to stop the drug trade. It was a lesson in the daily routine of police officers assigned to that precinct, but it was hardly a response to what the people thought should have been a war-like mode. They wanted specifics, not generalities. The crowd began to murmur among themselves, and the murmuring became steadily louder.

Finally, Captain Nicholson perceived that his message was not getting through or was thought to be inadequate. "I think I detect a level of dissatisfaction with the police activities I just outlined," he said. "Does anybody here have a question about what we're doing or can do, and maybe I'll be able to answer that for you. We know your problems, your fears, and how you feel about this issue. I want you to be absolutely comfortable that the police are doing everything possible to protect you and your children." That statement unleashed a loud reaction. A few people even applauded but almost immediately felt out of place.

Over to the side of the gathering, a large hand shot up. It was Michael O'Hara, a burly Irishman who had migrated to the United States from Cork in Ireland some thirty-five years before to find a better life for himself and his family. "All my life," he began in a hoarse, gruff voice, "I've been working to provide a better life for my kids, a life that they can enjoy, a better life than I had in the old country. Now I see all this drug crap all around me. Kids walking around with empty eyes and faces, like zombies. I hear all about the break-ins and daylight robberies in the neighborhood. Everybody says it's drug-related. The police shrug it off as just drug-related. That's not enough. That's not good enough. I think you have to do more than that crap you just told us about. You have to be more aggressive. These people are selling drugs in plain daylight…right under your noses. Your guys have to see it. They're not blind. You have to do something. Now!" There was loud applause. Sometimes the deepest and most explicit thoughts came from the less educated.

Across the auditorium, another unidentified voice yelled out, "Yeah, you guys have to get off your asses." More applause.

Another voice yelled out, "He's right." Then another shouted, "We want something done for all that pay you're getting!" The crowd was now very noisy, talking among themselves.

Finally, Jim Wright, the President of the Holy Name Society stood up and held out his hands and called for order. When the group had hushed somewhat, he faced Captain Nicholson and said, "Captain, I think you can hear our concern. We're worried about our families, our neighborhoods, our homes. You do have to listen and do something and right away. I could send my teenage son down to the Junction right now and he'd be back in ten minutes or less with drugs he bought there. They're all around you. The police have to wake up. They seem to be turning a blind eye. What can you do?"

Captain Nicholson was flustered. "Well…," he stammered, "…I can see and hear your concern. It's our concern, too. Believe me, nobody on the force is turning a blind eye. I believe you when you say it is widespread and out in the open…"

The crowd began to shout back. "You're not listening.", "Do something, now!" were the shouts as the noise got louder and louder. The people at the dais table called for quiet. Monsignor Bates whispered something to Jim Wright. The president gaveled loudly, but the crowd continued. It was a steady, but loud drone now.

Finally, in response to the president's gaveling, the noise abated.

"Let me continue," Captain Nicholson said, somewhat fearful now. He could see the evening's public relations attempt finishing in a public relations debacle. He didn't want that. "We're going to do everything we can. I can assure you, we'll continue our efforts and, you'll see, in a very short time the problem will be curtailed. We won't stand for it either. We are sworn to protect you and uphold the law. We know our job and we're going to do just that. When you're not happy, we're not happy. I'd listen to any suggestions you may have. What do you want us to do beyond what we're doing? Anybody?" He looked around.

There was silence for a moment, and then a number of hands shot up. It seemed that every family had a suggestion. "I'd like to see you start arresting those dealers, right now, tonight, tomorrow and every day thereafter. Don't let 'em make jackasses of your patrolmen." There was loud applause.

"We want action," one voice shouted. Another said, "We don't know police work. Don't ask us how to do your job. You're paid to do it and supposedly trained for it. Do it, quick." Many people had an opinion but wanted to remain anonymous. Almost every shout drew loud applause. Monsignor Bates, Captain Nicholson, and Jim Wright were obviously uncomfortable.

The Monsignor looked around the huge room, hoping for some way to halt the proceedings, to save Captain Nicholson from further embarrassment. Over in the corner, near the doorway, he spied Ellen Coburn. Ellen was a volunteer in the parish. She was one of those ladies every parish has, the lady who quietly did just about everything,--cleaned the altar linens, put out flowers, matches for the candles and took care of all sorts of parish needs. She attended just about every parish function. As a widow with no children, she had lots of time.

Ellen was very interested in the proceedings. She had a direct connection to the drug problem, her husband Eddie having been a detective in the Narcotics Squad for several years. He was killed one night in an abortive drug bust in Harlem and she inwardly held the department responsible. She believed strongly that the police had not furnished the help and support her husband and his partner needed to complete the action successfully. It was true, as she was told repeatedly and tried hard to believe, that nobody could have possibly anticipated such an unusual thing happening as the explosion of the police car her husband was sitting in that night. In her heart, she thought differently. But she was not bitter, at least outwardly.

Catching the Monsignor's searching eye, she pointed with her hands to the tables of cakes and cookies stretched before her and the hot coffee steaming in pots. Monsignor Bates caught on immediately. He was happy for the gesture she had made. He knew how much the parish relied on Ellen Coburn and was even more appreciative at this moment.

Rising from his chair at the dais, he turned to Captain Nicholson. "Captain, I want to thank you and the Department for coming here tonight. I am personally glad you had an opportunity to hear firsthand from our parishioners exactly how they feel. I want you to take away from this meeting the strong feeling that something must be done, and now. It is an extremely urgent problem. We can't wait any longer. We have to turn this drug thing around, for the good of the children of the parish, for everybody's good."

He reached down into the unbuttoned part of his tunic, and pulled out a paper. "Captain, this is a Certificate of Appreciation the Holy Name Society of St. Vincent Ferrer Parish has asked me to confer on you. We appreciate your time and effort. Thank you for coming and thank the Department for sending you. We are going to adjourn now for coffee and cake. You're invited to join us if you wish."

There was a loud murmur of disappointment from the crowd. The entire meeting had lasted only a little over an hour. The people expected more...a lot more. Captain Nicholson rose to accept the certificate. He thanked the Monsignor and the people present for the opportunity to speak to them. He tried again briefly to reassure them he would take their message to heart and give them swift action. It was obvious they didn't believe him. He decided not to stay for the coffee and cake.

4

The funeral Mass for Margaret Barnes was a somber affair. Monsignor Bates correctly anticipated a large turnout and was not disappointed. To make it as orderly as possible, he had asked the Bereavement Committee to attend and act as ushers. He knew that Ellen Coburn would be there anyway, and would do a great job on the seating of parishioners. Ellen served several functions within the church itself. She seemed always to be around.

Therefore, it was nothing exceptional to see her gliding silently across the sanctuary area behind the altar at St. Vincent Ferrer Church that day, as the parish prepared for Margaret Barnes' funeral Mass. She had worked out an elaborate seating arrangement she had expected her minions to follow as parishioners arrived for the Mass. Everything was expected to be orderly, despite the large crowd that arrived. Ellen could be seen occasionally, giving directions to one member of the committee or another from time to time, with a simple nod of her head. She wanted this funeral Mass to go as smoothly as possible, aware of the sadness of this particular occasion, mainly out of respect for Frank and Arlene Barnes.

After what seemed like longer, but only ten minutes after everyone was seated, the hearse arrived bearing the mortal remains of Margaret Barnes. The event was going like clockwork. Almost immediately after the hearse stopped in front of the church doors on East 37 Street, six brawny men dressed in black, most likely off-duty policemen or firemen, jumped out of the next limousine and walked rapidly to the back of the hearse. Within seconds, they had the back door lid up and had removed a collapsible aluminum porter from the back and opened it. Carefully, they pulled the coffin from the back of the hearse and laid it on the wheeled porter. They rolled up to the open doors of the church and paused.

There waiting for them was Monsignor Bates dressed in priestly vestments, surrounded on either side by young altar boys. Monsignor Bates intoned the greeting that Catholic ceremonial regulations required to be said on greeting a body entering a church for a funeral Mass. When he had concluded, he sprinkled some holy water on the coffin and turned to go back to the altar. As he did, the black suited men gently lifted and rolled the wheeled porter into the church and down the carpeted center aisle. Reaching the altar area, they turned the coffin a quick right and used that move to maneuver the coffin around so that the head of the body inside faced the altar. Quickly, as if they had done it a thousand times, and this time was no different, they spread a large white cloth bearing a huge black cross over the casket, and quietly walked away.

Everyone in the church waited in hushed silence, for Frank and Arlene Barnes to appear. Without seeing him enter, they knew he was coming as they could hear the wheels of his wheelchair rolling over the carpet. Frank rolled by on his wheelchair, head stooped over and staring straight down. One could tell he was overcome with grief and tears were rolling down his cheeks. Arlene was no better, pushing the chair along with a tear-swollen face, in obvious pain over the horrible turn of events that had stolen their only child from them.

It was a tragically sad and solemn affair. As his chair reached the front of the coffin, Frank signaled Arlene to stop pushing. Frank waited for a short time next to the casket with his hand underneath the covering sheet, as if he was reaching to hold hands with his much beloved daughter for the last time. He stayed in the aisle without getting out of the wheelchair and Arlene squeezed into the pew next to him.

The Mass went along rhythmically and well, the homily by Monsignor Bates driving almost everybody present to tears. He described what Margaret had meant throughout her brief life to those who knew her, and most of all to her grieving parents. He tried as much as possible to avoid any details about her passing and actually achieved it. Communion was received by almost the entire parish that day, shuffling silently up to the altar rail, some touching the coffin or Frank as they passed. Then Monsignor Bates launched into the closing ceremony. When he reached the point where he said, "...and may the angels lead you, Margaret, into Paradise," Frank and Arlene sobbed loudly and uncontrollably. The sobbing sounded even louder, and more eerie, in the echo-like acoustics of the otherwise silent church.

In a rare scene, most of those present accompanied the family to Holy Cross Cemetery, where a grave in the family plot had been opened. Frank and Arlene had never envisioned the plot being used for anybody but them. The mourners gathered around the opened grave as Monsignor Bates led them in several prayers. He blessed the remains and sprinkled holy water on the coffin resting on the roller tapes. The Monsignor then went over to Frank and Arlene to try to comfort them as much as possible.

Later, left alone by the graveside, Frank and Arlene were still speechless and could only mumble through their tears to each other. Finally, the driver of their limousine prevailed on them to leave the gravesite and they got into the car with difficulty. It rolled away silently, leaving Margaret, alone, on that lonely hill. Frank could not keep from looking back until the scene disappeared from sight.

That night, at home alone, would be the loneliest night of all for Margaret's parents. They sat, huddled together in mournful silence, a silence that would overwhelm them in days to come. For reasons and causes they couldn't begin to fathom, the light of their lives had been snuffed out. Religious people, they kept silently asking God for an explanation. Their reason for living had been taken from them. Their joy and happiness now and in their old age was gone, forever. They would never understand why this had happened to them, on top of all the other problems life had dealt them.

5

Ellen Coburn deeply felt the anguish of the Barnes' in the horrible and untimely death of their daughter. She knew how much Margaret had meant to them and knew they would grieve long and deeply, and might never overcome the sadness of the entire affair.

Ellen also knew the entire parish knew the same thing. Everybody admired Frank and Arlene for their pluck and determination in overcoming the paralysis of Frank and the drastic change that had made in their lives. Now, their shining light, Margaret, had been taken from them unhappily. Ellen, the Barnes', and the entire Parish would blame Margaret's death on the impact of the drug dealers and the drug related problems they brought to this neighborhood.

She knew that, and also knew something had to be done. The police couldn't do it. The politicians didn't want to. It was time for action. She would consult with the Bereavement Committee.

The Bereavement Committee was comprised of a group of mostly retired parishioners who had the time and inclination to serve the Church's needs.

The solid anchor of the Committee was Ira O'Malley, a retired fireman. He was a huge, brawny man of about sixty, very athletic and strong, with a large head of pure white hair. He made an imposing presence wherever he went and would stand out in crowds or groups, and he often wanted to be heard.

Also on the Committee was Joe Wickham, a former police officer who had gone through the Police Academy with Ellen Coburn's husband, but went into precinct work. He was also a huge man but had taken early retirement when he injured his right knee badly. It happened in an incident involving a hostile crowd in Crown Heights in Brooklyn during a dispute between the black population there and the Hasidic Jews who had begun to move into that area in great numbers. Wickham's knee was so badly injured, he took disability retirement and so, at fifty-five, was the youngest person on the committee.

Joe married his sweetheart Mary he had met at one of those Catholic School mixers. They had three children, but the youngest had been a problem for them. He had several brushes with drugs and minor criminal escapades, but escaped unscathed, permanently. He righted himself and one day announced he wanted to be a priest. He was enrolled in Mt. Saint Alphonsus, the Redemptorist Monastery in Esopus, New York, graduated, was ordained and was now on missionary work in Peru, searching for converts to Christianity.

Joe enjoyed the stature having a son a priest brought him. Monsignor Bates called on him frequently and he served by appointment on the St. Vincent De Paul Committee as well, distributing food and money to Parish families in need, under absolute confidentiality.

Another member of the Committee was Jim McCormick. A lanky second generation Irishman, he had only recently retired from New York Life Insurance Company where he had enjoyed a quiet career in the Actuarial Department. He was not an actuary, but he did collect the statistical data they needed. A person like him was very important in the days before computers became the watchword in all types of computational things. The actuaries relied on Jim to produce the material they needed to make the important decisions affecting the Company's economic success.

When computers began to assemble, sift and spit out the statistical data electronically and swiftly, Jim was quick to recognize his position was a dinosaur, soon to be extinct. . Pushing for an early retirement deal, he got one, and took it with alacrity. Still in his early sixties, Jim thought about the best thing you could do with your free time was to work for the church. He loved working with the Bereavement Committee and thought it a high honor to be invited to join.

Perhaps, the most incongruous of Committee members was Rodolfo Saviano. He was a short, burly Italian, very muscular, with large hands. He was a stone mason or bricklayer, whichever job was available. A tried and true union man, he put great store on loyalty to whatever cause he was connected with. Rodolfo, or Rudy as he was called, was not religious, and strangely, neither was his wife Maria. Affable and outgoing, he could be seen almost daily during the warmer evenings, walking the sidewalks on Farragut Road for the two blocks in either direction from his house, talking with the various neighbors who were sitting out, mainly the Doyles and the McGraths.

Now a proud grandpa of sixty two, a shop steward in his union, and not required to do heavy manual labor anymore, he had plenty of time. Unfortunately, one of his grandchildren had gotten in with a bad crowd, tried drugs, and then found he couldn't get off them. One day, a policeman came to Rudy's daughter's door and told her they had found her son dead of a drug overdose.

Rudy inwardly seethed at a society that could allow their children, their future, to become victimized so easily. He hated drugs and drug dealers and complained openly to anyone who would listen about this evil cancer growing untouched within their neighborhood. He launched himself into parish activities to keep his idle time busy, partly to allow himself freedom from those thoughts. Having been seen so openly and often at parish functions, and around the neighborhood, he was a natural to be selected by Ellen for the Bereavement Committee.

The committee also had several transient members who came and worked at various functions, but not all of them. Only O'Malley, Wickham, McCormick and Saviano could be considered 'permanent' or 'regular' members. The others came and went on occasions that worked well with their activities and were not members of the Steering Group of the Bereavement Committee, the important policy-making body that governed committee activities.

Ellen Coburn stayed in the background, but was the most important member of the Bereavement Committee. She was the one who organized all meetings and committee activities, calling various people from time to time, asking them to help out on one thing or another. She had set up a calling ring, so she only had to call a few people, and those people in turn would call others, the number determined by how many people Ellen thought she would need at the particular function.

As a younger widow with no children, she had time to spare and seemed almost always to be in attendance, quietly in the background, at all parish functions, serving in one way or another. No parish job was too small or too big for her. There was no question she was the soul of the parish itself. She would lead the committee to clean up the problem.

6

Carroll Gawloski had performed this ritual many times before. For nearly precisely 38 years he had driven his car to this corner, parked in the bus company parking lot, and located the bus that was to be his vehicle for the day. The company almost never changed his buses. The one he had the day before was almost always the one he would use the next day, and the next, and so on. The seat almost had his grooves formed in it.

Today, though, the ritual was something more significant. After all those years, he was close to retirement. This week's trips would be his last. The end was in sight for his career but he had no clue as to what life would hold in store for him after retirement began. He had no plans, no hobbies and no prospects for working another job and, frankly he didn't want to. He was a man who believed that when you reached retirement, your pension and other benefits should satisfy your needs and there was nothing more to it. That was life.

So, with an air of the approaching inevitable end to what he considered his life's work, he approached the bus assigned to him with almost reverence. He stood in front of it, spread-legged and with hands on his hips, facing its headlights, as it sat silently in the cool August morning air in the company parking lot. As he measured it, there, that day, he was impressed with the air of stability, of reliability, the vehicle gave off. He was satisfied the bus was up to its assigned task for the day, and for many more days, and he viewed it with pleasure.

The bus was enormous compared to his five-foot one inch stature, but it was also enormous when measured against almost every other vehicle. That size advantage was something he liked--a lot. He tried to use that advantage as he guided the bus across its designed route throughout the day, taking pride and enjoyment out of intimidating car drivers whenever the opportunity presented itself. In the driver's seat, he owned the road.

He began his slow walk around the bus, taking note of a few dings and dents picked up along its travels. He was sure none of them could be attributable to him because he drove and maneuvered the bus with such loving care. It was difficult going in and out of traffic, turning at traffic lights through many lines of cars headed in the opposite direction. Then there were the tight turns and the problem of the stops made almost every two or three blocks. The bus had to be swerved into the curb area so passengers could get off the bus and new passengers board.

That was no easy task, what with cars parked illegally in the bus stop spaces, or others double parked with their motors on or off, but with someone in the car waiting. Gawloski, affectionately known as "Pat" to his regulars, would often lose his temper over such interferences with his job, but he never vocalized his intemperateness. He kept it all inside, simmering. He would not miss that aspect of his job after he retired.

He continued his walk around the bus, inspecting with pride the double tires on the rear axle and noting that they were fully inflated. He gave the outside tires a kick just to make sure and was pleased with the results. He ended his inspection trip when he reached the front door of the bus. Gawloski sneaked a peek at the sign in the illuminated panel at the top of the bus and read it with pride. "Kingsway 37". His route. He turned the key in the latch and the door sprung open so he could enter.

Once inside, he slid his body behind the large, almost horizontal, steering wheel and adjusted his seating to be as comfortable as possible. It was going to be a long day. He placed his lunch pail down beside his seat in the area near the exterior of the bus, to his

left, so as not to interfere with the passengers. Then he pulled the toggle switch to turn on the heater and turned the key to activate the motor.

The motor came on with a roar. It pleased him, sensing that it meant power to push this big baby for the entire day across a whole lot of Brooklyn geography. After touching the brake to make certain the air compressor was working, he tapped the brake pedal several times, getting joy out of hearing the hiss of the escaping air and feeling the tug of the bus against the brake. He took a devilish delight in being able to alternately push on the accelerator pedal and then the brake pedal, forcing the bus to leap forward in tiny leaps. He only did that on rare occasions when he was alone, mainly.

Finally, it was time to go. He had a schedule to keep, and people were depending on him. Looking left before he exited the sanctuary of the parking lot, he eased the giant bus out of its parking space and onto Ralph Avenue. He turned right onto Ralph Avenue and headed north. The trip went smoothly and uninterrupted and he reached Glenwood Road without having to stop for a light or anything.

The area, known as the Flatbush section, consisted of almost entirely one family houses, built on plots that were twenty feet wide and about eighty to one hundred feet deep. Not a lot of space. Houses were attached to one another, at least on one side, so they shared a common wall. They also shared driveways since there was generally speaking not enough space for each home to have its own driveway. The closeness amplified the neighborliness required for families to get along with one another in such close quarters.

The houses were well cared for, each having a small patch of land in front of them running towards the sidewalk. That passed for a lawn of which they were justifiably proud. Contrary to popular belief, there were trees planted along the way, large, old trees that created a country-like atmosphere in a teeming city. Brooklyn really had more than one tree.

Mostly white shingle, or stucco-covered, the houses created an aura of quiet comfort. It was generally speaking an Irish-American neighborhood, although several families of Italian descent lived among them and got along well. There were parks for kids to use swings and climbing bars, and wading pools. There was also the neighborhood club-the Farragut Pool, that provided welcome summer recreation and relief from the blazing summer sun.

The neighborhood was changing. The Irish-American families had children, most of whom attended the parochial school at St.Vincent Ferrer Church. As those kids grew into maturity, they went away to college, married and lived elsewhere. The community was aging and the neighborhood began to slowly yield to urban diversity, causing some white families to flee to real suburbia, possibly out of some fear.

Developers bought up some of the private houses along Newkirk Avenue, and, with city and state subsidies, developed the property assembled into high rise apartment housing, known as the Vanderveer Houses. Diversity accelerated. Now the neighborhood changed more quickly. The entire area was in flux and the influence of the parish, and the pastor, diminished, although parish events continued to be the center of life for a large number of the populace.

.

On Glenwood Road, Gawloski headed west toward East 52nd Street, where he knew his first passenger, at least, would be waiting for him. He was not to be disappointed. As he approached he could see a slight smile of recognition wind its way across her face. She was a largish black woman, Ella Perkins. She had been riding with him on this bus for several years, back and forth to her job at Kings County Hospital, where she worked in the hospital kitchen. She was the only person waiting at the bus stop, as usual.

Gawloski swung the bus into the bus stop area and the door slid open simultaneously with the stop. Ella Perkins managed with some difficulty to lift herself up the large steps toward the waiting farebox. Dropping her fare in the box, she paused to catch her breath and stared at the driver. "Last week, huh, Pat? We're gonna miss you on this run. It just won't be the same."

"Heck," Gawloski said back, sheepishly, "you'll fall in love with the next driver too. You young gals just love us guys in uniform." They both laughed. Ella Perkins' days as a young woman were long gone. The fifty plus years she had accumulated along with the added weight from years of over-indulgence, had taken her short, stocky frame well beyond the young woman stage. She was still laughing as she reached her seat. Only after she was safely seated did the bus start forward again.

Gawloski smiled to himself. There were many regular riders like Ella Perkins, who came on the bus for long or short runs to transfer points. Lots of them knew him and he liked them all. He was sure they were all aware of his pending retirement and he looked forward today to getting a lot of good wishes for health and happiness in whatever he decided to do.

There was a stop at East 48th Street, but nobody was there. He cruised along Glenwood Road to East 45th Street where he picked up two young male riders. They were strangers to him and didn't say much, just got on and walked to empty seats. Once in their seats, they seemed to fall asleep.

To his right, he could see the Farragut Pool, the neighborhood water hole, now quiet and empty at this early hour. Nobody stirring. There was another scheduled stop at East 40th Street but that also had no passengers waiting so Gawloski continued on.

He could see ahead to Brooklyn Avenue now, but not very clearly. At Brooklyn Avenue, he was due to make a left turn and head south to Kings Highway which he then followed west again until the end of his route, then turn around, and head back. Eight times each working day.

It was going to be kind of a rainy day and daylight had not quite manifested itself fully at 6:10 AM. He could see St. Vincent Ferrer Church coming up on his left at East 37th Street. Beyond the church, also on his left, was Monsignor Gately Auditorium, the modern building that served as an auxiliary church, a meeting hall and a basketball court for the parish youth. An example of Catholic economy--three buildings in one! There was almost no activity on the streets, nobody out walking yet.

Passing the church buildings, the traffic light at Brooklyn Avenue was now more clearly in his view. As his eyes scanned the horizon ahead, he could see something obstructing his lane of traffic, hanging down from the street lamp on the corner. The traffic light was red against him so he prepared to bring the bus to a stop.

As he peered more intently through his windshield, the obstruction came more clearly into focus. "Holy shit," he thought to himself. "Is that--is that a body hanging there.?" Then, within seconds, he exclaimed "Jesus Christ! It is a body. Ella!," he shouted... "come here! Is that a body I see hanging from that lampost?"

The large woman shuffled up out of her seat and towards the front of the bus. She could tell from Gawloski's exclamation that he was disturbed. By the time she reached the front where he was sitting, he was already bathed in sweat and little droplets were running off his balding head. She squatted slightly, like a frog on a lily pad, to look through the windshield, too.

"God damn, Pat," she shouted at him. "It is a body. God damn! That's awful. Hate to see crap like that. Damn," she repeated, obviously very disturbed at the sight. "What do we do about that? We can't just go right on and leave it there. Alone."

"I don't know what we're supposed to do. I don't know. Never had anything like this happen before. Not in almost forty years on the job." He looked at Ella, studying her face. She was sweating now, too. No answers came.

Finally, he said, “I guess we'd better call the cops. They should know what to do. I'll go call them.”

“Where you gonna get a phone to call from--right here at this hour?” Ella asked with a practical judgment.

“I'll go over to that dentist office back there, Dr. Senreich. He should be in there at this time. What do you think?”

“Hell no,” she answered stammering a little. “He won't be there now. You know doctors and dentists. They hardly work when they're supposed to nowadays.”

“Then I'll walk over to St. Vincent's Rectory up there,” pointing up on Brooklyn Avenue to his left. “Somebody ought to be up in there by now.”

“Good idea”, Ella agreed. “I'll go with you.”

“No,” Gawloski shot back excitedly. “You stay here with the bus.”

“Hell no! You're not gonna leave me here alone. I'm not staying here by myself, not with no dead body. No sir. No way,” Ella replied. “I'm goin' with ya. Let's get going.”

Outside the bus, they stood staring at the site of the limp body hanging from the lamppost. It was an awful sight. The head sloped over to one side with the neck obviously stretched and distorted. The face looked painful, it wore a grayish black beard and long unkempt hair. The body was robed in what looked like designer blue jeans, a t-shirt and a denim jacket, black shoes--hightops.

Those two looked like an odd couple, out there alone on the sidewalk in slowly coming dawn. He was a short stubby, chubby guy in a too small and grey uniform, shiny from constant wear around the seat area and partially down the legs, and her, bowlegged and waddling along beside him, trying to keep up as they walked toward the Church rectory.

Gawloski was still sweating profusely from nervousness when they reached the rectory door, she sweating from the briskness of the walk as well as the excitement.

Just as they reached the rectory door, about to ring the bell, the door opened and they stared straight ahead into the face of Monsignor Bates. The sudden shock of seeing people unexpectedly in front of him at that hour surprised him, too.

"Who are you two, and what do you want?" he asked, puzzled as well by the unusual nature of that couple, standing there before him, sweating and shivering with nervousness.

"I'm the bus driver, Pat Gawloski," Gawloski blurted out. "There's somebody hanging from the lamppost down there," he said pointing toward the intersection. "We don't know what to do so we came here, to call the police."

Monsignor Bates stepped out onto the small landing outside the door and turned to look down at the Brooklyn Avenue intersection. He was dumbfounded, too, at what he saw. "I'll be damned," he said. "It is somebody hanging from that post. That's an awful sight--if it really is a human body and not just a prank of one of those Brooklyn College fraternity kids. I'll go call the police. You two go back to the bus."

Relieved, Gawloski and Perkins turned to head back down to the bus. They went reluctantly, stepping slowly, as they wanted to spend as little time with that body as they could. Suddenly, Gawloski remembered the other two passengers on the bus. He felt he shouldn't have left them alone as he had done so he quickened his pace to get back. Perkins trailed behind him, not able to keep up as he moved out more rapidly. He needn't have worried, they were still asleep in their seats, oblivious to everything around them.

Once back in the bus, Gawloski and Perkins sat in passenger seats opposite one another as they waited. They were reluctant to even sneak a peek at the limp form hanging in front of the bus. Looking back, they saw the form of Monsignor Bates leave the rectory in great haste, the red pom-pom ball affixed to his four-cornered hat bobbing as he hurried along to be as 'on-time' as possible for the 6:30 Mass. His cassock, halfway open to the waist, flowed along behind him, reflecting his quick step. Only the red piping on the cassock marked his rank as monsignor and distinguished him from any other curate in the parish. He had done his job, summoning the police.

In what was only minutes but probably felt like a lot more, the police began to arrive. First it was a squad car with two uniformed officers inside. They stopped their car at the intersection corner and looked at the site through the windshield for a few minutes. Then, one got out and walked slowly over to the bus. He was a tall, lanky young man in his early thirties. He peered into the bus through the open door and talked to both Gawloski and Perkins. It didn't take long for him to realize they would offer little help to any investigation. He asked them to wait until the detectives arrived before he could let them go. They were happy with that thought of going on their way, away from there.

Now it was a police matter and they began to take charge with their customary aplomb. Another squad car quietly arrived, then another, then a private car with two plainclothes detectives inside. The intersection now was teeming with police and spectators began to accumulate along the sidewalks to watch with both horror and deep interest what was going on. It was a newsworthy event in that neighborhood.

Finally, a fire truck arrived and the firemen raised a ladder to the top of the lamppost and began the process of untying the rope that held the body and then lowering it down to the waiting policemen and medical personnel that had arrived from Kings County Hospital. Everybody looked efficient and worked together, albeit slowly, to bring the scene of horror to a close. The body lay on the roadway for a short while covered by a sheet with morning traffic slowly moving around it and the police cadre who were there. The drivers were rubbernecking, taking a look at what there was to be seen.

It was slightly after 7:30 when Gawloski and his bus with the three passengers inside were allowed to leave. The body was already down and the number of police cars had whittled down to two.

Once the scene was gone, Brooklyn Avenue returned to normal. Traffic moved well again, the spectators went home and pedestrians walked by, ignorant of the scene that had been there only a short while before, almost like it had never really been there, never really happened. They were on their way to the Flatbush Avenue Junction, to catch subway trains to their daily places of business. The city was like that, full of constant change. The routine of city life didn't have time for individual events. It was virtually insensitive.

Even the police treated the incident in a commonplace way. Of course, it was unusual for a body to be hung from a lamppost, but other than that, it was just one more murder in a city where murders seem to happen with regularity.

The police followed their routine which had evolved simply because of the seeming regularity of such events. The body was removed to the morgue at Kings County Hospital and a full autopsy performed. A record was made of the entire set of statistics to be derived from the study of that body. The brain was removed and weighed, its vital organs examined and swatches of blood were taken and coded.

These things and the report that included them indicated the deceased was a black male in his early to mid thirties. He weighed one hundred seventy two pounds, exactly, and had no marks or scars on him to indicate he had been beaten before he met his demise. He had been a heavy drug user.

His clothing was relatively nondescript but was sent over to the forensics lab at Police Headquarters for examination and study. The ropes that bound his hands and circled his neck were sent to forensics, too. The report concluded that death was attributable to strangulation or death by hanging, and came suddenly.

There was no mention of the incident in the Daily News, the Daily Mirror, or the New York Post, the city's most popular tabloids that ordinarily thrived on such news items. There were just too many of them for all of them to be newsworthy. The New York Times, primarily concerned with global, international and national news emanating from Washington, D.C., would never consider reporting on such a minor incident.

The police were left with the unhappy tasks of identifying the body and notifying the next of kin. It turned out the deceased was hardly a model citizen, having a track record of several run-ins with the police during his thirty-four years, and having spent three years as a guest of the state prison at Attica for drug related crimes. His name was Amar Jihadu, obviously a name that had been changed from the original when he became a follower of Allah.

Nevertheless, his mother, Berniece Gumbs, loved him, she said, and screamed at the police who brought her the news, demanding that his murderers be caught, tried and executed. The incident, though, was headed for the files of unsolved crimes, waiting for some clue that might come from forensics or be developed by some tangential investigation. It would have to be solved by some unexpected witness coming forward and that usually only happened after a long period of time had elapsed and the tip came from the investigation of another crime. Otherwise, it would languish there, unsolved.

7

If the police treated the Jihadu hanging lightheartedly, because it was apparently being a part of a routine drug incident, they didn't react similarly the next day. That morning, the precinct at Newkirk Avenue got a phone call at about 6:35AM informing the desk sergeant that another dead body was on display in public. This one was hanging upside down with a rope around its feet, dangling from the marquee of Ruiz Bodega on Avenue D and New York Avenue--same general area in Flatbush. But now the problem was widening and could no longer be dismissed lightly.

Chief Henry Garcia, Precinct Commander, was notified and he came speeding in from his home in Belle Harbor. He had grasped the significance of the notice immediately. He was hell-bent on putting a lid on whatever was going on as soon as he could, before it got even further out of hand. Two similar deaths, of unknown authorship, would certainly get the hot breath of both the print and TV media on his neck.

His first step was to make a personal plea for immediate assistance to the Medical Examiner's Office. Garcia wanted to know the details on the victim, personal details such as his name and age, so that he could get the detectives rolling in the proper direction right away. The Medical Examiner's Office wanted to be cooperative and promised quick results. Unfortunately, between the order to perform a prompt autopsy and the actual performance of it, the order received considerable civil service nonchalance and it didn't get underway until late that evening.

Garcia, meanwhile, had gotten other balls rolling. Patrolmen were sent out in the area trying to dig up anyone who had any information whatsoever on the event. After an exhausting search, they failed to turn up any witnesses or persons who had seen anything, significant or otherwise, that would shed even the slightest light on when and how it had happened. People seemed afraid, more than the usual unwillingness to help the police. The perpetrator, or perpetrators, had performed their deed in absolute secrecy, probably hidden by the darkness of the night, when most people were in bed. They were still unknown.

Garcia had much more luck once the body was identified. It turned out to be a thirty-eight year old black man with a long dossier of police involvement. One common thread noticeable at that early stage, was that he and the victim of the day before had both served hard time in the same prison at the same time. Could this be the common denominator police always look for when the *modus operandi*, (the "MO") fits the pattern of two or more similar incidents? The problem had now definitely taken on racial lines, so his first thought that it was a race war was a distinct possibility to be part of the motivation. However, that possibility was problematical because it did enlarge the group of persons from whom suspects would have to be pulled.

If anything, Garcia was determined to confine this incident to the Flatbush locality. He had high hopes that heavy police reaction would impact whoever was involved and terminate any further activity. To that end, he huddled with his detectives, trying to impress upon them the importance of prompt investigation activity involving the public. He wanted the actions of the police to be highly visible and well-known, increasing the likelihood that fear of detection and arrest would hinder any consideration of further activity, if any such additional activity might have been planned.

The detectives assigned to the incident were senior people, veterans of over fifty combined years of police work. They had paid their dues and were well schooled in the ways of the streets and the activities of drug dealers, prostitutes and thieves, either those driven to burglaries and crimes to support their drug habits, or those who needed no additional motivation to commit crimes. They were the so-called 'naturals'.

Nevertheless, even these concentrated and well-publicized efforts turned up nothing useful. Forensics and the autopsies had added little to the body of knowledge about the crimes, although they were helpful on personal material about the victims. This latest one was named Pierre Toussant. He had emigrated from Haiti over twenty years before. He and his family had almost immediately drifted into the welfare routine and received their sustenance over the years from various government programs.

He left a wife and three children but he had been separated from them for several years. In fact, the wife expressed no surprise or grief when told about his death, saying it was expected sooner or later. She went on to describe a physically abusive husband, more often than not under the influence of drugs with a very expensive habit. She described a man, sometimes desperate for money to buy drugs that he seemed to badly need. She knew he had been in prison for a while, had committed crimes and was still doing them. Often when the need was greatest, he would show up at the house and physically beat her to get whatever money she had. He was a dirty, vile guy and she was not at all sorry he had died.

Toussant's mother, on the other hand, described a loving son, one who was always faithful to his family and good to them. His problems with the law were on trumped-up charges, the usual anti-black stuff, designed only to punish someone-anyone-without trying to find out who the actual culprit should have been. His prison time was an injustice, but, she said, he never lost faith in the system. When confronted with the wife's description, the mother simply dismissed her comments, saying she was an unfaithful tramp and that the last two children were not fathered by her son. Naturally, the mother was in extreme grief over the news of Pierre's death and wanted justice--total, complete justice, but doubted the police really cared enough to do that. "After all," she said, "it's just another black man killed. They don't mean nuthin' to you guys."

8

Chief Garcia now knew he faced a major dilemma. He had two murders, finished off in grotesque style, but almost with the same MO. He had done all he could to keep the media from creating their typical frenzy over something like that and, for all he knew, he had succeeded. Nothing had been mentioned in either of the daily papers or on the television news. He did worry, though, that sending out all those uniformed police into the neighborhood to try to track down any evidence or information at all was likely to raise some political or media eyebrows. That was a chance he had to take, and did. He was disappointed that effort had turned up nothing, and he called it off.

Now, he would have to solve those crimes through dogged police work. He thought there were several possibilities. It could be a race war; after all, both victims were black. The fact that the MO's were essentially the same didn't rule that out since one side could simply begin answering the other with the same dose of medicine.

Then there was the possibility that it was a drug war. The area surrounding the location of the bodies was a heavy drug scene, producing lots of neighborhood complaints. Drug lords were well-known to jealously guard their turf, and could be sending a message to other drug prospectors to stay away from their base of operations.

There was also the possibility that some nut was on the loose, taking out his frustrations on whoever he located at the time he was ready to kill. That could be the worst of all scenarios because those people walked the streets almost unaware that they had done anything wrong. They melted into normal society and didn't stand out until caught in the act. If that was the case here, the murderer would have to be a very cautious person, acting without witnesses in the dead of night. That was an unlikely scenario here, because the weight of the bodies and their presentation to the public would require almost superhuman strength on the part of such a person. Not likely.

There was always the possibility of vigilante efforts, citizens acting on their own after dissatisfaction with police efforts, to rid a community of a dangerous and spreading evil. That would provide the strength needed to lift and place the bodies where they were, since more than one person would be involved. This neighborhood had generated many complaints against drug activities at the Junction, especially of late, and the residents had been very vocal and, occasionally, angry. However, the neighborhood was a relatively tranquil one, consisting mostly of private houses and religious families, and was mostly crime free except for drug related or sponsored crimes.

Of all the possible scenarios, Chief Garcia favored a race war theory. Racial confrontations occur frequently, an almost never-ending saga of cultures trying to live among one another. As a Hispanic himself, he was aware of the pushes and pulls of daily life in the area where he worked and around his home in Belle Harbor. He readily noted the different manner in which he was treated when he appeared in regular street clothes as opposed to in his uniform. It was also a fact that fast food establishments in purely black areas didn't want to serve non-blacks, a sort of holding together, one for all, type of demeanor. Since racial events were more common, he felt that scenario was the more likely.

Analyzing the situation thusly, he began to formulate a methodology of attack to dig out information and solve the crimes before the situation got too far out of hand. He was too late.

The very next day, the third in a row, a body was discovered lying in the gutter at Farragut Road and Rogers Avenue. This one wasn't hung but it was trussed up in a wrap of rope, suggesting a similar

MO and leading to the conclusion that a gang was involved and the message was clear—to someone.

This body was a young black man, in his late thirties, and of almost nondescript character. Except for identification found in his wallet, there was nothing else they could find to uncover any information about him quickly. Later efforts would determine that he was a heavy drug user and an occasional salesman of drugs, but was only at the inception or beginning of that phase of his life. He had a record of police confrontations and some short jail terms, mainly as an end user of drugs and having them found in his possession when stopped for suspicious activities. As far as the police knew, he left no next of kin to notify and was not known to have been married or to have fathered any children. He was almost a phantom.

This event did produce the repercussions that Chief Garcia feared. The call first came from police headquarters, from a Chief Marsh who served both as division chief, and as a liaison between the police and the black and Hispanic communities.

"Henry," the Captain began, "I hear things are happening out in your command. What's going on? What is all this stuff about three killings?"

"Wendy," Chief Garcia began, "I don't have much to go on just yet, but it's a real problem. I've had investigations going but so far haven't turned up anything. There've been bodies found every morning for the last three days. As far as I can tell, the activities take place during the middle of the night and nobody seems to have any information to help us, not even a little. We've had all-night prowl cars cruising the neighborhood, but nothing. We're stumped thus far, if I have to admit it."

"I know some of what you're up against," Captain Marsh said. " When I was in charge of the three five two, we had a similar situation, a little like it, anyway. The MO's weren't as consistent as you seem to have, but there was some organized effort going on to achieve some purpose. It seemed to be racial, too. Is yours a racial matter?"

"It could be," Garcia replied. "There's some indication it is and we're actually working on that theory. We're pursuing the investigation just as if it is a racial thing. You know, I don't have to tell ya, those things get out of hand quickly, and call down all sorts of political problems for the boys in blue. I don't want that to happen here."

"Neither do I," Marsh came back. "Do you think you can control the situation, just a little?"

"I'm doing what I can to do just that," Garcia replied somewhat testily. "There's only so much I can do to control it but I'm investigating the hell out of it. I'll get some clues, I hope, pretty soon. This is a big item out here in Brooklyn, and a great many people must be involved, especially if it's a two-sided war. Somebody has to stumble, sooner or later."

"I hope it's sooner. I know the commissioner knows about it and will want to be kept fully informed. Once this hits the news media, it'll be all over everywhere. Then there'll be a lot of pressure to find someone."

"You don't have to tell me that--I know. What do you think has been my biggest worry? The victims aren't much in the way of model citizens, so we haven't lost a lot from that point of view, but they are dead bodies, and the public gets all excited about that. I know all about that stuff. The way they've been served up would make a big wad of grist for the media mill."

They ended the conversation with the promise to stay in touch. Garcia adjusted his position in the chair nervously. He was sweating a little and could feel the hot seat he was sitting on. He pondered his options. He knew he had to do *something* fast, something calculated to produce some results. When the media blitz hit, all hell would break loose and he needed answers for them. The routine police

work had sort of failed him to date, and he had to consider other options. He needed someone who could dig into the facts here and turn up some clues on which to base some action, someone sort of special, a tenacious, determined policeman.

Now that headquarters was involved, he knew he could count on them for special assignments if he could decide what he needed. As he turned over in his mind the names of policemen and detectives he knew as he came through the ranks, he realized that the vast majority of them had retired. They had felt left out in the cold, stymied in the possibility of promotions as the force conceived its obligation to promote women and minorities to positions those others would have gotten in the regular course of events. The department had lost a lot through that commitment but it was the public policy and the department had to respect that. Recognizing that didn't make it any easier for Garcia to figure out his options on what to do, who, if anybody, to select. There weren't many choices.

9

Tony Monteverdi seemed to be just the right man for the job. He was an experienced police officer, having worked his way through a multitude of assignments to the gold shield of detective. From his beginning days as a beat patrolman on foot in the Bay Ridge area of Brooklyn, he had wanted to establish himself and his reputation as the consummate cop, one who took nothing that could possibly be considered a bribe, a payola, or anything that he could be criticized for. He never even accepted so much as a free cup of coffee from overwilling restauranteurs on his patrol during the cold days of Brooklyn winters.

Whatever he did, it seemed to work. Precinct commanders he worked under held him in high esteem, some almost worshipping his work habits that so clearly distinguished him from his peers. As the near perfect policeman, he garnered the best of assignments as the years passed. Whenever anyone was requested from City Hall or Headquarters for a special assignment with dignitaries or celebrities, it was Tony Monteverdi who led the group from his precinct. The oddest thing was, he was so well respected, that the others didn't seem to be jealous or to even expect to compete for those high profile assignments.

Soon, he was being requested by name for those tasks. His reputation grew, not only for 'cleanliness,' but also for his willingness to take on difficult assignments and to accomplish them quickly and well. He had become the cop's cop. He was transferred to headquarters and promoted to detective sergeant. The rank helped a lot, but mostly economically, since the raise it carried allowed him and his wife to live better, to take vacations, and to enjoy life a little more. The new police duties did not allow for relaxation, though.

During the late fifties,the drug trade had begun to flourish in the United States and, of course, in New York City. Monteverdi well knew that his work habits and his honesty would eventually earn him promotions to higher rank and status. He also knew, though, that progress along that path would be slow and limited. To reach the real lofty elevations in the police department hierarchy, and progress quickly, he would have to distinguish himself in the actual tough, day to day, street crime activities for which patrolmen won citations and awards, and occasionally received publicity. Rising through the ranks as he was doing, would be acceptable, but too slow, and he was aiming for that loftier status of Inspector, Deputy Commissioner, and even possibly Commissioner, if things fell his way and he played his political cards right.

To achieve that, he would have to enlist in the street crime war, 'earn his stripes' as they say. He had long ago talked frankly and openly to a detective named Mulligan, who Monteverdi looked upon as somewhat of a mentor.

Mulligan had established his reputation as a hard-nosed guy and had volunteered into the anti-drug arm of the NYPD. He was so tough, he quickly rose to be the head of the unit, small as it was in those days of its infancy. But Mulligan was good and he was able to assess the strategies of the drug dealers and their methods of distribution. He learned to distinguish the meaningful drug dealers from the users who were forced to do just about anything to maintain their habit.

As drug use increased, so, too, did crime. Mulligan was the first policeman to establish that crime, drugs and money went hand-in-hand. Stop drugs and you would lower the crime rate, but you couldn't cut off the money. He worked hard and deliberately to halt the drug trade but he eventually came to realize it would not ever happen, at least on his watch, or in his lifetime. It was a losing battle.

He saw that there was so much money in that drug trade, it would operate to infiltrate even the most honest of drug warriors. He began to take notice of the types and frequencies of the arrests being made. He could see that at most, only medium to low level operatives were being collared. Most of the arrests were made of the end users of the drugs, the real druggies, who were caught in petty crimes they pulled to get money to fund their habit. They were the dumb ones, too, those who didn't know that drug money was easily within their reach through liberal government largesse, by just signing a few forms--through Social Security Disability. The big guys, and their international suppliers, always seemed just beyond reach, and could, would and did buy off any threat to their operation. He could not in good conscience join them, so he did the next best thing.

Mulligan theorized he could never beat them entirely. Too much money bought too much protection from all levels of government operation. Without government at all levels fully engaged in the anti-drug war, there could be no final victory. Even with that, only on a state or city level, victory would be highly unlikely, too. He worked with the system and actually did arrange large drug busts. They garnered heavy publicity. It was all to please the public, the public that was paying huge sums for salaries and pensions to its anti-drug army.

It worked and worked even better with law enforcement. District attorneys reveled in the announcements of drug busts. They routinely displayed huge cakes of heroin and other drugs to the TV media and the newspapers to feed the public craving for action, and the media's ravenous hunger for news they could photograph. The district attorneys always made well-publicized announcements of these events. They translated the captured drugs into street values to inflate the number tremendously. That created the impression they had put a huge crimp into the drug cartels' ability to function, in the near future anyway. It worked to some extent. The public was fooled, but the events actually meant little.

The district attorneys received the glaring publicity they craved. They would benefit from that publicity, having their names be well known, a useful tool when they tried to climb to higher elective office. The police and detectives, Mulligan among them, benefited too. Awards were doled out liberally and citations awarded for what was called 'outstanding' police work. Everybody connected with those operations saw some benefit and the public believed they were winning the war on drugs. But the cartels knew better.

Knowing it could not be ended, Mulligan worked as best he could within the system. Year after year the frustration worked its toll on him and he began to show his age in the job. He began to look for a possible successor so he could retire, confident the war would go on, with at least someone holding his finger in the dike. Monteverdi would be his man.

He impressed on Tony Monteverdi that only continued success, such as it was, in the drug war could provide a meteoric ride to the top. Routine police work, no matter how many criminals you collared, or murders you solved, could never provide the magic carpet for the ride to the highest levels Monteverdi aspired to, and Mulligan spoke about. And Monteverdi listened, and Monteverdi believed.

Before long, Tony Monteverdi was transferred to the anti-drug unit. Being fair skinned, he was never considered seriously for the dangerous undercover activities the unit carried on regularly. Entire squads of policemen went under cover to arrange for sting operations and to infiltrate the channels of the drug trade. That trade naturally crossed all lines of criminals, from new entrepreneurs trying to get rich on a new product, to the mafia operatives who muscled their way into all aspects of crime, including, of course, drugs.

Monteverdi operated almost exclusively on the tail end of the sting operations. On prearranged signals, he would lead a group of plainclothes officers, badges gleaming from their chests, into the bowels of the underworld warehouses, seizing packaged drugs and caches of currency. His face became a fixture on the evening news, standing off in the background as the district attorneys proudly displayed the results of the police stings, as if they had done them themselves.

Monteverdi became a well-known cop. He received decoration after decoration and after a while seemed to be the most decorated officer on the force. Now he was in the big time he always had wanted. Now he could make it pay for him in lots of ways, not only those that were legal.

Drug wars were common as drug lords battled over turf, to sell their wares to more and more people, concentrating on neighborhoods where the kids could afford the habit, at least in the beginning. As one drug lord's activities spilled over onto the turf of another, actual wars would take place. Murders and beatings became commonplace in their societies. It seemed that whenever a drug lord was killed in a shootout with police, the officer who acted as the triggerman was Monteverdi. Sometimes it wasn't so clear the victim was a drug lord, and maybe they were 'connected' some other way. Nobody really knew, and fewer even cared.

Then there were the never-ending rumors about the huge drug bust and shootout Monteverdi had been involved in a few years back, that had gone horribly bad. It was a real pitched battle, with guns being fired back and forth by the cartel goons and the police. The shootout began as the police advanced trying to help one of their own who had been in a parked car waiting for the signal to go in to help on the bust. The car had been blown up, bursting into consuming red flames, and the cop inside incinerated. The rumors were that the bust squad arrived late, or got the signal to advance late, or that there was some tipoff or other fix involved, and left the dead cop exposed, all alone. There was something always fishy about Monteverdi's role in the delay in giving the signal, some suspecting he had conflicting loyalties, or some other reason nobody could come up with. The bust had been a bust for many reasons.

Chief Garcia had heard all these rumors about Monteverdi, but couldn't come up with a bigger or better name otherwise. Garcia knew the media would believe he meant business in solving these murders on the mere mention that Monteverdi had been put in charge of the investigation. His was a name they knew, and respected as a tough law enforcement person, and they would be satisfied then. He dialed Marsh and asked that Monteverdi be assigned to his precinct for the investigation. He got his wish.

10

Tony Monteverdi had learned his lessons well. In his first interview with Chief Garcia, he sensed correctly that Garcia feared most of all the involvement of the media. It was not uncommon for a person in Garcia's position to wish for tranquil times throughout his precinct leadership career, hoping to have violent crime stay at a minimum, and certainly to avoid high profile cases. He realized that Garcia feared the three murders discovered in the unusual positions they were could be the high profile sensation he so much wanted to avoid. Such notoriety could propel him and his command into a spotlight they could not endure, from which they could not, under any circumstances, escape unscathed in department thinking.

In recognizing this, Monteverdi knew he had the elements of a very good position from which to work his magic, whatever it was. He had the unconditional loyalty of his chief, on whom he could count for unlimited support. It was a very good situation for him, one from which he could achieve great things for himself as well as the department. He was just the man for that job. He did not consider himself stuck with the chief's theory that the killings were the result of a racial war. He had an open book, and mind, and would proceed to dissect the available information and measure it against all patterns.

The neighborhood was the key, he thought. "Someone in this neighborhood has his ear to the street, knows what's going on, and can be of enormous help," he thought. "I just have to find that person, or persons." Walking the streets from Newkirk Avenue south to Avenue J, taking in the entire cosmos of stores and houses of all types, he quietly admitted to himself he had taken on a formidable task. There were stores of all kinds typically found in residential neighborhoods,--candy stores, hardware stores, travel agents, real estate offices, restaurants, and doctors and lawyers of course. There were two churches that served the area, Little Flower Church that was located on Avenue D, and St. Vincent Ferrer Church located on East 37th Street and Glenwood Road. The area was predominantly Catholic so the churches could be the key.

Monteverdi decided to try to enlist the pastors of both churches to help him ferret out information that would be helpful. He decided to call on Monsignor Bates at St. Vincent Ferrer Church first. Monsignor Bates was almost shocked when Monteverdi called on him. "I don't know if I can be of any help," Monsignor Bates said. "If I can be of assistance to the police and bring an end to this very strange crime wave, I'll be happy to help, within my clerical limitations, of course."

"Of course," Monteverdi replied quietly. As the two of them sat in the coolness of the rectory receiving room, they were almost forced by the quietness of the building to speak in hushed tones. "I understand, completely," he said. "I would never ask you to violate any confidences or your clerical privilege. If you ever think that anything I ask you will in any way require you to do that, just tell me and I'll back off. I intend to respect your collar in every way. Don't hesitate to tell me if you just *think* it might require that type of disclosure."

"Good," Monsignor Bates answered, somewhat relieved, but still wondering just what might be asked of him.

"I understand the bus driver and a passenger reported to you that the death had occurred, that there was a body hanging from a lamppost at the Brooklyn Avenue intersection. Why did they come to you?"

"I don't really know," the Monsignor replied. "It was early in the morning and perhaps they didn't know what to do otherwise. I just don't know."

"Did you know either of those people before that day?"

"No. I had never seen either of them before. They weren't parishioners here as far as I know. They were both terrified, I could tell. They were sweating profusely and spoke very nervously. I guess it became clear they were looking for access to a telephone to call the police. It was early in the morning. They asked me to do that, and I did."

"Did they hang around, or go back to the bus?"

"I guess they went back to the bus. I saw them walk in that direction. I was just coming out of the rectory when they rang the bell. I was surprised by a visit at that hour and had coincidentally just started to open the door when they rang. We all seemed surprised to see the other. I hadn't even heard the bell yet. I was on my way to celebrate the 6:30AM Mass. When I left the church after Mass, there were several police cars at the intersection, the body was down and possibly gone but the bus was still there. I didn't go up there to see myself what was going on then."

Monteverdi shifted in his chair. He didn't know where to go from here, what he should or could ask the Monsignor next. He had gotten nothing of any significance but had at least started a dialogue that could blossom into something helpful later on. Shifting uneasily, Monteverdi asked, "Father, is there anybody in this neighborhood who serves, you know, like a neighborhood ombudsman, sort of a person who touches lots of lives of the people?"

"Well, there's the doctors and dentists who come in contact with a lot of people. You could try them. They might be helpful in some way. I don't really know how, or what you'd expect from such people, but you could try."

"Is there anybody else?" Monteverdi asked. "I've been told lots of the kids in this neighborhood get into little legal scrapes. Who do they go to for help? That might be a better person to contact if there aren't too many of them."

The Monsignor stroked his chin and pondered the question. Finally, he began, "There is a local lawyer who probably represented most of the kids around here when they got into any kind of trouble. He might be just the one for you to talk to. He's probably got his ear to the ground far more than I do, and far more, probably, than the doctors and dentists around here. Almost everybody knows more about the area than I do. I'm relatively new here."

"Who would that be, Monsignor?" Monteverdi asked.

"Go see a lawyer down towards the Junction, on Glenwood Road and Nostrand Avenue. His name is Willie Mitchell. He does most of the law business around here. I dare say he's closed all the sales and purchases of homes around here in the last ten years or so and probably has a huge will business from parishioners. He's a pretty good guy, and very well connected politically. He's in the Holy Name Society and his wife is a big shot in the Rosary Society. It wouldn't hurt for you to get to know him anyway. I'm sure he'll want to be helpful."

"Thanks, Monsignor," Monteverdi gushed. "That could be a good idea. Even if he just represented some of the kids, he might know something about what's going on around here. Thanks a lot."

"From what I hear, most people around here think it's a drug war. You don't think it's anything different than that, do you?"

"Probably not," Monteverdi shrugged and got up to leave. It was apparent Monsignor Bates was relieved the interview was over. He wanted Monteverdi to leave, but now he had a double reason. He wanted badly to call Willie Mitchell and give him a 'heads up' that Monteverdi might be dropping by. "Nothing wrong with keeping your fences mended," he thought.

Out on the street, Monteverdi stopped to ponder what he had gotten from the interview. He had not progressed at all with any tangible clues to the problem, but he might have gotten a new and better source of information to search out.

Contrary to what Monsignor Bates had thought, Monteverdi did not directly head for Mitchell's office. Instead, thinking it might be better to have the parishes on his side first, he headed for the Rectory of Little Flower Parish on Avenue D. There, he was to be disappointed. Father Bruno, a priest who had come to the United States from Sicily, wasn't used to the police dropping in to see him. Despite being in this country for over ten years, he still had the basic Sicilian distrust of the police and avoided contact with them as much as possible.

Also, he still had a difficult time with the English language and so used it sparingly. As a result, his interview with Monteverdi was a string of one word answers, mostly 'yes' or 'no' and sometimes just a shake of his head. It was clear to Monteverdi the priest was very uncomfortable and determined not to be overly-cooperative. The interview trudged along in this disappointing way in spite of Monteverdi using what little Italian he knew and constantly referring to the two of them as *paisanos*. Father Giuseppe Bruno didn't see it that way.

It was nearing four o'clock now. The sun was starting to slip beyond the treetops, making its way toward the horizon, heading west. Monteverdi thought he could at least drop by Mitchell's office to start the ball rolling. He had struck out in both places so far really, but more so at Little Flower from which he had gained nothing. He desperately wanted to report some progress to Chief Garcia if he could, but so far no such luck. Maybe Mitchell was going to be the answer.

Pulling his unmarked police car into a parking spot next to a fire hydrant, Monteverdi then pulled down the sun visor to reveal his status as a detective on a card attached to it. He was right in front of

Mitchell's office and he could see some activity in there. Entering, he was surprised to find Mitchell inside, working away on something that required large mounds of paper. Mitchell looked up from his work as Monteverdi entered, and asked whether he could be of help.

Monteverdi answered pleasantly. "Hello. I'm Detective Monteverdi from the Newkirk Avenue Precinct. I'm assigned to investigating some dead bodies that have been discovered around here. I thought you might be able to help me a little. OK?"

"Sure. Come in," Mitchell said. "I'll do whatever I can. I've heard about them. Awful things. I've seen hordes of police combing the area and asking just about everybody if they knew or saw anything. They had even come in here. I wasn't much help to them and neither was my secretary out there in front."

"Well, you know," Monteverdi said, "you might not think you have anything that'll be of help but you might just know something anyway. I understand you represent a lot of the families around here from time to time. Do you?"

"Sure I do," Mitchell answered. "That's the skin and bones of a neighborhood law practice. You have to be available for all sorts of things,--closings, wills, accident cases--we even sell insurance."

Monteverdi and Mitchell discussed the events surrounding the murders and the probable cause for them. Both seemed to latch onto the easy and plausible theory that it was a war between drug lords, probably minor ones, over the turf of Flatbush. It was a relatively new area for drug sales and was probably coveted by the drug dealers, both men and women, who sold their wares in that general location. Those people knew that profits meant cash in their pockets and people would stop at nothing to protect their monopoly over the territory.

Mitchell was not as forthcoming as Monteverdi had hoped. Relying on professional ethics, he refused to give any names of people he had represented but suggested Monteverdi could use his easy access to court records to look up what he needed. Mitchell did not think it would be of any help to him because he thought, like Monteverdi, that it was a war between drug lords over turf and did not directly involve the neighborhood residents.

Monteverdi was puzzled. After leaving Mitchell's office, he sat for some time in his car at the curb, trying to fathom the problem. He understood that police theory was that the incidents were drug crimes, probably between drug dealers, and would have to be solved or stopped that way, by the participants themselves. He pondered his next step.

Instead of driving away, he left his car there and walked to the Junction. He had hoped to find some obvious drug dealers he could question about the events, hoping to turn up some fresh leads or even some evidence. To his surprise, he found the area virtually abandoned by the drug dealers. There were none to be found and his efforts only turned up a few frightened young people who were in the vicinity, probably trying to make a 'buy' for their own use. It was not his day. Nevertheless, the absence of drug activity meant something, and it stuck in his mind as a fact to be remembered for later use. It confused him.

11

Then a fourth body was discovered. Like the others it was trussed up, mummy style, and this time suspended from the overhead canopy of the subway entrance at the Flatbush Avenue Junction. This body, though, was suspended horizontally by ropes tied to both its head and feet so that it sagged in the middle. That created a block over the entrance, an awful sight for its discoverers.

The perpetrator had become more brazen and creative, suspending the body in that way and in such a public area. Once again it appeared to have been done in the dead of night, swiftly and quietly, with no apparent witnesses.

Similarly, the body turned out to be a black man in his early forties, one who had a police record for drug arrests and convictions. His prison terms were short but he had sort of made the rounds of the available prison sites throughout New York State. He had fathered children by at least four different women, none of whom he had married. And he had AIDS. Except for the fact it numbered four among the deaths that had turned up in that general area, his passing was hardly of note and he would not likely be missed by any relatives or society in general.

Chief Garcia's worst fears had come to pass. This body had been discovered by one of the attendants at Kings County Hospital as she left for work that Monday morning. A huge black woman, she had tried to duck under the suspended body but couldn't quite make it. She shoved the suspended corpse upward to get more room and a hand and forearm fell out through an opening in the canvas. She stumbled back, fainted and fell onto the sidewalk. Several others were hurrying to their jobs behind her. A slight melee ensued as they tripped and stumbled trying to get around her and under the suspended body before anyone thought to sort it out, and order of a sort was restored.

But the damage had been done. Someone made a hurried call to the police, and one of the stringers for the press on duty there, gave out the information. In minutes, the subway entrance area had been roped off and was swarming with police and police cars, circulating lights blazing away. It made an eerie sight in the usually calm morning and before long TV reporters and their cameramen were jostling for position to provide a good backdrop to their story.

The daily commuters, typical New Yorkers, were unimpressed and gestured and cursed openly, complaining of this temporary interruption in their daily schedules. Now they had to walk several blocks back to the other Flatbush Avenue subway station to get to work. New Yorkers pride themselves on being stoic in the face of disasters, and this case was no different. Except for the complaints of inconvenience, they didn't seem fazed by the human event that had just taken place.

Chief Garcia was fazed, though, and upset. Now he was besieged by police brass descending upon him in person and over the phone. At the same time he had to handle the constant inquiries of a media that had now become energized by the fresh smell of a hot story in their own backyard. The media was in a feeding frenzy, pointing fingers already at the police because of their seemingly having covered up the story on the other bodies without letting them in on it. The media was almost always concerned about their getting a story more than the public's right to know, the constitutional 'right' they flaunted publicly whenever they weren't clued in on something.

Garcia's office in the precinct house was an untidy affair, not decorated with any flair whatsoever. The fading lime green paint on the walls gave the atmosphere an air of decay. It was not helped by the pattern of official directives and handwritten notes pasted on the wall with scotch tape. The room was dark, too, appeared dingy, and smelled of stale air.

The room now was crowded with media types and police brass clamoring for answers from the chief who sat behind his desk, obviously uncomfortable, but straining to maintain control of things. The room hummed with a buzz of half-whispered exchanges between both sides.

Near Garcia stood the division chief, a large man dressed in a uniform that must have fit him several years ago, before nature and a more sedentary lifestyle took its toll. The chief, an Irishman named Wendel Marsh, with a ruddy complexion and facial skin that looked like a road map with small veins running all over, stood mainly silent. He nodded from time to time to help Chief Garcia by providing directions.

The questions came fast and furious, too fast to give much of an answer. Even worse, the questions were not connected to one another although they covered the same general topic. They were shouted out and seemingly all at one time in harmony with one another. Garcia had a difficult time selecting one question from the drone to answer. Finally, the telephone rang and Chief Garcia reached for it hurriedly, happy to get some relief from the pressing newsmen, at least for a while. He held his finger in his right ear as he listened intently to the caller, answered "sure, sure," several times before hanging up.

He then stood up behind the desk, facing his adversaries and gestured for quiet. "There's gonna be a press conference at headquarters at four o'clock today. You should alert your superiors so they can make arrangements to attend. It will begin at four, sharp. They will need credentials to get in, the usual stuff will do. I'm instructed to end this little meeting now. I'm sorry but I will not take any more questions." He turned to look and the burly Marsh was smiling. He was happy, too, for that moment anyway.

12

Bill McKenna had come up the hard way. Born into an Irish immigrant family, he was taught the ethics of always working hard, being loyal to your employer, and being honest and faithful to your church, above all. His father had supported him and his eight brothers and sisters while holding down many different jobs, always seeming to be the odd man out whenever layoffs came around. The depression of 1929 that dragged on through the thirties hurt people on the lower end of the social spectrum the most.

His father knew little of politics or economics. He just knew he needed a paycheck to bring home to pay the rent and minimal living expenses of the family. All he knew about politics was encapsulated in three words—Franklin Delano Roosevelt. As the national economic tailspin continued and dragged on, FDR's name became almost that of a deity around the home. There was a photo of FDR above the table where they ate their simple meals. He was a constant presence in their discussions and the senior McKenna would curse the opponents of FDR as "ungrateful bastards."

Getting that paycheck wasn't always easy. Many times the family had to subsist on baked beans on bread and use lard to make sandwiches that were mostly ketchup sandwiches anyway. The family was doing good when peanut butter or apple butter replaced the ketchup. Mostly, though, he was able to find work as a janitor in the skyscrapers that adorned lower Manhattan, or as a street sweeper for the City of New York. Occasionally, he would have to sign on to work on a WPA project, but that required him to stay in billets away from the family. He didn't like that.

From these circumstances, Bill McKenna resolved that he would climb the social ladder. Education, he thought, would be the means of locomotion through the social strata. Early on, he showed considerable promise as a student, and he took advantage of the accessible options available to him. He ran track in Trinity High School and excelled. The priests at Trinity fastened onto him as a possible future somebody, and suggested he could obtain a college scholarship through track at the Jesuit school, Georgetown College in Washington, D.C. He would be furthering his formal education through the talents the good Lord had bestowed upon him.

Since that suggestion came from the rectory, his father thought very well of it. It had the imprimatur of the church on it, so it had to be good. Ordinarily, he would have had to leave school at an early age and earn a living for himself while helping out the family. He would be different, though, his father thought. His case was an exception and the Almighty had almost signaled it himself by helping young Bill discover this natural talent and express it so well. Once the decision was made, the family, through the Trinity High priests, pursued the Georgetown possibility with great fervor. Finally, one day, the mail contained a letter offering him the scholarship they so coveted.

Washington D.C. was an impressive place, even back then in the early forties. Not knowing much about politics-local, national or global-he was stunned as millions of others were when Japanese naval forces bombed Pearl Harbor, Hawaii to start World War II. He wanted to enlist immediately, to help win the war, but his father thought the McKenna family would make the contribution required of any one family through the service of his four brothers. He was urged to stay on and finish his schooling.

Military needs dictated that many servicemen obtain background training at colleges and universities. Georgetown was no exception and the school was suddenly flooded with servicemen. However, the war had taken a great number of the young men who were otherwise available for jobs in the government. Bill found himself

being encouraged to take a position after school hours at the Congress, to help out with government requirements. He did, and caught on with a relatively young and obscure congressman from Texas, Lyndon B. Johnson.

This was a man who worked unlimited hours and constantly harangued his staff, Bill among them, to do more, and more. Bill's studies were neglected as a result, and his grades began to suffer. Since he spent more and more time in the halls of Congress and less and less at the school, his track activities also were neglected. He was in danger of losing his scholarship. When he mentioned this to the congressman, somehow a letter got through to the school authorities and the pressure was eased. He continued to receive his scholarship, track activities were suspended and, even though he did not increase his efforts at study or attendance at school, his marks improved. He carefully noted, then and there, the magic of political intervention.

When he graduated from Georgetown in June 1944, the war was still going on, but now the United States was plowing forward to victory. The D-Day landings were a huge success and the German Army was in full retreat, a defeated and undisciplined mob. The War was almost finished in Germany and the activity in the Far East against the Japanese Empire accelerated. McKenna was due to be drafted since his deferment had ended, and he actually looked forward to it. Congressman Johnson, now fully enamored with this young man from New York, wouldn't hear of him just entering service as a buck private. Instead, the congressman maneuvered an appointment for McKenna with the Office of Secret Service, the mysterious OSS, the hidden intelligence unit of the country. McKenna again took note of the subtle magic of political power.

He never went into military service and did next to nothing with the OSS, but it would forever give his resume a definite mystique. In later years, people would often ask him about his service with the OSS and he would politely decline to say anything, claiming top secret confidentiality. Following that brief tenure, he returned

to the safe haven of Johnson's office as Johnson was preparing a run for the United States Senate seat from Texas. He was up against a clear favorite local Texan, "Coke" Stevenson, a former governor of the state, whose name was a household fixture, while Johnson was relatively unknown. To top it off, Johnson's guiding light, President Roosevelt had died that April and his successor, President Truman, himself an unabashed and crude Missourian, couldn't abide this crude, impolite Texas cowboy.

Nevertheless, Johnson was as confident as ever and worked long and tiring hours in the campaign. At the end, it came down to some locked polling boxes in southern Texas to be counted. They were deposited in the ballot boxes in an area that would have ordinarily gone for Johnson's opponent strongly, but strangely, when they were counted, they tipped the election scale to Johnson. McKenna played a huge role in that "counting" process and Johnson felt he was forever indebted to him.

The career of a native New Yorker with a Senator from Texas was somewhat limited. Johnson, therefore, procured an appointment for McKenna with the New York State Investigation Commission, using the local Democrat Party connections he had, the Democrats being virtually unbeatable in New York City elections.

One day, a shy and retiring auditor with the commission came to McKenna with the startling results of his nursing home industry audits. The nursing homes were supported by State funds, mainly to provide free care for indigent New Yorkers. That occurred on the Labor Day weekend while McKenna was the only assistant commissioner available over the holiday. McKenna understood what it was, and immediately sensed he had the springboard to greater things by using this scandal as much as possible.

Even though it was a holiday weekend, he scheduled a press conference immediately for that Friday. He announced the scandal for what it was, a theft of taxpayer money, and it caused a huge splash in the papers. McKenna got the credit for uncovering the scandal, although the efforts of the State after that day were undertaken entirely by others who worked for the commission, and eventually the New York Attorney General. Now his name was well known.

By this time, it was early 1953 and Dwight Eisenhower had been elected president on the Republican ticket in a landslide over Illinois Governor Adlai Stevenson, probably the most intelligent candidate ever to run for the presidency. The former five star general was convinced, that in case of a war on United States territory, the infrastructure of the country would have to be improved with better roads. He reached an uncomfortable but strong rapport with Senator Johnson, who guided the highway bill through the United States Senate.

When that bill was signed into law by President Eisenhower, a Republican, naturally consulted his new ally, Senator Johnson, a Democrat, on appointments for positions with the Interior Department that controlled the billions in highway funds. One of those patronage dispensing appointments went to Bill McKenna, who ran the enterprise in New York. There was money to be made here and McKenna handled it well and wisely, developing lifelong followers who were willing to contribute funds to political campaigns on request and almost without limit. That, in turn, endeared him to the politicians elected through use of those funds.

Although he never ran for elective office, McKenna used his highway funds role to bankroll several other political campaigns, not all of them in New York. Senator Johnson received the major share but even he didn't use them for his own personal campaigns, because he had more than enough from Texas oilmen and the contractors, Brown & Root. McKenna observed the background funding role Johnson played across the country and adopted it as his own *modus operandi*. Virtually the entire Democrat group of politicians in the Congress, both the House and the Senate, owed him a huge debt of gratitude.

McKenna did relish the spotlight, however, and his father, to his dying day, was most proud of his accomplishments. McKenna was bewildered when Senator Johnson agreed to run for vice president on the ticket with John F. Kennedy. He thought his concerns were borne out when the office Johnson attained turned into a mere nothing. Why did a man like Johnson, by then Senate Majority Leader, with all the pomp and patronage and power that went with it, want to chuck that for a back office position, out of the spotlight? Johnson answered that by saying "vice presidents get into history books more than senate majority leaders."

Nobody believed it, until that fateful November day in 1963 in Dallas, Texas. The sudden and unexpected death of President Kennedy catapulted Lyndon Baines Johnson not only into the presidency, but also clearly into the public spotlight. He had achieved his lifelong dream to be the President of the United States. An emergency swearing-in of now President Johnson took place that afternoon with only a few persons in attendance aboard Air Force One on the tarmac at Love Field, Dallas. However, there was another more expansive, but still somber, swearing-in held back at the White House a few days after, very private. McKenna was an invitee.

In a private moment with now-President Johnson that day, McKenna was asked about his own aspirations. He went on at length describing how the Irish immigrants had flocked to jobs in New York City, mainly to the police department. He confessed that he always wanted to be well known and respected in Irish-American society and that his dream job was to be Commissioner of the New York Police Department. Johnson promised him then and there he would see his dream come true. Only one year later, in 1964, that position opened up amid some minor scandal in the department, and President Johnson prevailed upon the Mayor of New York City to appoint Bill McKenna commissioner.

It was as commissioner that McKenna attended and presided over the press conference held at police headquarters at 4:00PM that

day. The room was jam-packed with television and print media personnel, all clamoring loudly for a position from which to shoot questions to the podium. McKenna had moved the conference from a much larger conference room they had available, just to make it as uncomfortable for the media as possible, thereby making it easier to cut off questions when he wanted. It was an old and very common political trick, and the veterans in the media knew that.

13

McKenna had arranged things skillfully. The room was hot, especially with the thirty-five sweating and anxious bodies crammed into the little chamber, with klieg lights and camera equipment turned on and operating. He was getting the reaction and control he wanted. It was difficult to breathe clean air in the room and it was uncomfortable to say the least.

McKenna began the conference with a slight introduction of the personalities on the stage with him, 'just in case some of you present don't know them.' Then he launched into the history of the four murders, discussed at length how each of them was discovered suggesting they had been left that way to add to the impact of discovery. He mentioned forcefully there was a great likelihood that they had been placed there strategically and purposefully during the still hours of the night when almost nobody was likely to be stirring.

He described the efforts Chief Garcia had taken with his patrol force to try to discover evidence of the perpetrators but the hours of the events, and the emptiness of the streets at those hours, most likely eliminated the availability of any eyewitnesses. Similarly, he mentioned that efforts to turn up evidence through investigation of the backgrounds of the four victims and their activities had proven to no avail. He pledged to keep the media fully informed as efforts to untangle the mess and discover the perpetrators went forward. He promised no quick results but that, through continued dogged police work, the matter would be solved.

Answering questions about theories the police were using, he emphasized that their principle theory was that it was a war between drug dealers or drug lords, they weren't sure yet, but they had just about ruled out a racial war. He mentioned that the Flatbush area was a relatively new territory for drug dealers, probably a most profitable one, and the dealers or drug lords wanted to protect their turf.

He stressed the absence of clues uncovered thus far. It was his purpose, and he achieved it, to create the impression that the police department was taking all action possible to obtain clues that would lead to the apprehension of the person or persons responsible and bring them to trial. His discourse was a litany of efforts undertaken by Chief Garcia in his precinct, where all of the murders had occurred.

Most of all, Commissioner McKenna tried to paint a picture of four killings that were unrelated to any possible racial motivation and described it mainly as a war among drug lords. Then the commissioner discussed the efforts the department had undertaken to clear that fine residential area of drug activity, although it was pernicious and almost immune to the strong police effort there. He emphasized 'turning the corner'.

The conference had been going for about an hour when the telephone on the desk behind the commissioner began to ring. Chief Garcia was closest to it and picked it up quickly, hoping to cut off disturbance of the commissioner's talk as much as possible. Chief Garcia's face reddened as he listened to whoever was speaking on the other end of the phone. Then, he sheepishly gestured to the commissioner that the call was for him, "very important," he shrugged.

McKenna took the call. He said almost nothing in reply to what was being said to him, and ended the call abruptly with "I'll be right over." Turning to his audience, by now sweating hard and patiently waiting for more facts, he said, "It's the mayor. He wants me to come over for an immediate conference—not connected with this matter, by the way. It's something else entirely that I can't

disclose right now. This conference has to end, now, and you have my promise that I will see to it you fellows are kept in the loop from here on in."

14

On his arrival at City Hall, Commissioner McKenna could see that something hot was on the fire, and hoped it would not be him. The public relations staff was huddled in a corner of the mayor's anteroom, not even acknowledging his presence. From inside the mayor's office, McKenna could hear something going on since the people inside were speaking loudly.

Pushing open the huge oak door, he saw that the mayor and several other advisors were engaged in a heated exchange. The mayor looked up as McKenna entered, seemingly angry and flustered, and said, "Bill, we really need you *here!* What in hell is going on over at the department? What are you guys doing over there?"

Walking toward the huge desk that dominated that room, McKenna shrugged his shoulders and said, "I assume you're speaking about the four bodies found in Brooklyn."

"You're damned right we are," the mayor screamed. "Why wasn't this whole saga brought to my attention so we would know what to expect? You've brought just about the whole damned world down on my ass, and I don't even know about it, don't know what's going on or what to say."

McKenna was obviously disturbed and his face reddened. "I wish I could tell you about it, but I didn't really know about it myself until the fourth body showed up and it became a news story. I know I have to get after my chiefs to get them to bring stuff like this to my attention so I can keep you ahead of the media turmoil, but I just couldn't do that here. Sorry. I guess I was out of the loop, too."

"Well, let's get into it now," the mayor said disgustedly. "Tell me what's going on, what we're doing, and how we're going about trying to bring this to an end, and catching the perpetrators," the mayor said angrily.

McKenna responded, "I'd have to say that we're doing everything possible right now. There's damned little evidence to go on. The killings were done without apparent witnesses, in the dead of the night. The bodies were trussed up and put on display obviously to get as much media attention as they could. I have no idea right now who is doing what to whom."

The mayor slammed down his palms on the desk. He was getting angrier. "You mean to tell me you don't know a damned thing, is that what you're saying?"

McKenna shuffled his position, obviously defensive now. "I guess you could say that. We have identified the bodies at least, but they don't give us any clues. We have some theories.. . "

The mayor interrupted him. "Theories," he screamed, "theories!! I can't live with theories. I need some rock solid information. I have to hold off the entire black community since all the bodies were minorities, or do I have to remind you of that?"

"No," McKenna answered. "I know that full well but can't do anything about that. The chiefs seem to think it may be a drug war over new territory. One detective thinks it's a mafia hit on other gangs trying to squeeze into that territory. Nobody thinks the killings were unrelated. They were not isolated events."

"Look," the mayor said exasperated. "I have to have something to go on besides good wishes and theories. I've got to handle the Reverend Windall in a few minutes. You know him. He thinks he speaks for the entire black community just because he's loud and out front. He'll want me to kiss his ass here before he leaves. He'll be here in a few minutes. You'll have to stay with me through that. You may even have to do a little kissing yourself."

McKenna winced at the thought. "We'll have to be up front with him. I know he won't accept that and will want to make a lot of noise. That's his style. We'll just have to bear with it and play it out until we catch a break or it loses steam."

Mayor McPhilliamy was a nervous sort of man. He was almost perpetually grumpy and smoked like a chimney. His office was always filled with smoke and smoking odors. People hated to have to stay in there for long. He had been elected to that office twice, the first time by a fluke when the Democrat primary ballot was filled with many candidates. He just happened to be the only white one on the list and got the biggest vote, although by no means a majority. Winning the Democrat primary in New York City is equal to winning the election, there were so few Republicans in the city.

He was just past sixty-four when he ran for a second term. He knew he couldn't win a primary against a minority candidate. The city was now populated with a near majority of blacks, and they were a huge political mass. He had to avoid a risky primary fight. He did that through judicious appointments to city jobs, filling the ranks with minorities who were well placed in the various party echelons. They guided the clubhouses into a peaceful period so that no primary candidates opposed him.

Despite all that, he barely won the election against a well-known black Republican candidate who seemed far better qualified. That candidate, though, was naïve about politics and thought the votes would come based on his policies, not believing as he was told, that party loyalty in New York City would be so steadfast and control the event. He was wrong and shocked and angry when he lost the election. It was a victory for machine politics over a clearly better candidate. The democratic system had failed this time so city government would continue in the shaky hands of Mayor McPhilliamy.

The meeting continued. Without any solid theories to expound on and without very much evidence to work with, it was clear to everyone that the police were doing exactly what they could, to the limit. Nevertheless, it was frustrating and even more so to the mayor who would bear the heat of the media and the activist public figures. Mayor McPhilliamy couldn't come to grips with any idea as to how to handle those focus groups. A lot would ride on his handling of the affair he and the police knew very little about.

"One thing we did do, mayor," McKenna continued. "We did assign a special investigator to try to find out what he could about the crimes and who was responsible. Right now he's our best hope to uncover information that may lead to an arrest soon."

"Who is that?" the mayor asked imperiously.

"Tony Monteverdi," McKenna responded. "You'll recognize his name. You have to know our confidence in him is justified and he's a name the public will know, too."

"That's great," the mayor said. "At least it will show we're going somewhat in the right direction. Monteverdi's a good man, the best man for the job."

There was a knock on the huge oak door and the secretary poked her head in sheepishly. "Reverend Windall is here. He would like to see you as soon as possible."

"OK", the Mayor said exhaustedly. "Send him in."

15

In what seemed like seconds, the huge black man came into the room. He was very large, with a belly that protruded well ahead of him, forcing an almost imperceptible lean backwards as he walked. His hair was slicked straight back and there was plenty of it, making a pointed mass at the back of the head. It was jet black except for streaks of gray that came through. He spoke with a hoarse voice and gestured wildly as he spoke.

"Mayor, we have a disaster on our hands. The black community is up in arms about these killings and they want something done, and now! We think there's something sinister in the police trying to squelch any publicity about these murders. It wouldn't be the first time, you know."

"Why don't you sit down, Reverend, and we can discuss this matter in a gentlemanly way," Mayor McPhilliamy said.

Reverend Windall stared at him silently. Then, after studying the mayor for a brief moment, he went to take the seat that had been suggested.

"Reverend," the mayor began, "we're taking this matter very seriously. We have had the police combing the neighborhood in the search for witnesses to anything about these killings. We are NOT sitting on our hands." The mayor studied the reverend carefully, trying to measure the impact of his words.

"As you can see," the mayor continued, "I even had Police Commissioner McKenna come here to be in on our discussion. That should tell you how seriously we take such matters."

The reverend looked puzzled. "How," he thought to himself, "was the mayor able to get the commissioner to come over there when the mayor had no notice the reverend was coming to see him? Could that be attributable to the savvy of an experienced politician or just dumb luck and coincidence?"

Commissioner McKenna leaned forward in his seat. His eyes were transfixed on the Reverend Windall, trying to fathom what made such a person tick. He was unquestionably one of the most outspoken of the black leaders who presumed to speak for their people. He injected himself into every black issue, whether or not the cause was meritorious or whether there was actually anyone at fault.

McKenna knew the reverend did not represent any fixed constituency and yet he could raise a group of followers to be his audience at any time and place. He was a force of some degree but just how much of a force was never fully ascertainable. Yet he had staying power and, once he injected himself in an issue, he tried to become the focal point, often mouthing the most outrageous and obviously contrived rationale for the racial aspects of any possible dispute.

The reverend had vaulted himself into a case upstate involving a teenage black girl who accused the local police of beating and raping her. Despite what became overwhelming evidence to clearly indicate her charges were a hoax to cover up her consensual sex escapade with some friends, he steadfastly stood behind her. He even secreted her to a place down south, safe from subpoenas and court papers in New York. He never flinched from backing her story and continued to plead her cause long after it was publicly exposed as a hoax.

"You know, Reverend," McKenna started, "these killings took place in the dead of night. It seems there was apparently nobody on the streets in that somewhat quiet neighborhood and nobody seems to have seen anything that's helpful. Now, we've assigned one of our leading detectives, Tony Monteverdi- I believe you know him-to try to dig out something that will open a door for us to a lead."

"All I know is that four gentlemen of color have died and someone has to be responsible for this," Reverend Windall seemed to shout out, pounding the desk. "Something has to be done, and quickly. We can't wait for the poh-lice department to fudge around and show action with no results. We need results. The black community deserves justice."

"We know they do," interjected the mayor, trying to control the meeting, "and we're gonna give it to them. We'll find the perpetrators and bring them to justice. You'll see, but we do need time."

"You have to remember, Reverend," McKenna spoke, leaning even closer to the reverend's chair, "these victims weren't the cream of the crop of the black and latino community. All of them had a criminal record of some sort, they had served penitentiary time, they had children out of wedlock they were not supporting, and they had records, some of them even physical assaults on their bed partners. Not the best of the lot."

"That's no reason not to seek out their killers. You know that. You have to take it as a crime against a human being and find their killer or killers. Even a prostitute has to be respected for that by law enforcement. She has to be paid. That's your obligation."

"We know that," McKenna replied, leaning back, a little angry. "We know our obligation, but their criminal and anti-social history makes us believe it may be a drug war between drug lords over a new territory. That's the purpose behind telling you that. You may be thinking the perpetrators are white men, but they very well might not be. This might not be a racial incident at all. Do you understand that?"

Reverend Windall leaned forward towards the mayor again and pounded the desk. "Mayor, we cannot tolerate this wait-and-see attitude. We have to..."

Mayor McPhilliamy interrupted him. "Now hold on, Ed! You and I have been through a lot of these episodes together. I know what drives you and you know the same about me. Let's not have any histrionics or show here. Save that for outside, which I know you will. You know that we're doing all we can and we'll continue to do just that. The commissioner here is in full charge and will do the very best the department can manage."

"That's right, Reverend," McKenna said. "You can count on that, now and in every case. *Every case.* That's our obligation and our commitment."

The Mayor again broke in. "There, you have it, Reverend. Now why don't you just let us alone to get down to the solution of these cases so we can satisfy you and what you call the 'black community'."

The reverend was silent. His face was a study of someone trying to mull over his chances and his options on what to do next. After a short period, he spoke again. "I believe you, Mayor. I'm quite sure you mean well, but actions will speak a lot louder. Hear me now. The 'community' will not tolerate inactivity--so there had better be some action and fast." He got up to leave and extended his hand to both the Mayor and McKenna.

As he left through the huge oak door, the Mayor said, "Good to see you again, Reverend, as always. My door is always open to you. Come again soon."

That was disingenuous. As soon as the door closed behind the reverend, the Mayor said, "That bastard. He knows full well that we're doing all we can. He knows that these people killed were drug addicts, pushers and had terrible family situations. They fathered children then left the women, generally just girls, and sometimes

beat them up for good measure. We shouldn't even have to do anything to anybody who rids society of such garbage. But you know, Bill, that we can't just do that, don't you?"

"I sure do," McKenna replied, but the Mayor wasn't listening.

"We could balance our budget in a wink if we didn't have to clean up the slop from those kinds of people, if we didn't have to pay for their housing, their food, clothing and all-- medical treatment and everything. Then they send in someone like Windall to ask... demand... more. All the time, more. When will it ever stop? We have to stop appeasing those people and let them fend for themselves for a while."

McKenna knew the conference had ended. He stood up and took his leave of the Mayor. As he walked out through the reception room, he could see the same huddles of public relations people in the same clusters. They appeared relieved to see him going, knowing that aspect of city government life was done for today.

McKenna exited from the elevator, walked through the rotunda and out into the open air. It felt good to be out there, away, at least momentarily, from the pushes and pull of political stresses. The outside felt good, but he could hear the drone of someone speaking over a microphone to a noisy bunch of people.

McKenna peered out through the archway. There, he saw the Reverend Windall at a microphone inciting the group with him to carefully watch for police action and to make sure they don't let up on their investigation. He was telling them he had just made demands on the Mayor for prompt action, and he meant it. The crowd cheered. McKenna shrugged his shoulders and walked across the roadway to the police department building and headquarters.

16

Ellen Coburn wasn't sure they had done enough yet. She hadn't seen any overly active police effort in quite a while. She had noticed that it seemed like business as usual at the Junction whenever she ventured down there. They had already done quite a bit but it did not seem to have the public reaction she wanted to achieve. The goal was to somehow, either through fear or police action, clean up the Junction area and rid the neighborhood of available drugs. She and the rest of the committee thought that would be a giant step in saving the neighborhood children from running afoul of the drug siren. She would have to reconvene the Bereavement Committee again to see how they all felt about carrying their activity one more step, to get the necessary result. As customary, she would talk to the members separately after Mass on Sunday.

Ellen felt in her heart of hearts that they would all agree to go along with whatever she wanted to do. Therefore, she thought she would always have to exercise good judgment and line up the reasons for or against any action she was suggesting. She knew she couldn't do it alone, she needed the help of the others, if only because there was heavy lifting to be done and she couldn't do that by herself. But then again, there was also the desire to be fortified by the collective wisdom of the committee, something she avidly sought all the time and, in her conscience, needed badly.

The committee had held together very well. Nothing in the way of suspicion had come within any distance of any of the members and, the way it was going, nothing would, unless they slipped up somewhere. There had been no loose talk even as the deaths became a matter of general public interest and concern as the days passed and became weeks. There was no show of glee on the part of the committee members, and no out-of-line comments to anyone that she knew about.

Except for meetings which included all members of the Committee, both transient and the four pillars, as she called them, Sunday Mass was the only time there was usually any communication between them, and that was always secretive and oral. As the wife of a deceased policeman, Ellen was accorded a lot of respect by the other members of the committee. They believed she knew a whole lot about police methods and that would keep them safe from the long arm of the law and discovery. It seemed perfect.

After Sunday Mass, she separately cornered Joe Wickham and Jim McCormick. Both of them cautioned against doing anything more just now, hoping to let the prior events stew awhile and sink into the public mind. They were for caution, thinking that anything more might just be an opportunity to screw up and let out a clue that could tie them to the killings.

Jim clearly did not want any more killings, just now, anyway. He reminded her that the media was now on the backs of the police and that was making it hot for the police officials. He had seen the Reverend Windall on the tube, haranguing his followers with his usual racially edged speeches and told her he thought that would stir up the action she wanted. If it didn't, then they could consider more action. It made sense. Wickham seemed to agree with McCormick.

Having spoken to both McCormick and Wickham, she felt duty bound to speak with both Saviano and O'Malley. Ellen was somewhat surprised that the two men she had conferred with had not gotten her hint that she wanted to nudge the situation a little more. She would not get that feeling from either Saviano or O'Malley.

Saviano was eager to do more. He had a genuine hatred for drug dealers and political and police figures who allowed the pushers to function almost without any harassment. He felt they were the murderers of his grandson and wanted revenge on anyone he could identify as a drug operative, big or small-it made no difference.

On the other hand, O'Malley would go along if the others did. His was a public contribution motivation. He had the fatalistic feeling it would all come home to roost some day anyway, so why not continue until the result that motivated them in the first place was achieved. The major point he made, though, was that no action should be allowed to split up the committee. If the proposal for action wasn't unanimously received, it should not be done, as that could lead to disintegration of their comradeship and from there to criminal responsibility early on.

Disappointed but not outwardly affected, Ellen Coburn would wait to raise the question again. She would watch the proceedings from afar, through the media that criticized loudly but told you so little. When the time came to have agreement on governmental inaction, she would bring it up again and keep the pot boiling that way. She was determined that such vigilante action would eventually lead to the action the entire neighborhood wanted and needed. She didn't have long to wait.

17

Tony Monteverdi admitted to himself he was stuck. Nothing he had a hunch about had panned out with any lead whatsoever. He had thought the churches in the neighborhood would be able to produce some information, if only to stop what seemed like senseless and indiscriminate killings in their neighborhood. He was wrong apparently. The local attorney who worked the parishes for business hadn't offered anything either and Tony was half-way convinced the attorney probably knew nothing anyway.

Police have a difficult time nowadays anyway. The inroads made by Supreme Court decisions on the time-honored police methods and traditions had turned the job into a lot more than it should be. Now a police officer or a detective had to turn over to a sensitive district attorney a case that was built with evidence they had pieced together from sources other than the defendant. Confessions were almost verboten now and it was harder and harder to make them stand up in court. True, there had been professional excesses throughout the past but they did not merit the vast change that had come about in the criminal law. Nowadays, an officer had to almost be a lawyer.

As Monteverdi drove along Farragut Road, he seemed to sense some acquaintance with the area. Then he realized that his old partner in the patrol car, Eddie Coburn had lived somewhere along Farragut Road. He had been to dinners and parties at Eddie's house before he died so tragically. He thought he would remember the house when he saw it, even though it had been a long time. He wondered to himself if Eddie's wife Ellen still lived there. He wondered too if she would remember him, and if she did, would it be a fond memory.

Nearing 40th Street, he began to slow the car down to have a longer look at both sides of the street. He knew their house was right around there somewhere and wanted to see it at least. As he passed 38th Street, still on Farragut, he recognized the house, he thought. There it was, number 3718. It was well maintained and looked nice. He felt sure it was the house because it was the only non-attached house on the block. Eddie Coburn was always proud of that.

He had to swing a u-turn to bring the car in front of the house to park. Exiting, he stood on the side of the car taking a long look at the house. This was it, he seemed even more sure now. It was neat and well cared for meaning that Eddie's widow or whoever else might live there now kept it in good repair.

It was getting along to four o'clock in the afternoon and the sun was heading west with what seemed like breakneck speed. The days were getting shorter and shorter as Fall was giving way to cooler air of Winter. Monteverdi decided to try knocking on the door so he climbed the steps in front of the house.

It took what seemed like a long time for someone to answer the door. As soon as Monteverdi heard the voice from inside, he knew it was Ellen Coburn, Eddie's widow. She didn't seem overjoyed to hear his name after he responded to her question. "Why should she," he thought, "I'm a reminder of a memory that might still be very grim for her. She might still be trying to deal with Eddie's sudden and unexpected death."

The door opened. Monteverdi would always remember his thoughts as the door unfolded before him and he saw Ellen Coburn standing there. He had always considered her to be a beautiful lady, almost too beautiful for a cop's wife. Now he stared at her, thinking that she was still beautiful, maybe more so now.

Ellen seemed cold to him as the conversation started. She stood in the doorway in such a manner as told him he was not about to be invited in. He was surprised by that, but understood. After

all, he was the partner of her late husband who died in an aborted drug raid, a raid at which he was only to be an out of the way coordinator. The patrol car Eddie Coburn was in, watching the proceedings, suddenly exploded and burst into flames. There was no hope for Eddie who was immediately immersed and consumed by the flames. It was a horrible way to go, although there is no good way.

Ellen and Monteverdi engaged in very small talk, reminiscing slightly about old times. Ellen had to be coaxed into those discussions and purposely kept them brief. Finally, Ellen tried to call it to an end, but Monteverdi wanted to ask a few questions about the murders.

"Ellen," he asked, "did you hear about those murders that happened around here just a few days ago?"

"Sure," she said, " I would have to be deaf and dumb not to hear about them. They're the talk of the neighborhood."

"Do you have any ideas about them? I've been assigned to the case and can't seem to get a lead on anything that would help me."

"Tony, I only know they happened. This is a troubled area now, lots of drugs and drug dealers lurking around all the time. The Junction is filled with them. It must be a drug war, you know, the kind you and Eddie worked on when he was alive."

"Yeah, I guess so," he replied. If you hear of anything, anything, please give me a call. It's still the same number we always had. Do you still have it?"

"Sure, Tony, sure. I'll call you at that number if I hear of anything suspicious. OK?"

"Yeah. Thanks, Ellen. I might stop by to see you once in a while as I progress with this. I'll probably be in the neighborhood a lot and

if I get any leads, it might be good to talk over things with someone I know and trust."

"That's Ok Tony, but I've been out of the police business several years now. I probably won't be of any help but you're free to stop anytime."

"You still look swell, Ellen. Real swell. It's great to see you after all these years. Stay well."

Ellen closed the door and leaned back against it. She stroked her chin. "This is a very unexpected development," she thought. "This could either be a very good thing if managed properly, or a very bad thing if not managed well." Her thoughts ran the gamut from fear of exposure by accident of the activities of her and the Bereavement Committee, to the intended result of having the neighborhood cleansed of drug problems. She realized she was perspiring a little. The visit had unnerved her, it seemed, and she would have to think about how to share this information and development with the members of the Committee. She needed time to think about that.

18

It was not so easy for Tony Monteverdi either. The reception he received during that impromptu visit to Ellen Coburn was not warm, and possibly unfriendly. He didn't have long to dwell on that just now, because his radio crackled to indicate he was being paged.

"Monteverdi, are you there? This is Chief Garcia. How're you making out on your investigation? I have to know very soon because the commissioner is calling me for a progress report. He's being bugged about it by the mayor who, as you probably know, is getting bugged by everybody--the press, the community groups and lots of just plain citizens. Call me back as soon as you can."

"Damn...," Monteverdi thought,"...this is just going to be one of those jobs. You have to keep as careful an eye on communications with the brass as you do on searching for clues and evidence. This was going to be a difficult job."

Monteverdi reached for the radio and called in for the chief. Garcia sounded terribly disappointed that Monteverdi had not uncovered any type of lead. Garcia hated the thought of telling Commissioner McKenna he had nothing new to report. He knew the commissioner would become unraveled and berate him over the phone for sloppy and careless police work. It was not that so much, but the brass and the politicians always thought that anything short of success was attributable to police indifference or negligence of some sort.

However, Monteverdi had really hit a brick wall. He didn't know exactly what to do next. It was rare for him to be stumped, but stumped he was. Absolutely nothing to go on, no leads, no evidence of any kind. Whoever had committed the murders had done a good job. It seemed as if they had gotten away clean. He knew the difficulty the chief was in and that a lot of pressure was building up all around from all sources. The media was the worst. They kept pressing for developments and there just weren't any.

Before he knew it he had arrived near the Junction. He was a little surprised at how close it was to the Coburn house and the church. He should have noticed that before but hadn't. He pulled his car to the side, put down his department credentials to fend off any overzealous parking attendants, and got out and walked.

In a short time he had arrived at the Junction proper, where Nostrand and Bedford Avenues cross. It is a well-known location for anyone familiar with Brooklyn. Tony walked slowly toward the actual nexus of the two streets, both of which ran generally north to south across the entire borough. From there, he could take in the entire busy area without going any further.

It seemed like business as usual. The day was overcast but a nice fall day and it was good to be out on the streets. Tony noticed that plenty of Brooklynites felt the same way, as there were a large number of shoppers filling the sidewalks. The Ebinger's Bakery had its usual long line of waiting customers to buy their wonderful pastries. He could see a few people here and there standing in the doorways, he suspected they were drug dealers, waiting for their 'customers' to come by.

The neighborhood was exactly as Ellen had described it. The dealers were operating in plain sight, seemingly unafraid of police activity. Tony noticed there were no policemen within his view, although that was not uncommon. In these later years, the police had pretty much given up the walking beat cops and went to responding to complaints by car, or just riding by in cars.

Tony walked north along Nostrand Avenue. Within a block he came to the office of Willie Mitchell, the attorney, but it, too, looked busy with several people visible through the plate glass window. Going a little further, Tony came upon a young man, obviously of Latin descent, standing in a doorway and smoking. Tony stopped to talk with him.

He found out the young man's name was Jaimie Gonzalez, by coincidence. He was from the area and just watching the traffic, he said, not doing any drugs at all. He said he had nothing to do with drugs. He claimed to be an out-of-work computer programmer and was looking for a job through headhunters. It sounded reasonable.

Tony walked on and could see other young men standing in doorways, too. As his eyes fell on them, they would huddle away from his gaze, probably worried about being recognized. As Tony walked towards them, some of them would hurriedly walk away. Instinctively, Tony knew these were likely drug dealers but he wouldn't disturb them right now. He had another mission.

Shortly, he surprised another young man in a doorway. He started to walk away as Tony approached, but Tony grabbed him by the arm and held him still. "What's going on?" Tony asked. The young man, somewhat disheveled and unkempt, needing a shave, told Tony "nothing." Tony asked about what was going on with the druggies in the area, were they afraid because of the killings? Yet the boy stuck to his story of knowing nothing.

Tony suggested he could run him in to the precinct as a suspected drug dealer. "Maybe I should search your pockets, what do you think of that? Would that help your memory?"

"Aw, man," the boy said. "I ain't doin' nothin'. I got nothin'. What do you want from me?"

" Just a little information," Tony said. "Just some idea about what's goin' on around here. Who's doing the killings."

" I told ya I don't know nothin'," the boy replied, worried. "I don't know nothin' about that."

"You don't even know there have been a few killings around here? Don't you know even that?"

"Sure I do. Everybody knows that. We figure you guys are on top of it and its gonna be safe for everybody. What do you want from me? I'm a nobody. A nobody."

Tony angrily let the boy go. He knew he was going to get nothing important from him. The kid was right. He was a nobody.

But Tony was frustrated. "Somewhere," he thought, "there has to be a break. Somebody around here must know something. He needed help."

Tony lit a cigarette. As he let the smoke come out through his nostrils, a car pulled up at the curb. A short, stubby, olive-complexioned man got out and approached Tony.

"The boss wants to see ya. Soon!" he said poking Tony with his elbow. "Cabeesh?"

Tony nodded. "Tell him I'll be around there later today. I'll stop in at the Club."

19

Mulberry Street runs north from Canal Street for a few blocks in Manhattan. It is a cobblestone paved street with narrow sidewalks that seemed to slant away from the buildings towards the roadway. Here and there the sidewalk grew slightly wider and then narrowed, but such oases were few and far between. Essentially the street was quite narrow and cars parked along both sides making the roadway lane appear even more narrow, but considerable traffic flowed through. On the south side of Canal is Chinatown. They are that close.

Little Italy, as it was called, was actually a tourist stop. Many visitors to the city would wander down and through the area, some after a visit to the extremely crowded Chinatown that ran for several blocks south of Canal Street as well as along Canal Street. Chinatown was spreading.

The visitors came and were largely disappointed with what they found in Little Italy. It was mostly cafes and restaurants that bordered the narrow roadway, and even narrower and sloping sidewalks. They had expected to see more stores selling native Italian wares, such as many of the tourist stores did in Chinatown. They just weren't there in Little Italy.

However, if they came for the food, they were not disappointed. Italian food is probably the most popular in the world, far surpassing American, Spanish or French cuisine. Most of the dishes in the Mulberry Street restaurants were native Italian, usually with some type of tomato based sauce spread over them, then topped with an imported grated cheese. It was great food with many selections ranging from simple pasta to veal, chicken and beef. Eggplant was a favorite as well. Most of the waiters were imported too, speaking with a heavy Italian accent woven throughout the English they were learning here.

For the Italians who lived in the squalid, tiny apartments above the stores and restaurants, and others who did business other than restaurants in the area, it was difficult to understand what lured the tourists. Perhaps, they thought, it was to see the site where Crazy Joe Gallo got whacked while having lunch in the garden in back of the Foccacceria Bologna. Normal people are intrigued by stuff like that. That was a celebrated Mafia hit, two gunmen walking brazenly through the restaurant into the garden, each pumping five bullets into Crazy Joe at point blank range, and then lowering their pistols and nonchalantly walking back through the restaurant and out the door. They were watched by about forty stunned noontime visitors having their lunch. Nobody could move. They were in shock and their eyewitness accounts given to the police who finally arrived were worthless as evidence. Eyewitness accounts are usually unreliable anyway.

Tony Monteverdi would not have to use his police department plaque today, the plaque that signified him as a policeman on duty so that ticket personnel would not ticket his car. No identification as such was needed in Little Italy because the police rarely ventured in there. Little Italy was also well-protected by the Cosa Nostra personnel, the dons, the capos and the soldiers who came and went to the various social clubs located there.

Monteverdi parked his car halfway on the sidewalk near the front of the Palermo Social Club entrance. He could see the loyal soldiers of the Don Miglio family, standing around on the sidewalk, smoking, some hanging out against the building, all on duty to protect the Don inside. Monteverdi was noticed as he got out of his car and even nodded to a few of them. They weren't terribly friendly and showed it. The soldiers didn't ever trust anyone who came from the 'other side' as the enemy was called. It didn't matter if he had the blessing of Don Miglio or not, he was a cop, and they didn't like any cop, and didn't trust them.

He found his way into the club blocked by a huge man dressed in a suit that looked like something from the zoot suit era, brown with large lapels and grey stripes running through it. He wore a tie that clearly didn't match his suit or shirt and stood out like a sore thumb. His hair was slicked back, and he continued to slick it back regularly with his right hand, a nervous sort of gesture.

"Can I help ya?" the man in the doorway asked.

"I'm here to see Don Miglio. He sent for me," Tony replied.

The door guard looked him over top to bottom and then back again, saying nothing. After a few puffs on his cigarette, he nodded with his head, motioning Tony to go in through the door. He followed Tony in.

It was dark inside but Tony could see down the hall to a somewhat large room where several people were seated around a table with a lighted lamp hanging down over it. As he got closer, he could see the participants were all men, somewhere above fifty, and dressed casually. They smoked those tiny black twisted Italian cigars called stogies, and the room was filled with their smoke, and the sour smell of tobacco.

As he approached, he saw Don Miglio who motioned to the others to leave them alone together. They all got up to leave, almost at once, as if their movement had been scripted by some playwright. Don Miglio demanded that type of respect and he got it. There was a rustle of chairs as they rose and left the room.

"Come in, Tony, so glad to see you," Don Miglio exclaimed. "Please sit down."

"Glad to see you too, Don Miglio, Tony replied respectfully. Approaching, he took Don Miglio's left hand in his two hands, raised it to his lips and kissed it. "Really good to see you."

"Tony, I'll get right down to the reason I invited you here. I've been getting complaints from my capos that somethin' is rotten out there in Flatbush. I'm sure you know about it," Don Miglio smiled as he said that. He knew darn well Tony knew about it, and was knee-deep in trying to get to the bottom of it.

"What do you mean, Don Miglio?" Tony asked playing coy. "Are you talking about the recent killings out there in the Flatbush area?"

Don Miglio recoiled. Tony noticed that motion by the otherwise unflappable older Italian man, and made a mental note to try not to be a wise guy. "Of course, of course, I'm talking about that. The capos tell me their runners are afraid to go into the area. That's a lucrative spot for them. They have to be able to do their business there. Business is business. Cabeesh?"

"Yeah, I know about it. I've been assigned as the detective in charge to try to turn up the responsible parties. I haven't had too much luck in getting any evidence to count on. I've..." Don Miglio interrupted him with a gesture telling Tony to lean closer to him as if there was someone listening in on their conversation. Tony leaned forward and Don Miglio very gently wrapped his hand in Tony's jacket lapel and pulled him down toward him. They were almost nose to nose.

"Look," Don Miglio spoke in an almost whisper. "I like you Tony, like you a lot. But I gotta attend to my business. Can't let my personal likes and dislikes interfere with business. Cabeesh?"

Don Miglio puffed his stogie and let the smoke waft out of his mouth toward Tony's face. "Business. That's what I'm interested in," Don Miglio said after a short pause. "Business. I have a duty, you understand, a duty--to protect my capos, to have them do the business they do. They have to make a living. Cabeesh? That's why you're here."

"What do you want me to do Don Miglio?" Tony asked.

"Tony, you were never very smart, just good at what you do. You have done a lot for me already so I almost don't want to ask you to do even more. Just your share. This killing has to stop, now. Do you understand? It has to stop now," he said slapping the table. "Now!"

Tony started to answer and then decided to think for a while. Finally, he said, "I don't know yet what I can do. I don't have any evidence to go on. The chiefs are saying it might be a race thing, you know, between the blacks and Hispanics. Some of them think it's the mob, you know, the Cosa Nostra trying to take over somebody else's territory. Now that you spoke to me I think I can rule that out. I…"

Again Tony was interrupted. "Tony, I don't think you understand. It has to stop now. I don't care if it's the blacks killing themselves or the spics. I don't care. I just want it stopped. You have to stop it. *Now.*"

"But, Don Miglio,…" Tony offered, a little more low-key as if he was afraid, "…I can't do anything without some information about who is doing it and why. I have to get that before I'm able to make a dent in the problem."

"You work on it. You'll come up with something. That has to stop and we have to clean out the area for the capos and their runners. That's what's important. You do it. Get it done right away or else I'm gonna have to do something you won't like out there. I'm not trying to scare you. Just trying to motivate you, as they say, ---- give you a reason to get it done. I can't wait long. That's all. Get it done! Don't listen to them when they say we're involved in a war or something like that. We ain't. They always try to blame us, the Guinea immigrants, for everything that goes wrong around here. You just get it done, Tony, cabeesh?"

Pausing, Don Miglio thought for a while, smoked on his cigar, and finally said, "And Tony, don't fuck this up like you fucked up that thing in Harlem a few years back. We don't like it when a cop gets killed, no matter how he gets killed. That's trouble for us, unpleasantness. We like to be left alone."

Tony started to reply but Don Miglio raised his hand. It was his way of announcing the interview was over. Tony had his marching orders and would have to work hard at it. He didn't know what Don Miglio meant when he said he would have to do something himself out there, but was worried that it might result in harm to him. He got up, bowed slightly and left the room.

After Tony was safely out of the room and Don Miglio heard the door slam, he motioned to someone standing in the shadows of the room. "Cosmo…" Don Miglio said, "…go tell that car repair guy we did the favor for back a few years, what was his name….yeah, Sabella, tell him I want to see him."

20

Bill McKenna was feeling the heat, too. The talk shows were inviting anybody and his brother to debate the cause for the killings and the lack of leads turned up by the police to locate the killer or killers. They kept up a steady drumbeat, stoking the flame that the police were either incompetent or racists, saying they didn't care because the victims were off-white.

Naturally, that theme was picked up by the black and Hispanic leaders who always pushed the racial card as much as possible. They were trying as usual to foment a backlash that would gain them something more and tangible than what they already had as public benefits. The leaders would then be able to point to those new gains as gains they had achieved for the communities. They were like elected congressmen although they were self-appointed and had no electorate basis for their claims to leadership. They were loud, brash and outspoken and those traits, and the media's hunger for any sort of news, propelled them into the limelight and gave them considerable TV time.

One of the ways they kept up the pressure was to continually call upon the public representatives elected to serve their communities. They were in excellent paying positions with huge retirement and health benefits and did not want to lose them, or opportunities to move up the ladder. Therefore, they responded to the heat from the leadership exactly as the leadership wanted. The representatives used their entre to the mayor's office to continually push his buttons to get something done. The mayor was exasperated and frustrated. He then started the ball rolling back down the other side of the hill, and came down hard on the police, and Commissioner McKenna.

McKenna's reaction was almost the same as the mayor's. He came down hard on the chiefs who came down hard on the detective force and ultimately Tony Monteverdi. As with the dung beetles, the dung ball rolls downhill all the time.

When Chief Garcia couldn't give the commissioner any satisfactory answer, not knowing exactly what Monteverdi was up to, McKenna decided to go straight to the horse's mouth. He called Monteverdi. McKenna had a hard time and a long wait to get through to Tony, but finally succeeded.

"Tony," McKenna said, "I don't ever want to be interfering in police investigations, I don't want to be known as a meddling commissioner, but I'm getting lots of heat from all sides on those Flatbush killings. We have to have progress soon. What can you tell me?"

"Yeah," Tony thought to himself. "You don't want to be known as a meddling commissioner! Bull shit! That's exactly what you're doing now!"

"Well, Commissioner, I haven't been able to turn up any real hard lead. Forensics has come up with nothing. Every detail of the killings seems to have been well planned. They've left nothing behind, no DNA, no threads or hairs, no blood stains, no pieces of evidence we can trace to a seller or dealer. The rope they used is nautical rope, specially wound, but around here, so near the yacht basin and the ocean, there are just hundreds of places that sell it. It seems to be just airtight. You would almost think whoever is doing these killings has a police or forensics background. They've been so careful."

"Do you know if it is one person or more than one?"

"No, not for sure. But the weight of the bodies and the manner in which they've been delivered for public inspection and discovery would make you think it had to be more than one person or, if not, at least a person of terrific strength."

"Tony, is there anything I can tell the media about progress on the case so far?"

"Well, nothing concrete. You can suggest that we know it's more than one person doing it. You can tell them that we are continuing our search for evidence and suspects and will continue to pour our efforts into that. Whenever possible, they should become a platform for saying the police can use the public's help. They should understand that we're doing all we can. We still haven't decided whether it's a racial thing or just a drug war. I think it's the drug war, but that's just my hunch. Nothing to go on. I know that's not much but it's the best we can tell 'em now."

"Tony," McKenna said pleadingly, "I want you to do a favor for me. Put all your effort into it. Don't stop at anything. We have to solve this crime spree before it blossoms into a real war and we lose control entirely. I want you to work especially hard on this. I'll remember it. You'll see."

"I'll do everything I can for you, Commissioner."

But it was already too late.

21

After Monteverdi sort of bowed his way out from Don Miglio's club parlor, the don sat and weighed the events that had just transpired and what was happening out in the world. He felt he had been flimflammed, handled, by an expert. He had actually accomplished nothing more than giving Monteverdi a warning to get on his horse and stop the killings and find the culprits. But he had no warm feeling that Monteverdi was going to do any more than he had been doing and that he really had no resources to get the job done. Monteverdi would continue to let him down, he thought.

After a short while, his bodyguard, Cosmo, came back into the room. "He's here, Don Miglio," he said. "The car repair guy you wanted to see. Sabella."

"Show him in."

Sabella was a tiny but somewhat rotund man. Grey had begun to weave its way into his jet black hair. He was a man of about fifty. He felt sheepish about appearing in front of the respected don in his grease stained overalls and plaid woolen shirt. He approached the table where the don was sitting, in an almost crouch or bowing way. It was obvious he was not comfortable with the situation he unexpectedly found himself in.

"Sit down, sit down, please" Don Miglio said motioning to a chair at the table. Sabella sat slowly, taking the don's hand in his own, hoping that the almost perpetual grease in the fingerprints and under his nails would not disturb his host.

"Relax...," Don Miglio told him, "relax."

Sabella could not relax. Instead he almost whispered, "You wanted to see me, Don Miglio?"

" Yes...Yes I did. Do you remember the favor I did for you a couple of years ago with your daughter. What's her name, Josephine? Her problem? I asked you to come over here today because now I have a favor to ask of you. I want you to do me a favor. Can you consider doing that for me?"

"Sure, Don Miglio, sure. I can do a favor for you. Just ask."

Don Miglio leaned forward, planting his elbows on the table. As he did so, he gestured to Sabella to come closer. "What's your first name?"

"Joe--Giuseppe," Sabella replied, taking care to tell his Italian first name.

"Well, Giuseppe, here's what I want you to do for me. Remember this is to be kept completely between you and me. Nobody else is to know, cabeesh?"

"Sure, sure, Don Miglio, I cabeesh."

"Good," Don Miglio said. "Now come closer—listen..."

22

Jaimie Gonzalez could sense something was up. There seemed to be an almost total absence of police cars cruising the area of the Junction. It was just too quiet without any police nosing around. For some reason all that activity that had become an overkill in a search for information, had stopped. Sensitive noses picked up such things.

It was not a lack of pushers selling their wares, standing in doorways trying to look invisible to normal passersby. There were still plenty of them available. It was just the lack of governmental activity that stirred the empty feeling in Gonzalez' gut. He was entering the world of a supplier now, no longer just a routine-type pusher, the little guy who lives on the sales of the ten dollar glassine packets to the end users, the flotsam of the entire drug business. The throwaway people.

He was about to be a big shot now and didn't want to think that anything could derail his advancement. He now had a source of supply and cut his own drugs into the glassine packets in his apartment. His sales now were to the pushers and that made it a lot easier. He didn't have to be face-to-face with the typical habitual user who desperately needed the stuff. He wanted to avoid that class, the class where sometimes, the girls especially, wanted to pay in 'trade' as opposed to hard cash. He couldn't use all the 'trade' he was offered.

It was the almost total lack of that activity that gave him that queasy feeling. Something had to be up. He just didn't know what. He did feel it would be something from the government, either the feds cracking down for a drug bust or the local police doing the same thing. He was aware of the pressure being put on the government guys because of their failure to make an arrest in connection with the killings, but nobody he spoke to seemed to know anything about them. Almost everyone admitted the dead guys would not be missed. It was actually a cleanup.

Gonzalez knew just about everybody hovering in the doorways, trying to push the dope. He didn't have personal relationships with them, or know their pedigrees, but he knew enough. He knew, for example, that some of them were the 'wise guys', the 'made men' from the mafia, who were soldiers in the Don Miglio family. Nobody touched those guys. Nobody interfered with them. The retribution would not only be swift if they did, but it would also be terribly harsh. Surviving the treatment was thought to be even worse than being whacked by them for any transgression.

The others weren't organized enough. They competed with one another ferociously. Those people were concerned with distributing their packets to the junkies and getting back the money they had invested. Then they could eat and feed their own habit which made their exit from the drug scene almost impossible. They never got better, never tried to kick the habit or clean up, unless they were picked up by the police and got to do jail time. No, they couldn't be the cause for the current *agita* Gonzalez felt. It had to be more.

Therefore, he surmised it had to be some form of governmental action. He knew that stoolies would turn in certain sellers to government agents when they wanted to make a routine drug bust and net a few guys like Gonzalez and their stash of drugs. It would do almost nothing to the drug scene that existed in the vicinity but the police and the DA's would look good on TV and get a lot of praise and publicity. The police knew just what they were doing. They were in on it, too, and profited from the continued prosperity of the drug sales. You just had to avoid being one of the people the stoolies fingered. To avoid that, you had to lie low, try to be invisible and not irritate or cross any of the likely stoolies.

Gonzalez patrolled the four corners of the Junction as if he owned them. He was careful not to look too smart but he wanted to cast the aura of a regular citizen just out for ordinary business or a constitutional walk for his health. He did not want to stand out but he wanted to be noticed in a non-offensive way to certain people. He would stand for a while in some doorway on each corner, waiting to be approached for a 'buy' by one of his pushers. He would routinely reach into his pocket when approached, pull out a ten-pack of glassine envelopes and swiftly hand them over, all the while holding onto the folded bills in the buyer's hand. It was for cash, nothing but cash, no checks or credit cards here. Cash only, and it spoke loudly or there was no speaking at all.

The sales were made without anything such as a kind word passing between the two participants. Each knew what the other wanted, had what was needed and concluded the silent transaction with a few head nods and a swiftness rarely seen in a business transaction. Each knew and trusted the other and needed each other to play their roles in the drug scene. It would be bad for business for both of them if they tried to pass bogus stuff to the other. They would be found out and business would suffer, and so might they, depending on who the victim was.

Once in a while, Gonzalez would buy a newspaper. He fingered the pages slowly, mainly starting from the back, the sports pages. It was coming on to fall now, and the air was just slightly more brisk. You had to dress up a little more, wear a little heavier clothing. The newspaper gave him an air of legitimacy, standing in the fronts of stores, or in doorways. It was World Series time and the somewhat newly-minted Baltimore Orioles (they had recently moved from St. Louis where they were the Browns) were playing the Los Angeles Dodgers. It was late in 1966 and the Dodgers couldn't handle the Orioles and their great pitching staff. The Dodgers would lose in four games, the last three by shutouts.

Gonzalez was no longer deeply interested in the fate of the baseball teams. His interest, which had been very heavy, had faded as his

drug business increased. Nevertheless, he would huddle against storefronts near to the newsstands from which you could catch the play-by-play descriptions of the games above the din of the street traffic at the Junction. The World Series deserved everyone's attention.

From that vantage point, he could survey the scene very well. He was disturbed and somewhat unnerved by his conclusion about what was going to happen. He thought about absenting himself from the street for a while to let the thing blow over. He also hated the nauseating odor of the car and bus fumes that overwhelmed the Junction. It would be great to get some relief from that. However, he couldn't bring himself to do it because he feared losing his clientele who would have to make other connections in his absence, especially since they wouldn't know how long he would be gone. He would have to stay and risk it, but he wasn't happy.

That slight run-in he had with Detective Monteverdi had scared him. It was close, and, if the cops hadn't been preoccupied with turning up evidence on the Flatbush killings, it could have been disastrous. He could have been one of those turned in to satisfy the public that the police were doing something good about the drug problem in the neighborhood. He could've been the anonymous sacrificial lamb to appease the public's appetite, and with hardly any effect on the drug scene itself. He considered himself lucky in an odd sort of way.

23

Ellen Coburn had noticed the virtual absence of police activity, too. She had been uneasy since her heart-stopping run-in with Tony Monteverdi, but thought all the committee had done could be for naught, or very little. The killings had not brought the public wrath down on the police to force them to do something to solve the crimes, at the same time eliminating the drug problem in the neighborhood. Aside from some slight nervousness, the killings hadn't disturbed the drug sellers either. The drug problem, if anything, was coming back and had even grown in dimension, and more and more of the neighborhood kids were yielding to the temptation to "just feel good."

News was getting around the neighborhood, little by little, confirming the already-known background behind the Margaret Barnes suicide. Most of St. Vincent Ferrer's parishioners knew her parents and a good number of them had known her, too. As the gritty details leaked out, the news disturbed the parishioners even more. At Holy Name Society and Rosary Society meetings, as well as Home School Association meetings, people vented their growing anger and their disappointment with police protection. Something had to be done.

Monsignor Bates was feeling the heat, too. As pastor of the parish where the drug problems were hitting hardest, he knew he had to do something. As an old line parish priest, he was not really up to dealing with this latest menace and the way it wove itself into the fabric of the families he shepherded. It was as if some great plague had descended on the families and the disgrace of it all forced them to tough it out, while hiding the ailing victim within their close family circle. But even though the families tried to keep their inner disgrace within their family unit, the word leaked out through neighbors and friends so that any secret was soon public knowledge.

Now, knowledge of the drug problem was rampant. It was the subject of public discussion before and after Mass on Sundays, and among those loyal churchgoers who made it to daily Mass. People stopped to visit with neighbors sitting out on their front steps to commiserate with them on the depth of the drug problem and how far it had penetrated into this once great community.

If the drug problem had hit hard on the good families of St. Vincent Ferrer Parish, it had also hit hard on the 'made men', the capos and soldiers of the Don Miglio family. Their business had at first been seriously cut into by the growing Latino population that brought with it the competition from Latino pushers and sellers. Now it was something different. The murders, and the fact that they evaded solution, made everybody uneasy, made them worry where the killings were being ordered from. Each group suspected the other.

The heat was coming from the so-called bottom up. Don Miglio had stoked the fire by calling Tony Monteverdi on the carpet and giving him a warning. The heat came from the top down, too, by way of Commissioner McKenna relaying the pressure from Mayor McPhilliamy. The mayor was getting lambasted in person, in print, and on the TV media about the lack of action. McPhilliamy's peptic ulcer was now a matter of constant discomfort for him and some deep concern.

Now, Tony Monteverdi really felt the need to generate a lead of some type, but nobody was talking. There was no news around anywhere about what was going on, no hints, no breaks, no leads. Tony knew he was in the best of positions and that he would profit the most, in one way or the other, by solving the crimes. He would be a public hero, the police would cover him with glory and awards, he could become the favorite of Don Miglio and the media celebration would be grand. But he had no leads.

Unknown to Tony, forces were in motion that would bring something to a head. Don Miglio was taking action in response to the complaints of his soldiers. The police, with the commissioner as the driving force, were thought to be readying an assault on the Junction to clean out any and all pushers, sellers and users that happened to be unlucky enough to be in their way when the police sweep began. The citizenry of the parish were beginning to mobilize in a vigilante type of way to clean out the area themselves, thinking the police would never get around to doing it.

24

Tony Monteverdi knew an opportunity when he saw it. As he cruised along Flatbush Avenue late that October, he spied a young , husky, black male dressed with his pants almost falling down his behind, shuffling along lazily, headed north towards Newkirk Avenue. He stopped the car and got out to speak with the boy.

"Hold it right there, young man," Tony said respectfully. No use in being accused of racial slurring or anything like that. "I want to talk with you for a minute. What's your name?"

"My name's George, George Widmore, sir." The young boy was obviously nervous and appeared a little slow-witted. "Some people call me 'Rabbit'. "

"Well, Rabbit," Tony said somewhat with deference, "I want to talk to you about those killings that took place around here a few weeks ago. I have a hunch you may know something about them."

"I don' know nuthin' bout them. Didn't even know there was killins."

"Oh, come on,..." Tony said facetiously, "...everybody around here knows that there've been some killings. You trying to shit me?"

"No suh, ahm not trying to shit nobody. No suh. Ah just don't know nuthin'."

"Listen, Rabbit. I'm a police officer. A detective. See this badge? That means you have to answer my questions and not bullshit me. You have to tell me the truth. Always."

"Yes suh. Ahm tellin' you the truth. Ah jus don't know nuthin'. Honest."

"Well, I just find that hard to believe. I just can't believe there's anybody around here that doesn't know there's been some killings."

Widmore could sense this interview was starting to go badly. He was scared and hung his head and shuffled around and definitely tried not to appear menacing, although he was big for his age.

"Listen Mr. Detective, suh. Ahm telling you the truth. Ah just don't know nuthin' 'bout no killins. That's the truth." Widmore knew enough not to appear impatient and to stay respectful.

"Then why were you looking around up here just now, right where one of the killings took place? Why?" Monteverdi demanded, now in a more confrontational tone.

"Ah wasn't doin' any lookin 'round. I was jes goin' to my grandmother's 'partment. She lives down here a ways. Honest. I jes don't know nuthin'." Widmore had heard of these things happening to black kids, being stopped for suspicion of crimes by the police. He knew he had to stay polite and not talk back or things could go real bad for him. He even knew kids who had been stopped and then ended up in jail for a long time, but he didn't know if they were guilty of what they were accused of doing, or not.

Monteverdi plunged ahead with the inquisition. "Yeah, I bet that's what you're doing. What is your grandma's name? What's her address?"

"I don' know her address," Widmore replied. "I jes know she lives in a 'partment down here on the corner, on Nostrand Avenue." Now he felt the interview was getting too deep for him and he started to sweat and stammer. "Ah, ah, don't know the actual address. Jes how to get there. Honest."

Monteverdi started to grab him by the shirt but thought better of it and brushed his hair with his hand instead. "You know I could run your ass into the precinct house if I wanted to, you understand that?"

"Yassuh, I knows that. I knows you can do a lot of things but I don't deserve that. I dint do nuthin'. I don' knows nuthin about any killins. Honest ah don't."

" I think you're a wise guy. I think you know a lot more that you're telling me. I think I'll run you in and get you to be more honest with me down at the station house." With that, Monteverdi pulled out his handcuffs and with only a little difficulty snapped them onto Widmore's wrists. Widmore began to cry. Tears rolled out of his eyes and down his cheeks. He hung his head in despair. He now knew he faced a tough ordeal but didn't know why. He didn't know anything about any killings. He didn't know why this was happening to him. He hadn't said anything wrong.

As Monteverdi pushed him into the back seat of the car, Widmore began to sob uncontrollably. He was feeling the impact of the desperate situation he was in. As he slammed the back door, Monteverdi said, "I'll get the truth out of you at the station house. You'll learn to not lie to police officers. You better be ready to tell the truth down there."

25

"He confessed..?" Chief Garcia shouted into the phone. "He confessed? That's great. Without much proof we really need a confession. Boy, the commissioner will be happy to hear that. He's been getting a lot of heat in the media."

"Yeah," Monteverdi said. "It didn't take a lot of doin' either. He wasn't as smart as he thought he was. He acted guilty from the start and he cracked pretty easily."

"Are you sure the confession will hold up in court? You know it would be a disaster if we went to trial and the judge didn't allow the confession in as evidence."

"Oh, yeah, it'll hold up all right. It's a good confession. He wrote down a lot of details. The English isn't too good, not foreign, but not too bright either, if you know what I mean."

"I do, don't worry about that," Garcia replied. "I'm sure you read him his Miranda rights, too, correct?"

"Yeah. First thing I did, right after I cuffed him." Monteverdi realized now he hadn't, but what the hell. Who was going to know or complain?

"OK," Garcia breathed a sigh of relief. "I'm gonna get on the horn right now and tell the commissioner. Is that OK with you or do you want to do it yourself?"

"You can do it. I'll probably get a call from him right after you hang up, or he'll probably call the mayor first, then me. Either way, I know he'll speak with me. I just know he will."

26

Commissioner McKenna practically ran to the phone. As he returned from another browbeating type meeting at City Hall, his secretary had told him that Chief Garcia was on the phone with some good news.

The commissioner fumbled with the phone but finally got it into position while still standing. "Hi Chief," he said. "I understand you have some good news for me."

"Yes," Garcia answered. "I think it is *great* news. Monteverdi has solved the Flatbush killings cases. He got the perpetrator and wrung a confession out of him. How about that?"

"Wow," the commissioner exclaimed, dropping down into his leather chair. "That *is* great news. Great news indeed. I hope to high heaven it hasn't been leaked to the media. I'm sure the mayor will want to announce it."

"Nothing's been leaked yet," Garcia answered. "I'm hoping we can keep it quiet until the mayor gets his act together to do it, but I can't promise how long that will be the case. I'll do what I can. You know that."

"When'll the arraignment be?" asked the Commissioner.

"We're planning it for late this afternoon. We have to do everything right, you know, dot all the i's and cross all the t's. We can't let this one get away on a technicality. Then the DA will probably want a grand jury indictment. He's probably gonna to be pushed into going for the execution penalty."

"Yeah, that's right," McKenna replied. "But are you sure we've done that so far. Was he read his rights on time?"

"You know Monteverdi. He's a smart cop. He wouldn't screw up on that. It's so fundamental."

"Are you sure the confession will hold up? They didn't beat up on this guy, did they? No bruises or hard knocks showing? Will he claim it was forced from him and not valid?"

"Of course, he will. That's basic public defender representation in these cases. I'm sure the confession will hold up. Monteverdi said the guy wrote out lots of stuff in his own hand. Things only the perpetrator would know."

"How old a guy is he?"

"He's about eighteen. His confession didn't really include any clear motive. Just killing for the sake of killing. He picked on drug dealers, you know, so he might have robbed them. That might have been his initial motive and it just phased into the murders. We just don't know yet."

"Well, I hope you're right," McKenna said. "Keep it quiet over there and I'll get the mayor in on it right away. You know how he is. He'll want all the details and he'll start worrying about them right away. Thanks for the heads up."

27

The mayor was skeptical, too, as McKenna had anticipated. It was delicate stuff. He pushed McKenna hard to commit to the statement that the confession was valid and would hold up in court. McKenna did the best he could to dodge that bullet and whatever he said seemed to placate the mayor.

"I've been burned before," McPhilliamy said. "I'm an old hand at being burned at the stake and I'm too old to take any more of it."

"I know, I know," McKenna replied. "This confession was gotten by our master cop. He knows what he's doing and he knows how to get confessions that hold up in court. You know Monteverdi. He's our best cop."

"Yeah, I know. He just may be too good. I just can't forget all those accusations of him as a mafia hit man. I know the grand jury cleared him and the police investigation backed him up. But I still have those nagging doubts. Those guys were killed almost mob style and the grand jury and the police probably felt it was a case of good riddance to bad rubbish. The public never got too excited because they were mafia guys anyway, wise guys. Maybe Monteverdi will get another pass here, too."

"I know all about that, even though it was before my time. I think he got the confession right and that it'll hold up. What more can I say?"

" I just want you to know that if it doesn't hold up, and it looks like we tried to railroad a young black kid, the black reverends and their so-called community will be out to hang my ass. You know that. I

want you to know, if that happens, your tushy will be hanging right next to mine, on the highest spot on the hill."

"I know all that. I just have to have faith in my men and Monteverdi is one of the best of them."

"As you say," the mayor retorted. "Be here at four PM and we'll have the ladies and gentlemen of the press, our loveable media friends, here for the press conference. Try to get here a little earlier so I can go over the facts with you a little more."

"OK."

28

The media was anxious for the details. As they assembled in the press room at City Hall, a few of them had gotten some sketchy details leaked from their personal close contacts in government. The total facts, though, were still somewhat of a surprise and the media representatives responded with alacrity to get all the details they could.

The message delivered by the mayor was short and concise and contained only a few of the salient facts. This prompted a feeding frenzy when the conference was thrown open for questions.

Who is this guy Widmore? How old is he? Did he work alone? Are there any more to be arrested that you haven't located yet? How did you get him? What led to his arrest? All good questions and deserving of a good answer.

However, the mayor, acting on advice from his cabinet, stammered a bit as he chose to rely on the limited message he delivered. His excuse for not giving more facts was that he didn't want to spoil the evidence that would be needed to convict the perpetrator, so he had to hold them close to his vest for a little while longer. In truth, he had very few additional facts.

The media, though happy that the case had been solved, was not content to get only those few facts the mayor gave out. They would question and probe and get deeper into the case and its solution as time went on. They were doing the proper job of a democratic media, exposing all the facts they could, while at the same time serving their hunger for sensational stories.

Mayor McPhilliamy was uneasy in the glare of that spotlight. He was suffering from stomach dyspepsia and that made his natural grouchiness all the more noticeable. Whenever he could, he referred the question to Police Commissioner McKenna, who was as agile a seasoned politician you could get. He was used to dodging bullets and continued to do so adroitly. More would be heard from the inquisitive press, though.

At the end, McKenna supported the good police work that had solved the case and arrested the person responsible. He was confident, and he said so, that there would be a conviction in the case and justice would be served. He intimated the case depended heavily on the confession and he felt certain the confession would hold up to judicial scrutiny.

After the conference ended, and after the mayor and others had walked off the stage, McPhilliamy stopped McKenna who was itching to leave. "Remember," the mayor said pointedly, "that confession had better be good or its your ass and mine. Both asses. Got that straight?" McKenna was speechless.

29

But the media was relentless. They continually pushed for more details and probed every possible source for more information on the solution of the case and the accused murderer. Widmore had a court-appointed lawyer named John Wilson working on his behalf. He took the traditional position that a defendant should say as little as possible, publicly or otherwise, to avoid complicating his position and losing some rights at his eventual trial. Widmore, accepting that advice, kept mum on everything, even with his fellow inmates at the Jay Street Jail.

It is a well known fact that inmates will try to get facts from other inmates about the crimes they were accused of and trade that information for leniency in their own trials or sentences. Those inmates, some of them undercover police in certain cases, would continually probe the accused and try to gain their confidence to wean from them those facts that would have trading value and be helpful to the police. Widmore was warned against them and just didn't respond to any of those questions.

Wilson kept a close watch on his client and visited him several times after being appointed. Wilson was a tall, rangy person who had been a moderate basketball star in high school. He had gotten a basketball scholarship to St. John's University and performed well there, if not outstanding. With no professional basketball career in the offing, Wilson stayed at St. John's, enrolled in the law school, and graduated.

As a lawyer, he drifted into the criminal bar area and carved out a reasonably good living for himself, but mostly as a court-appointed attorney for indigent defendants. He disliked the practice, mainly because most of those defendants were actually guilty, and the practice degenerated into working out the best plea bargain possible. He also hated the need to visit defendants in the Jay Street Jail, loathing the smell of stale urine that permeated the place, and the cockroaches that had free reign.

However, he sensed Widmore was different somehow. As he visited with him, he became aware that Widmore was a young man of very limited natural intelligence, just about a fraction above being retarded. He was slow-witted and unable to comprehend most of what was happening without a lengthy and laborious explanation. He seemed to Wilson to be malleable and a person who would be likely to confess to a crime he had nothing to do with, especially if pressured. People like that are willing to do almost anything that will relieve them from the pressure cooker of police interrogation, even to confess. Wilson began to conclude that was exactly what happened here.

Finally, after a few more days, Wilson announced to the press that he was asking the court to have Widmore mentally evaluated. When pressed whether this move was going to be a preliminary to a defense of insanity, Wilson replied negatively. He said he felt Widmore just didn't have the mental capacity to commit crimes like that and was likely innocent. Wilson also stressed that the crimes seemed to require the work of more than one person and Widmore had very few, if any, friends. He was unlikely to have been able to recruit anyone to work with him.

The psychiatric tests performed on Widmore confirmed Wilson's thinking. Those test results didn't sit well in City Hall either. Mayor McPhilliamy, upset over the possibility that the supposed solution to the crimes would be overturned, barked at Commissioner McKenna. "Bill, you and your police force had better not let me down here. You had better see that Widmore's confession holds up. I've warned you repeatedly that both our asses would swing if it came out badly. Remember that!" and he slammed down the phone.

That type of treatment upset McKenna, too. He was not used to it and reacted badly. He reached out directly to Monteverdi. "Tony, I hope you've done your homework here. That Widmore thing is becoming unraveled and people in high places are questioning the validity of that confession. It has to hold up. You know that. It will be a public relations disaster for everybody if it doesn't hold up. The police force would get a black eye and I don't even know what would happen to you or me under those circumstances."

He had reached Tony on his intercom while Tony was out driving around the Flatbush area. It was impossible to have a lengthy conversation on that intercom while Tony was in the middle of traffic, with the usual sirens and horns blaring around him. "Look, Commissioner, I'll call you back in a short while. I'm out here on the streets and will talk to you about it in a little while. I know you're upset. I can tell that in your voice. All I know is I did what I thought was right. I can't do any more than that." Tony continued driving but had that queasy feeling that trouble was brewing.

30

Notwithstanding the skepticism of the media on the arrest and confession of Widmore, Ellen Coburn knew she could not let it rest there. It disturbed her conscience that another person had been arrested for a crime she knew he did not commit. Even worse, he had confessed to the crime and she of all people knew the confession was false.

She recognized Monteverdi's hand was deeply immersed in that arrest and confession. She had her own private thoughts about his integrity, his honesty. She believed the ultimate trial and conviction would occur, with whatever penalty the judge or jury would want imposed. That would produce an unconscionable travesty and burden on her conscience that she might not be able to ignore.

Monteverdi's charisma would see to that. Monteverdi was a decorated and well-known policeman, probably the most easily identifiable of the entire force. Over the years, he had been through a lot of the different wars with the enemies of society. He had even been suspected of being on the inside, among the soldiers of the Cosa Nostra army from time to time.

The Monteverdi she knew, and knew well, was a diabolical person, but charming nevertheless. She didn't trust him and didn't like him. She had always felt there was a lot more to her husband's killing than had been told, and she blamed Monteverdi for it. She couldn't quite place her finger on anything in particular, but she had that gut feeling he was to blame to a great degree.

The media regarded him as somewhat of a god, a high profile policeman who made great copy and was always ready to engage in chatter with any person from the fifth estate. They were drawn to him like bees to pollen and seemed never to miss an opportunity to provide him with ink or TV coverage whenever possible. He seemed just made for the sound bites of the many news shows that graced the airwaves from the end of the working day to bedtime in the big city.

Ellen knew, and even feared, that his reputation would override the ultimate good judgment that was imputed to the media along with a less deserved reputation for justice and evenhandedness. They were after the story, or the headlines, without mercy and without concern for the ultimate fairness or justice that resulted.

These had been high profile crimes and the so-called leaders of the African-American 'community' had come prancing out with their customary inflammatory rhetoric. They flew the flag of discrimination like it was made for them by an African-American Betsy Ross. They tossed their challenges and claims of discrimination against them because of their race in contradiction of the United States Constitution and its amendments. They took free speech and unimpeded and unimpeachable rhetoric to new heights. And they almost always spoke to the same enthusiastic group of supporters who seemed programmed to respond to their call at any time.

Despite the fact that slavery had disappeared from the landscape over a hundred years before, and no living one of them had ever lived under that bigotry, they claimed it as their badge of honor. They strode like peacocks bearing that medal on their chests as if they themselves had been bought and sold, and been touched by the oppressive lash of the southern aristocracy, now long gone.

Ellen was a woman of deep religious faith and even deeper ethical standards. She felt the burden of leading her committee into that hazy world of crime to attract attention to the plight of the families living in the shadow of the Junction. Originally feeling absolutely justified in what they had done, especially since they had chosen

their victims carefully, she now felt the full impact of what the ultimate result could be. How could this have gone so far wrong?

None of those victims contributed anything to society, except as bad examples. Their lives were symbols of an underground society, living in a netherworld of drugs, crime and sin, fathering children already infected with drugs and beating their women and their children senselessly, and without shame. They took advantage of a social reality that was being murdered by high taxation, corruption in government and waste of assets, unable to hire enough policemen to fully counter the criminal elements that seemed to grow like Topsy. They just "growed."

Ellen's awareness of all of this now made her question the correctness of the things the committee had undertaken. She felt responsible for involving her committee members, taking advantage of their alacrity to strike back in some way against a criminal society and a government that ignored its obligations to its better citizens.

Those were reasons sure enough, but Ellen now mulled them over in her mind, almost without rest. Days and nights were spent in mental arguments with herself and laying out the possible end results of everything. She couldn't do that as well as she wanted and woke up each morning, very early, bothered by nagging questions of the outcome that she couldn't solve or answer, or didn't want. What to do?

31

Monsignor Bates felt good in the warm spring air. It was the day before St. Patrick's Day, March 16, 1967. The seasons were already changing, not being mindful of the date the humans had selected for the start of the spring solstice. He was happy within himself as he strolled from the rectory along Glenwood Road to the church. Crocuses had been budding out for some time now, their striped leaves flattening against the damp ground. Tulips were already beginning to peek through the surface.

The church seemed empty as he entered. There was a coolness in the air within the church and that gave the emptiness an even greater feeling. He opened the door to the confessional and settled in. He was an old-fashioned priest, one who believed that confession was truly great for the soul, and the pathway to heaven with a clean slate. Because of that, he continued to offer confessional hours faithfully even though the number of Catholics exercising that privilege had dropped off considerably.

Where once there was a strong feeling about confessions within the Catholic laity, now parishioners seemed to believe that the forgiveness expressed in the Mass was absolution enough for their sins. Parishioners going to Communion, however, had increased substantially, with almost the entire group of Mass attendees receiving the holiest of Catholic sacraments, far more than exercised the confessional rite.

The sanctuary of the confessional where the priest sat was always stuffy and smelled a little musty. As he made himself comfortable within the confines of that dark chamber, somehow Monsignor Bates sensed he was not alone. He could hear what sounded like a person breathing in the confessional chamber next to him, someone already there, awaiting his presence to have their confession heard.

He slid open the window-slide between the two chambers, a small portal about eighteen inches square, leaving a screen-covered opening between them. The screen was dark and the absence of any light permeating either chamber made his ability to see into the next chamber almost impossible. He sat with his face turned away from the opening anyway, as he had been taught.

There was a person there. The person began the confession ritual immediately, "Bless me Father for I have sinned. It has been several months since my last confession." Monsignor Bates could tell it was a woman's voice, almost whispering the words.

"I've done something very serious, Father, something in violation of one of the Commandments."

Almost incredulous, but thinking mainly of adultery, Monsignor Bates recoiled. He felt obliged to dismiss his darkest thoughts of what he was about to hear. "Now, now," he whispered back, "it cannot be as bad as all that. Please continue to confess the sin you feel so badly about."

" I've participated in murders, Father. I feel very upset about it now although I thought it was justified when I did it. Now, someone has been arrested and is likely to be convicted and punished for something he didn't do. I have to get this off my conscience. I have to get absolution from you so that I can feel better about myself. I will continue to pray that travesty of justice does not continue or happen."

"Murders!" Monsignor Bates whispered back somewhat loudly. "Murders! How can that be forgiven without full repentance and true sorrow for the sin? There must be some extenuating circumstances. What caused you to do it, what drove you to such an extreme?"

"Father, it's a very long story but my motivation was well-intentioned. I am repentant, truly repentant, and very sorry for my sins. Can you please forgive me?"

"This is very unusual, *very unusual,*" Monsignor Bates exclaimed, leaning closer to the screen divider in the hope of catching some glimpse of the face of the confessor. He could feel his heart thumping under his cassock. The voice sounded a little familiar but the whispering between them and the hollow effect of the confessional chamber threw him off. He couldn't place it, and he couldn't spend any time now trying to place it. He had to pay close attention.

"I know, I know," said the confessor, fighting back tears. "I can't live with this secret myself anymore. I had to tell someone. I had to cry out to stop the pain. I knew if I came to the confessional, the secret would be protected from disclosure, but I could get some relief from absolution. Do you understand that?"

Now Monsignor Bates was awash in horror, horror at the fact that such a secret had been confided to him. He leaned back against the wall of the chamber. He was puzzled about what to do, what to say next, what to ask. He had been a simple parish priest almost all his life. He dwelt in a level of sins where people cursed and used the Lord's name in vain. People had confessed to him over the years all kinds of domestic quarrels of varying degrees of severity. This was something different--something all his time in the seminary and all his experience as a curate, and now as pastor, had not prepared him for.

"Yes, yes," he muttered back, trying to buy some time, time to think, to put the puzzle together. He knew he could never get this genie back in the bottle. He needed time. However, immediately after he said that, he heard the woman start the Act of Contrition. "Oh my God, I am heartily sorry for having offended thee…"

"She thinks she has been forgiven, she thinks she has received absolution," he thought to himself. "I must stop her. I must detain her and discuss this more. I don't even know when she did this, who or how many she did it to and much more. I don't know what penance should be required."

As he leaned forward to ask her more, he heard her blessing herself. She had completed the Act of Contrition and was bolting out of the confessional. In an instant she was gone, out into the church proper. Now he was more perplexed. Should he peek out of the confessional to see who it was? No! The rules of the confessional promised secrecy and protection from disclosure, and, most of all, anonymity. He had to protect the sanctity of the confessional if he expected others to respect it. Curious as he was, with only milliseconds to decide, he let the opportunity pass.

He leaned back. He was relieved somewhat, but did not feel better as the seconds ticked past. He felt as if he had been with some sick person who had vomited all over him. They felt better now, but now he had the vomit on him and had to clean up the mess. He had to get it off himself. This would be a day he would never forget.

32

John Wilson was an old fisherman and he knew right away when he had a prize catch on the line. Thirty-eight years of practicing law among the criminal bar and their clientele had honed his senses. He knew the depths that could be plumbed of every case that came along, almost immediately. In Widmore, he knew he had a big one, maybe the white whale of his entire practicing years. And he knew how to land them.

Wilson had pressed for a preliminary hearing on the Widmore case. That would make the police and the district attorney put up at least a minimum of their case' they had to disclose enough to make a *prima facie* case as the law called it. It had to be the minimum, enough to warrant a jury trial, and the state was presumed to have even more evidence than that before bringing a case to court.

Wilson banked on his instincts that the state had only the confession. He also thought it had been wrung from Widmore under stressful circumstances, possibly stressful enough to warrant the court to exclude it from the body of evidence available, whatever that turned out to be.

He was right. The state presented the confession. But in the first instance, on their case presentation, they withheld the taped and photographed details of how the confession was prodded out of Widmore. Wilson was right, but didn't know it yet.

Wilson believed he had good grounds to challenge the confession's admissibility. The circumstances were stressful all right, as they showed detectives browbeating and hollering and virtually torturing Widmore as he sat before them. Wilson suspected that, and knew his chance would come if it went that far. He had an ace up his sleeve.

On the defendant's presentation of Widmore's defense, Wilson called the eminent but now ancient court psychiatrist, Harry Baierlein. Now somewhat feeble and finding it difficult to walk and to talk loudly, he nevertheless strutted to the stand like a fighting rooster. At eighty-five he still had the instincts of a battler, and was happy to answer the bell one more time.

Baierlein's examination of Widmore was forceful. He detailed his private examination of Widmore and told of his findings. The youth was of low mental ability, almost impaired. He could not read or write well and could hardly follow the simplest instructions or color in even the simplest of outlines. He was just above the level of being called mentally retarded.

Baierlein offered his opinion on the likelihood of Widmore committing the crimes he was accused of and had supposedly confessed to. It was an inspiring demonstration. Baierlein told how Widmore did not possess the mental capacity to construct a crime scene that had occurred when the murders were committed.

Moreover, his opinion was that Widmore had few friends, was reclusive and relatively uncommunicative. He had one major ally in life and that was his grandmother, who actually did live where Widmore said she did. He carried with him her name, address and telephone number on a scrap of paper, just in case.

Because of that, Baierlein found him to have been unable to recruit anyone to help him with the acts required. He was quick to point out the weight of the individuals killed and how it would have been difficult and nearly impossible for Widmore to have acted alone. With such low mentality, and virtually unable to conduct his own life, or recruit others to help, Widmore was not able to have done what he was accused of.

It was an encore performance by a tired old fighter. Following the completion of his testimony, Baierlein looked around. The spectators, including the district attorney personnel, appeared stunned. There was dead silence in the courtroom. The judge graciously told him to step down and thanked him for his testimony. The judge had been impressed.

As Baierlein rose from the chair and headed out of the courtroom. Wilson stopped him as he passed counsel table and shook his hand as he went by and mumbled his own gratitude.

The silence continued for a few minutes until Dr. Baierlein slid out through the huge oak door. Finally, the judge invited attorneys to approach the bench. "What do you want to do, Mr. Prosecutor?" he asked. "I think you've been had by this wily fox over here. I can't let this case go forward. It's impossible for this defendant to have done what you accuse him of. I can see for myself that he is mentally impaired. I don't think he understood a word of what was going on here today. I'm prepared to toss this case, dismiss it, and stop a serious miscarriage of justice. Thank God for lawyers!"

"Judge, I am going to have to speak with my superiors. I need a few days to do that. Can you put the case over until Monday and allow me to have that time? I believe, in view of what happened here today, they will agree."

"It's OK with me...," the judge replied, "...if counsel for the defendant will agree. My condition is that the district attorney himself must be in court for that hearing----personally, do you understand that ?" He leaned across the bench toward the associate district attorney for emphasis. Then he slammed his huge fist down on the bench loudly to further emphasize it.

"Well," Wilson replied slowly in his best conqueror's drawl, "... suppose we can do that. Can you release Widmore in his own recognizance, let him go free until Monday?"

" I don't see why not," the judge answered quickly. "He doesn't seem to be guilty of anything. OK with you?" he asked the prosecutor. The associate district attorney nodded his agreement.

On the following Monday, the parties met in private and the District Attorney, Leonard Skolnick in person, asked to have the motion to dismiss heard in chambers, the private robing room of the judge .

"Absolutely not," Wilson interjected hastily. "This is something for the public to see and hear."

"I agree," said the judge. "The prosecution's motion is denied. Let's go out into the courtroom."

When the parties had fully assembled in their respective places, the district attorney rose. "The People (the state) move to have the charges against Mr. Widmore dropped."

"With prejudice," the judge added. "I don't want to be back here with him on the same charges."

"Absolutely," the district attorney promptly answered, half hiding his chin in his chest. He was ashamed to have to make such an ignominious motion, to be associated with a case so easily dismissed. It would be an embarrassment for years to come. It would have a serious effect on careers and lives.

The judge was not about to let him off the hook that easily. "You, sir, and your minions have done this young man a great injustice. You were prepared to go to trial against him based entirely on a confession that was obtained from him under circumstances that would probably not stand up in court. It didn't seem to pass the test of *Miranda* and his rights were totally ignored. If it weren't for Attorney Wilson, a veteran *pro bono lawyer* appointed by the court and working generally for free or the modest stipend the government pays, you would have gotten away with it, and that

would have been unjust, wrong, and a shame on you and on all of us in this judicial system."

"'But on the facts alone, as we just heard from Dr. Baierlein, his mentality was so low as to be almost classified as retarded, and physically and mentally incapable of committing crimes of this complexity. You should have seen that, your staff should have seen that, the police should have seen that and all the elements of the People's system, the apprehenders and the prosecutors, never considered that but should have. There is the fault and what could have happened to Mr. Widmore under different circumstances. You must be more careful. You hold the keys of justice and you must use them fairly and properly and with discretion and judgment, not like you did here. You and your officers should be ashamed at what was done here. Don't let it happen again."

The old gray-haired black lady in the front row had been crying throughout the proceedings but now they were tears of joy. She stepped beyond the rail and hugged and kissed Widmore, saying, "See, I told you it would be OK. Let's go home now." She then turned and took Attorney Wilson's hand and lifted it to her lips. "Thanks, suuh, thank you. We owe you a lot. From the bottom of my heart I thank you. We will always revere you as a saint in our house." Wilson was blushing, but he liked the scene. A few tears made it down his cheeks, too.

33

John Wilson reveled in the aftermath of the Widmore case dismissal. He gave lengthy interviews to the media and appeared on talk shows as a mini-celebrity with current newsworthy material. He was expansive but cautious in his blame on the police department for having dug up Widmore out of nowhere, and for having fabricated a confession out of pure cloth. He detailed the way the police had browbeaten and terrorized Widmore until he was willing to confess to a crime he did not commit, just like the police wanted.

In Wilson's opinion, the Widmore incident was typical of police work. Their job as he claimed they saw it was to solve a crime by finding anyone who could be blamed, guilty or not. He charged misfeasance on the district attorney's office for their willingness to bring such a case to prosecution without standing back and viewing the evidence in its entirety and the source from which it came. Widmore, he said, was a simple lad who was obviously incapable of undertaking the killings as they had been done. The prosecutors should have seen that and refused to go along as they did at the urging of the police.

The case became a *cause celebre* and stayed in the headlines for several weeks before fading gradually back onto the inner pages of the newspapers. The TV media lost interest before that and did not carry any mention of it anymore.

Police Commissioner McKenna properly predicted that was what then would happen. He relied on the methods of the media to lose interest eventually, and let the matter die of its own accord. That did not suit Mayor McPhilliamy, however. He called McKenna on the carpet and yelled at him regularly.

"This Widmore thing is an embarrassment to me, to the city and should be to the police department. The African-American leaders see it as the police trying to railroad one of their own for a crime. They contend it's the usual police methodology and that's the reason behind so many black youths being in jail. I have to tell you I am very pissed off about how this thing was handled by your people."

"Look, Mayor," McKenna protested, gesturing wildly with his hands. "I assigned the most effective and high profile cop we have on the force to the case. He did his job. He picked up the suspect, he grilled him personally. The kid confessed. What was he to do? Ignore that?"

"Don't you dare ask me what he should do!" the mayor growled, pounding his desk. "You have no right to do that. You and your men are responsible for making the proper evaluation. You should have had the kid evaluated yourselves, rather than wait for it to be done to you, understand, in open court. You of all people can't expect me to be the expert on that issue."

McKenna protested but he knew it was futile. "I know it could have been handled better. I repeatedly asked Monteverdi if the confession would hold up and he assured me it would. You know that. I reported that to you all the time."

"Your ass is going to swing for this, Bill. The ministers are already calling for an investigation. You know what they want. They want a scapegoat, someone to blame and to take the heat, get fired or driven out of office. They want someone to be sacrificed for this event. You hear them. You know that. You've been around long enough to know that. You even know they're right in a way."

34

Ellen Coburn could relax a little now. She no longer felt the pressure of an innocent person taking the hit for her activities. It was a great feeling, almost one of euphoria, and she was once again able to convince herself that her and the committee had been right in what they did. It was justified in that it had raised the issue of drug matters in the public mind and she was sure something would be done about it now.

But not everybody was relaxed once the Widmore case was dismissed. The media had reawakened its interest in the Flatbush killings and was again fishing around for the cause. Their ready focus as usual was on the organized crime group, the mafia. Investigative reporters were writing speculative articles about how the whole thing looked like a Cosa Nostra battle. They intimated that because long time Cosa Nostra suspect Tony Monteverdi was the lead detective on the arrest and near conviction of someone who could not have committed the crime, it was a ploy to move attention off the back of organized crime.

Don Miglio did not fail to recognize the possible harm that could come to his organization. He knew that, from time to time, they had to endure heat from the media and even the police because of their activities. However, this was not one of their doing, he was certain of that. This heat didn't belong to them. His runner paid a visit to Monteverdi.

"You asked to see me, Don Miglio?" Monteverdi asked.

"Yes. I did. Come in Anthony. Come in." Don Miglio answered from the darkened area around the table where he sat alone. "Come in and sit down. I want to talk to you."

"What did you want to see me for?" Monteverdi asked, knowing full well why he had been summoned.

"Anthony, I told you. Don't fuck up. Don't screw around with this thing about the killings in Flatbush and make a mistake. Now the whole world knows you made a mistake. Now they seem all to be yelling about how it was our boys who did those killings. I don't like that. I don't like to hear that we're always in the paper or on the news shows. That's not good."

Monteverdi lowered his head. "I know. What was I to do?" He muttered lowly. "He acted suspicious. He confessed to the damned thing. What was I to do?"

"Anthony," Don Miglio responded, tapping his finger to his temple and leaning forward. "You have to use judgment. You have to use your head. That's why God gave that head to you. To use it."

"But Don Miglio..." Monteverdi started. Don Miglio interrupted him. "Don't argue Anthony. You fucked up. This is strike three as they say. You fucked up on the shooting of those two *capos* in the Bronx. Then you fucked up on putting the hit on that cop friend of yours. You said you could keep him quiet peacefully. You remember the trouble that caused in the papers and on the TV. And now this! Strike three! I'm very disappointed in you, Anthony. Very disappointed. You're lucky that right now the press is trying to hang that asshole Johnson and the war, and their focus is mainly on that."

Now Monteverdi was almost begging. "Please don't say that, Don Miglio. Please don't say that. Please give me another chance. Please."

"Don't worry, Anthony. I'm not gonna hurt you. I just won't ask you to do anything special for me from now on, at least for a while. You will have to earn my respect back. That's all. Cabeesh?"

"Thank you, thank you , Don Miglio. I will earn your respect and trust again. You'll see. I'll do it. It may be hard to do but I'll do it. You can count on that." Monteverdi was relieved that he was not going to be punished for his acts. He took Don Miglio's hand and kissed it. Then he backed out towards the door and left.

Outside, there was a slight drizzle falling, mistlike. It felt cool against his flushed face, almost medicinal as he had been sweating a little under the glare of Don Miglio. As usual there was the customary bodyguard standing in the doorway area, smoking.

Monteverdi went to his car and got in but the motor wouldn't turn over. Again and again he tried, really wanting to be out of there, to be somewhere else desperately. But the motor wouldn't cooperate and only responded with churning groans.

Finally, Monteverdi got out and went over to the bodyguard who seemed to be ignoring the entire thing. "Can you help me?" Monteverdi asked. "I think the engine needs a boost to get started. It must be the battery. Can you help me?"

The bodyguard said nothing but stared at Monteverdi and puffed on his cigarette. "I think there's a mechanic a few blocks away. We use him all the time and he comes. It's up on Canal Street. About two blocks. You can call him from inside. We don't have cables or any tools here."

Monteverdi went inside again, something he dreaded doing. The bodyguard inside had the name and phone number of Sabella's Garage and he called. Sabella said he would be right over, and he was true to his word.

The problem wasn't as simple as the battery boost Monteverdi thought he needed, but Sabella was up to the task. After a few minutes under the hood, he got the car started with the boost, and Monteverdi drove away at last. Relieved.

35

If Ellen Coburn was relaxed now, Monsignor Bates was just the opposite. From the day of his experience with the mystery woman in the confessional, he was haunted by the memory of the incident. Even more so, he was haunted by the implications of the confession he had heard. He tried incessantly to balance that knowledge with his obligations as a priest and his own ethical standards.

It was a complicated matter. He wrestled with the idea of going to the authorities to make the matter known. Then again, he was duty bound as a priest to honor the sanctity of the confessional. The confessional enjoyed a special status in the eyes of Catholics. Confession and absolution were basic tenets of the Roman Catholic Church, imbedded in the faith for centuries.

It even had its secrecy drafted into statutory law by protecting a priest from being forced to testify regarding matters in the confessional unless the confessor consented. It was a major recognition of one of Catholicism's basic tenets and a fundamental difference between Catholicism and other Christian religions. No other religion offered forgiveness of sins once confessed and given absolution by a priest, binding in heaven and on earth, forever.

It traced its history back to the New Testament. Jesus had said to Saint Peter that whatsoever the Apostles forgave on earth would be forgiven in heaven. Something that could be traced back to the Savior himself could not be lightly dealt away.

Monsignor Bates could not satisfy himself as to where his duty lay. It was a momentous thing for a priest to have enter his life. It was not the type of thing that he had volunteered into the priesthood to deal with. He was a simple man, a parish priest, who labored in the vineyards of Christianity, accepting anonymity for the right and privilege of dispensing religious sacraments and advice to the local parishioners. Momentous things, such as this confession, were not supposed to come his way. He agonized over his next step.

Finally, he decided to visit his mentor and old friend, Bishop Philbin. Philbin and Bates had been in the seminary together years ago. Philbin was much more of an intellectual and was well suited to the push and pull of church politics of the day.

Coming from County Mayo in Ireland, Peter Philbin had been born into a family of five. His parents eked out a fairly acceptable living on their farm. Peter grew up working hard on the farm, tending to the cows and chickens and helping in the harvests. When he was fifteen, he announced to his parents that he felt he had a vocation, a calling to join the priesthood.

His mother was overjoyed. It had been a tradition in Irish families that the oldest of their children would enter religious life, possibly laying the groundwork for the parents to enter into heaven. His mother had felt disappointed if not betrayed somewhat when her oldest son Patrick refused to enter the priesthood. Then, his sister Mary, the next in line, also refused, not wanting to accept the hard and anonymous life in a convent. Now, Peter had stepped up.

He entered Maynooth Seminary just outside Dublin where he quickly made his mark as an outstanding student and a person with a deep abiding sense of Christianity, its history and its global purpose and mission. He had no trouble adopting the noble mission of the church as his mission in the priesthood. From the beginning, he was favorably impressed with campus life. Maynooth combined both a seminary, that graduated young men as priests for service in the dioceses of Ireland, and a college for the laity that was co-educational, accepting both men and women in its rolls. Peter Philbin did not yield to the temptations of the flesh, although as a handsome and rugged young man, he received plenty of opportunities.

Some of its religious graduates were even sent abroad to spread Christianity through the missions and, of course, some of them even ended up in the United States. Peter Philbin was one of these and was sent for further study to the Theological Seminary of Mount St. Alfonsus in upstate New York—Esopus. High on the western shore of the Hudson and in remote circumstances, the Seminary at Esopus focused its students even more to the purpose and mission of the church. It turned out future monsignors, bishops and, who knows, maybe a cardinal or two and, hopefully some day, a pope.

There, Philbin met the affable Bill Bates, more a party animal than Philbin at that time, but nevertheless a dedicated servant of God. Though totally disparate in size, Philbin tall and athletic looking and Bates short and seemingly more likely to take his athletics in the form of bowling, they got along well in all aspects of advanced seminary life. They enjoyed themselves, too, at occasional social events. They became fast friends, friends for life.

Once in the United States, Philbin was assigned to the Diocese of Brooklyn and actually to the Parish of Our Lady Help of Christians. It was a progressive and very active parish set in the heart of Flatbush, an area young Peter had only read about but never thought he would see. From the beginning, the parishioners took to him and he was favored with many invitations to golf, to swim, and dinners at Breezy Point, a haven for Irish-Americans living in Brooklyn.

He immersed himself in the social whirl but did not forget his ambitions to rise in the church. His popularity caught the eye of the Bishop of Brooklyn, Brian J. McInteggart, who invited him into the higher councils of the Diocese and sort of became his mentor. To improve his chances to move up the political ladder, he was sent to Rome to study even more among the great religious thinkers of the church, among them the Bishop of Venice, Angelo

Roncallo who would become Pope John the Twenty-Third. That proved to be a wonderful association for young Peter, as he was now internationally known, and would be remembered when promotions came along.

He returned to the United States already a Monsignor and, after a brief stint as a pastor, he was reassigned to the Diocesan Office where he quickly made his mark. Naturally, when Bishop McIntеggart passed on, Peter was the logical choice for successor, even though he was further down the promotional line than others who had waited patiently for just such an opportunity.

It was Bishop Philbin that Monsignor Bates went to see that October morning. The world was waiting for the World Series game between the St. Louis Cardinals and the explosive Boston Red Sox. Although a good baseball fan, Monsignor Bates thought the chance to speak with the Bishop about this heavy matter was more important. So he went.

36

Bishop Philbin didn't wait for his old friend, Bill Bates, to be ushered in to his office. Instead, he got up from his padded chair behind the desk and walked out to the doorway, where Bates was waiting in the anteroom. It was a significant gesture for a man of Philbin's stature. It was no easy task either, because the bishop was a large man.

"Come in, Bill," the bishop said in a generous voice, a huge smile streaking across his face. "Come right in. It's a pleasure to have you visit me. You should do it more often, you know." The Irish brogue he brought with him to the new land leaked into his speech.

The bishop hugged Monsignor Bates. It was humorous to see the little monsignor enclosed in the arms of this huge man, both wearing the colored fringes to identify their rank in the church. "What brings you all the way down here today?" the bishop asked.

"I have a problem," Monsignor Bates said in a low voice, almost as if he were talking to himself. "A real problem. I think you can help me, maybe give me a little guidance."

"I'm anxious to hear it, and you know I'll help you in any way I can. I'm especially anxious to hear it realizing, as I do, that I can't think of any problem a man like yourself couldn't solve." The bishop intended to flatter his visitor as he did so many other visitors, motioning him to sit on the couch behind the coffee table.

The bishop sat across from him and peered into his face. "Now, what is it, my friend?"

Monsignor Bates drew a loud sigh and launched into the story. As he unfolded the details of that astounding experience in the confessional, he could see the alarm cross the bishop's face and knew he was pondering the deep problems such an event could propagate. Monsignor Bates recognized the face of the bishop was showing the signs of a problem that was fully understood in its ramifications and that he was puzzled over what to say.

"Well, Bill, that's truly astounding." In his bright purple cassock, the bishop made a truly impressionable figure. Now, however, that figure and face exuded a body language that showed it was puzzled and groping to come up with some suggestion for his friend.

"You know, Bill, my old Irish grandmother always used to say, 'Trust the Lord. He won't give you any problem bigger than you and He can solve together.' She was right. Come, come over to the altar here. We'll pray together on it. Something will occur to one of us, I'm sure."

They looked almost funny, the two of them, side by side, facing the large crucifix on the tiny altar. The bishop, a large man, kneeling, absorbed in prayer, next to his friend, Monsignor Bates, a small and somewhat rotund man. They were both princes of the church, in different ways.

37

The media kept up the barrage. They were insistent on getting more information and were hanging tough. When the media gets the upper hand in anything, they choke out the last possible bit of retribution, especially when it's a popular issue.

The idea was to get a scalp, someone to swing for the Widmore affair. They didn't care whose scalp they got, so long as it was a scalp, but the higher the better. This would be their victory and they wanted to have it no other way. Sooner or later they would zero in on the scalp they hankered for, then they would be relentless—and organized.

Right now, they were shooting for Police Commissioner McKenna's scalp. However, what they didn't realize was that he was an old-line politician, with roots in the federal system long before he returned to New York to head the force. His was going to be a difficult scalp to get, maybe impossible.

The media took daily and nightly shots at the ineptitude they claimed permeated the police department under McKenna. The Widmore affair only supported their view and gave evidence of the claimed lack of diligence they took issue with. But they were dealing with a force beyond their ability to comprehend. McKenna had been forged in the battleground of the media and had won before. He would not be denied now.

McKenna knew how to play it, and was not hesitant to use his knowledge to the best end. He was also patient, knowing that he had a full stacked hand and could play his cards when he wanted, not when the collective media, the self-appointed public educators, wanted. McKenna knew that he made the ink that counted; all else was simply speculation. The public would understand that.

As the incident continued to heat up, and the African-American reverends were applying their typical force, using their ability to attract media attention, he knew he would have to defuse the situation, at least a little. McKenna paused one night, on his way into a routine dinner engagement for some public cause, and engaged the media present. There was a rush to the commissioner's side by cameramen and interviewers caught unawares by this sudden news opportunity.

"You fellows have had pretty much a free reign, picking on me over the last few weeks. I want to remind you that you people were the ones who gave Detective Monteverdi such a great public reputation. He was literally our best cop to get into the investigation. I want to remind you of your happy headlines and stories when that appointment was made."

McKenna paused to allow his tangential attack to sink in. "You got exactly what you wanted. I want you to also be aware that Monteverdi did a great job, notwithstanding that he grabbed the wrong party. You have had weeks to ponder this situation. Remember that Monteverdi only had seconds to react, on the spot, in some dreary little corner of the city. He was alone, and had a likely possibility of a suspect not answer normal questions properly. He had to make up his mind, then and there, to follow through or not. What would you have done?"

Pausing again to grant them time to absorb his thought, but knowing that those people then assembled would have little to do with the final determination to air his interview, certainly not entirely, he decided to throw a few more snips into the fray.

"You and I know that you would have hanged him, literally, if he had let that possible criminal escape his grasp. You would have been out for his head, mine, the mayor's and everybody else's. The

black community would have been marching to condemn us for not prosecuting the murders of their community members. The black reverends would have been holding gatherings and marches of a different slant, and taking out a different kind of approach to the one they have now, all because we had let someone likely to have done the act get loose. They have plans to react either way, at any time. And you would have reported it all gleefully."

"You have to get over this stuff. The police department is working on the case and, who knows, at any time we may have a solution, may have an opening and may catch the person or persons responsible. You never know, and the pressure you bring does nothing to help. You have to behave more responsibly. You have an obligation to the public not to improperly foment public opinion to a wrong solution. Now print that. All of it."

McKenna quickly marched through the revolving door and on into the dinner. He knew he had them and they knew it, too. What they didn't appreciate was that McKenna had been through it all before. He had been personally involved in the great vote count scandal in south Texas, when Lyndon Johnson beat out the very popular "Coke" Stevenson for the senate seat.

He had weathered the withering fire of investigations and claims of voting fraud and ballot box stuffing. He had agonized through it while the investigations were holding forth but he never gave in, never withered under the fire. He came through it all, and endeared himself to a grateful Senator Johnson, eventually to be President Johnson. McKenna was a veteran, had been through the publicity wars, and nothing scared him anymore. The media didn't know what it was up against. They wouldn't get McKenna's scalp.

38

Now the powers that run the media knew they had taken on too much. They were not going to get McKenna's scalp and didn't really mind that they had run into a dead end there. They knew the iron-fisted police commissioner now was going to stand his ground and defend his force. They did not want to go to battle on that issue with him. So they sought a substitute. Any head or scalp would do. They just needed a scalp to satisfy their drive and justify their lofty and privileged position with the populace.

Tony Monteverdi was next in line. After all, it was his action in stopping Widmore on the street. He didn't seem to have any probable cause to stop him and inquire other than that he was alone going through the very area where the killings had taken place and, in Monteverdi's eyes, was acting suspiciously.

It was Monteverdi's error in judgment that led him to scare the devil out of Widmore and take him to the station house in tears. He should have known right off that Widmore was not mentally capable of any such planning, nor was he able to carry out such murders alone. Also, what could possibly be his motive? Certainly not robbery, or drugs.

It was Monteverdi who worked on Widmore at the station house. He applied such unrelenting pressure that Widmore confessed to crimes he didn't commit and knew next to nothing about. Nevertheless, Monteverdi, in a slip of zeal, obtained that confession from Widmore that was so easily dismissed when exposed to the light of the courtroom. Yes, Monteverdi was a real good candidate to lose his scalp.

The media dug up the old details about his history on the police force. They dredged up the unproven allegations of his mafia connections, how he apparently executed mafia *capos and soldiers* on what they thought were orders from the mafia kingpin, Don Miglio. Nothing certain, but certainly some smoke and likely some fire behind it.

Then there was the long ago botched up drug raid in Harlem that allowed the drug kingpins to get away safely from the police dragnet. Monteverdi had orchestrated the entire thing, right down to the timing and use of guns and tear gas to flush the kingpins and their operatives out of the building so the entire drug collection could be seized and destroyed. Nobody ever knew exactly what went wrong.

All that was ever exposed was that a talented police officer, Eddie Coburn, had been blown up in a unmarked police car as he waited for the signal to close in on the operation. It was a signal that some doubted was ever intended to be given. Coburn was immolated, of course. The details of the incident were so gruesome they seemed to overshadow the failed circumstances of the botched raid, and were lost in the after glow of the huge funeral of Officer Coburn in Brooklyn. Almost the entire force turned out and the investigation into the entire matter got lost in the media frenzy to cover Coburn's funeral and interment.

But the media remembered Monteverdi and his history. His scalp would make a suitable replacement for McKenna's. Monteverdi was a high up detective, probably the most celebrated police officer in the nation, and certainly the most decorated. There was talk of his running for Congress after his police career ended and he did little to squelch such rumors. Yes, he was a worthy replacement!

The media launched its campaign against Monteverdi almost immediately, once the decision seemed to have been made to go after him. Their insinuations about his mafia connections were highlighted, repeated and singled out for special treatment on an almost daily basis, with repeated news inserts on the TV media.

Mayor McPhilliamy was interested in this switch in stories and emphasis from McKenna to Monteverdi. Almost anything was OK with him as long as the buck did not come to rest in the mayor's office and force him to respond or defend his actions or those of his police commissioner. Anyone but him was all right.

But it was not OK with Don Miglio. He felt the enormous heat of the stories being written and spoken about on the news programs. The late night talk shows even got into the act, poking fun at the mafia and the way they did things. The jokes became nightly events on those shows, with David Letterman, particularly, naming the mafia personnel, whose names were publicly known, on his nightly list of "ten."

Don Miglio knew that this much public exposure of the mafia system and its personnel could not be good for the organization. "Imagine," he said to his loyal henchmen who were always with him, "that stupid cop has done the worst for us. He's gotten us into the papers and on the TV. We can't live with that. He fucked up once too often this time."

39

Tony Monteverdi was puzzled by the message the Sicilian messenger brought. He was the same messenger he had seen before several times from Don Miglio. The guy never seemed to show any familiarity with Monteverdi, even though he had brought him many such messages over the years. Always aloof, it was almost as if he was purposely acting as a stranger, and was very poor at it. It was strange to say the least.

This message was heartwarming to Tony, to a degree, and he welcomed the idea of Don Miglio giving him another chance, as the message said. He was to meet Don Miglio in his car at the Bay Parkway, Brooklyn shopping center next Thursday, at 3 PM. Tony had met Don Miglio there before, so the instruction to park in the usual place, on the parking row facing the bowling alley as you enter the center on the right, was familiar.

Tony appreciated that Don Miglio seemed to always deal with him personally. He felt that gave him a 'leg up' and a higher status than just one of the *soldiers*, or even some of the *capos*. That always pleased him and, of course, Don Miglio had always treated him as somebody special. This was only Tuesday, so there was ample time to prepare his schedule to be on time for the 'meet.' With Don Miglio, you always had to be on time or it was taken as a sign of disrespect.

Tony was able to read the papers, which he did avidly, and listen to the news reporters, the talking heads who regurgitated whatever the writers had written. He always had the impression that the news industry had gotten cheap, that they were following each other around, and reading their news pieces and then reporting on them themselves a day later. Nobody seemed to notice much so they were able to get away with it. It did take away respect for the reporters, though, and rightly so.

Tony was headed to the hockey game that night, to see the Rangers play the Flyers at the Garden. He didn't particularly like the Garden, it was inconveniently located, had dirty bathrooms and the stale smell of beer all over. He didn't like hockey that much for that part either, but they were the only game in town tonight so he would go. He got in free just by showing his badge, the precious tin, but most times didn't even have to do that. Most of the Garden personnel at the gates knew him.

In a way, Tony was vastly relieved that the pressure of the headlines and news stories had not turned Don Miglio against him. The don was capable of making judgments that were sometimes strange and illogical, so Tony was more pleased than he normally would be for this 'second chance.'

The hockey game went as usual, very dull, so Tony left early, getting to his car ahead of the rush hour crowd, and shooting out over the connecting roads to the Van Wyck, headed south and for home. It had been a good day, if not so great a night.

Thursday came in brightly, the sun came out early and strong and made it a nice late October day. Tony looked forward to his meeting that afternoon with Don Miglio, wondering what would be asked of him. Don Miglio always expressed it as a 'favor' so Tony knew it would be a personal request.

Tony bought his lunch at a McDonald's restaurant and took it with him. He headed for the shopping center early, to have time to eat and digest his lunch and wait for Don Miglio. He did not want to be late in the least as Don Miglio would certainly take that as a sign of disrespect.

Tony would recognize the car when it arrived. The don had eschewed the larger Cadillac and Lincoln Town Car he certainly could have afforded. He opted instead for a Lincoln, but the smaller Continental, without the big tire on the back, so as not to attract too much attention. The don loved anonymity and worked at preserving it to the fullest extent he could. The car was big and black, so it attracted attention anyway, since it was always so well-shined.

Don Miglio arrived just minutes to three, right on time. His driver pulled the big black car up next to Tony's car, just to its right. Tony quickly got out and slipped into the back seat of the Lincoln. Don Miglio, who always rode in the front, didn't want to attract attention, turned and greeted Tony.

"Anthony, it is good to see you," he said happily. "You're looking well."

"Always great to see you, too, Don Miglio," Tony said in a hushed voice. "Thank you, thank you for giving me an opportunity to serve you."

"Now, now, Tony," the don said, raising his hand to stop Tony from making his entry more effusive. "I've come to ask you to do me a favor, a great favor. Will you do it?"

"I will do anything you ask of me, Don Miglio. Just ask and it will be done."

"Tony, you know the press and the TV people have been concentrating on us, the family. I'm sure you know it because you're mentioned in some of the stories. I'm sure you've heard and seen them."

"Sure, sure, Don Miglio, I know about them. But what can I do about it? What do you want me to do?"

"I want you to retire. I want you to give up your badge and your life's work on the police force and retire. You can go to Florida, Arizona, Las Vegas or California-- just get away from here. The media guys are making you out to be the scapegoat of that arrest thing with that stupid kid. It's got to stop. I can't think of any other way to stop it. You could just leave. You'll have enough money with your pension and we would take care of you, as we always do. How about it?"

"Wow, Don Miglio, that is some favor," Tony replied almost astonished. "How soon would you want me to do that? How much time would I have?"

"I would want this to happen right away. The next two weeks or maybe less. The sooner the better."

"Don Miglio, can I think this over? I have to think it through. It's a big step, you know."

"Anthony, I know it's a big step. Is it too much to ask of you?"

"Well it is a lot to ask. Please let me have a few days to think it over. Is that OK with you?"

"Sure, sure, Anthony. Take your time. I know it's a big favor and I want you to reflect on it to satisfy yourself. I want you to be at peace with your decision. Let me know directly in the usual way, or just through the announcement. Cabeesh?" But the don was disappointed in Monteverdi's attitude.

Tony sensed the meeting was over. He started to say his goodbye and Don Miglio could see a glistening in Tony's eyes. It *was* a big favor to ask.

Tony climbed out of the car . As he did, Don Miglio said, "Just let us leave first, then you pull out. We don't want to attract any attention."

Tony understood. He got back into his own car and put the key in the ignition and waited, to give them a head start. He let out a big sigh, and shook his head. It was a huge favor to ask and he wasn't ready for that one. He watched over his shoulder as the big black car backed up and pulled away towards the shopping center exit to Bay Parkway.

Tony turned the key in the ignition. The car motor chugged and churned but the motor would not turn over. He tried again. "Shit," he said. "Of all times for this hunk of garbage not to start."

He turned the key again. Suddenly a big explosion rang out. A huge orange and red fireball and dark black smoke flooded the air. Tony's car had exploded and was a hot, burning inferno. Nobody could have survived it.

The big black car turned right out of the exit and went under the Belt Parkway overpass. Its occupants seemed indifferent to what had just happened. Then, it turned left onto the service road heading for the Brooklyn Battery Tunnel. Best to be out of the vicinity as soon as you could, disappear into the mass of humanity. As the vehicle made its left turn, one could already hear the emergency vehicles sounding their sirens, in an effort to get to the shopping center.

40

Bill McKenna had been through it all. The cumulative effect of what was going on in the very recent past now was getting to him. He had seemingly weathered the storm of the Flatbush murders. He had apparently come through the Widmore escapade unscathed, letting the hammer fall on Tony Monteverdi. Poor Tony. Now he's gone, too, and in the worst way. Blown up like that in the explosion of the car. He had no chance, the poor bastard.

Everything seemed to be crowding in on McKenna at the same time. He was tired of that dyspeptic, insecure mayor who kept up a continuous storm of threats and promises, trying to cajole some action out of the department that was just not possible to get. Evidence, after all, was evidence, and they just didn't have and couldn't find any. The entire scene was wearing on him.

Then there was always the predicament with the black ministers. They appeared at every opportunity, often with the same sycophants swallowing and repeating their message, without digesting or thinking it through. Then, after the situations they had imposed themselves in were proven to be the other way, they just disappeared for a while--no apology, no nothing. Yet when it came out their way, they demanded apologies and the heads of anybody even remotely involved. Any head would do.

He had had enough of this crap and was ready to move on. His friend, Lyndon Johnson, was now a lame duck president. The Democrat Party he once knew was no longer there. It had been replaced with totally political animals, greedy and self interested only. They were afraid of doing anything that might possibly offend anyone or cut off their contributions. Things that cried out for action were just left to die idly on the side, undone. There were no more fearless politicians who were statesmen and able to consider their franchise as securing their power from the consent of the governed. Now, they were afraid and unwilling to exercise that power, except to help themselves and special interests that funded their reelection campaigns.

It was cool that late September morning when McKenna appeared at his office. His routine was to go down to the snack bar, purchase a hot cup of decaf coffee and take it upstairs in the elevator, as he went through the mail. He followed his routine this day.

Usually, the mail had been carefully sorted and he only had to look at important letters that required action or a special reply. Ultimately he would pass them on with his comments to subordinates who would prepare responses for his review and signature. Today was a little different.

In leafing through the letters, his eye fell on one unopened envelope that seemingly had become stuck in the important pile. Usually those would be taken out and he wouldn't see them. They were generally crank letters anyway. This one seemed different somehow. It was addressed to him personally, but that wouldn't matter in the culling out process. It had the aura of something different, something important, so he tore away the sealed part and took out the written part.

The letter was carefully printed. The writer seemed to have spent a lot of time doing it very carefully. Every word was neatly placed and spelled correctly. It read, "If you want to solve the Flatbush killings, look up Ellen Coburn on Farragut Road and East 37 Street in Brooklyn." It was not even signed.

"My God," McKenna thought. "Could this be it? Could this be the break in that case the entire city was hoping for and expecting?" It was so accidental the way it had gotten through the culling process, and how succinct it was, and timely. McKenna thought, "This could

be a message from God telling me of a break in the case I so sorely need. I can't ignore it. I don't have a clue as to where it came from or who sent it, but I just have to look into it as quickly as I can."

41

Bill McKenna would follow up this lead himself. He wanted no more of the 'super cops' handling these items. Besides, he didn't want to look like a rank amateur, having policemen follow up on anonymous letters. He would look really foolish if it turned out to be a dud of any type and he didn't want that, so why expose himself to the possibility? He had had enough, too, of the carping criticism of the media and his dyspeptic boss, the mayor. He would do the leg work himself this time.

The morning air in October was already cool. It was only the eleventh, but fall seemed to have come on quickly. The air was fresh but the coolness made his nostrils itchy and he slipped into a police department unmarked car in the cool garage. Adjusting the temperature in the car, he turned on the radio and headed out onto the Brooklyn Bridge towards Flatbush.

As he drove along, he approached a McDonald's with its golden arches looming up out of the building it occupied. Turning into its parking lot area, he switched quickly to the "drive-thru" lane and ordered a cup of decaf—black coffee. It was delivered to him in a cardboard cup, steaming hot and tough to hold. He had to fumble through his pocket for the eighty cents it cost and, not finding enough change, offered a dollar bill to the gal serving. He noticed she was impatient at his fumbling for the money, although there were no customers behind him.

Sipping the coffee with some difficulty because it was so hot, he nosed the car out onto Flatbush Avenue and headed south. At Newkirk Avenue, he turned east to Brooklyn Avenue. He turned the car to the right and again headed south and stopped for the traffic light at Glenwood Road. That was where the first body had been found.

He realized he had passed Farragut when he saw the buildings of St. Vincent Ferrer Church and school to the east. He turned again on Glenwood, then drove back to East 37th Street and headed north again, the one block to Farragut Road. Ellen Coburn lived in number 3718. It would be on his side of the street and he didn't want that. He continued south on East 37th to Avenue D, turned right and then right again as he headed up East 38th Street to where it cornered with Farragut Road. It was one way south and the street was wide.

McKenna parked the car at the corner facing Coburn's house. He wanted to observe her when she didn't know anyone was looking. He noticed the house was white stucco with a brown shingled floor on top, as most of them were, but hers was the only detached house on the block. The others all shared a driveway. The house sat atop an obviously filled in lot that gradually ran down to sidewalk level as it reached Farragut Road.

He also noticed the outside of the house was clean and the grounds well-kept. The only modernization evident to him was that the large windows facing Farragut Road had been replaced with newer rollout windows. There was a large tree in front of the house in the grassy area between the sidewalk and the roadway. It was a nice house, he concluded. Although he could see large numbers of leaves strewn across the grounds in front of the houses, it was not any reflection on the homeowners, since the fall leaves had almost finished coming down with the colder weather. It could have been any policeman's house.

The coffee was still hot so he sipped it slowly. He unfolded the New York Times and began scanning the front pages of the four sections. He waited patiently for some signs of life in the house across the street, but it seemed lifeless. No lights were visible and there seemed to be no movement inside that he could see through the front windows, but he couldn't see inside very much. He decided to be patient and wait for a while, like any good detective.

After a short while, he finished the coffee. It seemed to get colder in the car now because he was parked in the shade of a tree, shielding the car from the sun. He was beginning to get impatient, especially because he could begin to feel nature's demands building up in his bladder. He didn't know how long he would have to wait and even thought that, if nature drove him to it, he could urinate in the empty coffee cup. He thought about the press he would have to endure if he was caught and reported by someone while he was doing that. Imagine, the commissioner of police peeing in a cardboard coffee container, and in broad daylight in a quiet residential neighborhood!

As these mundane thoughts played out in his mind, he noticed a slight flurry of action in what was the front porch area of the house he was watching. Then, the door opened and a youngish woman in her fifties stepped out and closed the door behind her. She was clad in a grey houndstooth cloth coat and looked to have a nice figure. As far as McKenna could see, she appeared very nice looking, probably a woman who was a real beauty in her youth.

She sprightly stepped down the three cement steps to the street and turned to the west abruptly. Then she walked quickly along Farragut Road and turned south to go down East 37th Street. McKenna surmised she was on her way to church, just in time for the nine o'clock Mass. He would see.

He started the car immediately when she was out of sight. He then nudged the car out onto the roadway, stopped, and pushed the accelerator to cross Farragut Road. He drove slowly up East 38th Street and stopped at the corner of Glenwood Road. He could see the corner between East 37th Street and Glenwood Road very clearly and he could see the church, too.

As he had surmised, the woman came to the corner, crossed and went into the church building. He was right--he thought-- probably making her daily Mass. It crossed his mind to go into the church too, but he quickly dismissed the thought. He would be noticed, surely, and he didn't want that. It was nothing he could explain away too easily.

Then he sat back and mused about what he had just seen. That woman was an ardent churchgoer, a good soul. She did not look anything like a typical murderer, much less a serial killer. McKenna couldn't see that woman committing crimes of that type. She also looked too small for the strength those crimes would require. She could have had confederates, he thought, but a woman like that, looking as peaceful and tranquil as she did, was probably guiltless. Just a stupid anonymous letter, he thought, as he drove away.

42

But McKenna's copy of the anonymous letter was not the only one sent.

Another one landed in the mail of District Attorney Jared Skolnick. He never ignored anonymous letters. They were the lifeblood of his organization that helped finger suspects for crimes anonymously, and very often they identified the correct person. Then, investigators and lawyers in his office would round out the edges and construct an airtight case, so it seemed. At least it was often sufficient enough to convince defendants and their attorneys that it was the better part of wisdom to carve out some plea agreement and cop out without a trial. The sentences were usually lighter, in some cases generously lighter, and it appeared as if justice had been served.

This letter was no different. Skolnick had been the District Attorney of Kings County, Brooklyn, for over ten years, more than two terms. Most often, the next step on the ladder for district attorneys was a Supreme Court judgeship but, if they were unlucky, they would simply retire. The pensions, like all other governmental officers, were extremely generous, so there was usually no reason to hold a benefit for them. In the case of Skolnick, though, he had his heart set on running for Governor, then for the Senate and, who knows, maybe the Presidency.

He handled this letter with care. He would later have it scanned for fingerprints that seemed to remain on paper longer than on almost anything else. It could be the key to the case that could be the answer to his dreams. He could solve once and for all the case that had the minority population transfixed, if not hypnotized, by the black reverends. He could escape from the stigma of the

Widmore incident in which his office had looked bad---very bad. Once that hurdle had been overcome, he would be a new cult hero to the black community, and the black community now represented the largest population block in a borough that was once densely Irish and Jewish. The black vote in his corner would make him an almost can't-miss candidate for lots of offices. It would be a major understatement to say the anonymous letter had little effect on his thought that he would be able to solve the case.

He decided to send for the most trustworthy and honest cop he had at his fingertips and entrust the entire investigation to him alone. That would be Carl Valentino, a detective for over forty years, one who knew his place and knew when to keep his mouth shut when silence was golden. For the last eighteen years, Valentino had been the chief of detectives assigned to the district attorney's office. He had earned a lot of respect for his patience, his wisdom and the manner in which he dealt with the accused, some of lofty position. Valentino was his man.

"Carl, this letter contains important news, I think. It fingers a person who may be responsible for leading whoever else helped kill those guys out in Flatbush. At least it says she may know something about those murders. You have to be discreet here, not let even the slightest hint of this letter leak out to anyone. I know you understand that."

"Chief, you know you can count on me. I'll dig into it as fast and as quietly as I can.

Nothing will get out." It was hot in the office even though it was cool, if not cold, outside. City buildings tended to be overheated in a total waste of energy that cost plenty to generate.

Valentino started to sweat, first a little then profusely. He never removed his jacket in front of Skolnick, no matter how hot he was, but Skolnick was in his shirtsleeves. He always worked in shirtsleeves, without a jacket. And like all politicians, he never

wanted to be photographed unless his jacket was off and his sleeves rolled up. Had to look energetic all the time.

"Are you OK, Carl?" Skolnick asked, concerned about his friend.

"Sure. Just a little warm in here. I'm OK. I'll go right to town on this and get you a report as soon as possible--good or bad. You OK with that?"

"You bet," Skolnick replied quickly. "You bet I am."

43

Valentino was a man of his word. Now nearing sixty, he was almost as energetic as ever and approached each assignment with great vigor. If you had known him back in the days when he started with the DA's office, you could hardly tell he had been there so long. When he was tapped for the position, he considered it a great honor. He would do his level best to make certain those who had recommended him for the job would never regret it, and would never be embarrassed by what he did or didn't do. Over the years, he earned the respect of the successive DAs he worked for and from the judges who heard the cases he was in on.

He never passed the buck. He seemed to gravitate to the most difficult of cases, choosing not to assign them to lower echelon detectives after he gained the seniority to do so. Even the assistant district attorneys, most of them just out of law school, and rarely from the top schools, or even high in their classes, had great respect for him. He helped them plenty, especially when they were new and trying to find their way in a chosen profession that did little at the start to give any helpful hints or training to rookies.

Valentino's trip to Flatbush was even more direct than McKenna's. He knew the way well, having been born and raised in Brooklyn. He played baseball for and against many of the parishes in the 'City of Churches' and knew them all and where they were located. He was a strict practicing Catholic and it seemed Brooklyn was a land of churches. In those days nobody asked what neighborhood you lived in; it was always what parish you lived in. Things have changed dramatically today.

Valentino parked his car in almost the same location McKenna did. It was a good vantage point to see across Farragut Road to the house he was interested in, number 3718. It was cool and he kept the windows shut to keep in as much warmth as possible. He could see someone working on a hydrangea plant in front of the house, cutting the spent blooms and some of the canes to give the plant a very austere look. Flowers would not be seen on it again until next summer.

The clothing the person wore while working on the plant made it difficult to tell whether it was a male or female. However, after a short time, the person sat down on the brick stairway for a rest. In doing so, the person removed the hat being worn to reveal a lot more of the face and hair. "It's a woman," Valentino mused. "It's probably the woman I'm looking for, Ellen Coburn."

"My God," Valentino thought. "It is Ellen Coburn! I know her! She's Eddie Coburn's wife. He was on the force with me. I never put the names together before. I knew him well, and her, too." Valentino was excited at the thought. He had identified the person as the one he was looking into. He pondered what to do.

In almost an instant, he had started the car and pulled around and came to a stop in front of the house. Getting out, he looked up at the woman. "Ellen, is that you?" he asked excitedly.

She could not see him well at first. "Who are you?" she asked, peering into the slight distance and puzzled at the thought some passing stranger had recognized her.

"I'm Valentino. Carl Valentino. Don't you remember me? I was on the job with your husband. We used to go to police parties together. Remember?" He began walking across the sidewalk to stand in front of her.

"Carl Valentino!" she exclaimed. She straightened up. "Of course I remember you. I just didn't expect to see you and didn't recognize you at first. You and I have both changed a little," she said, brushing back her hair to make it a little neater.

Back in the days they were active friends and attended police parties together, Ellen was a smart dresser and always looked stylish. She was not so stylish now, standing in old slacks and a windbreaker with gardening gloves on her hands. She withdrew a little into herself, thinking how sloppy and unattractive she looked now. She was slightly embarrassed at her appearance.

"Carl, what a surprise to run into you out here today. I never expected to see you again, let alone here, in Flatbush."

"I was just driving by and saw you. I had to look hard to recognize you, what with that hat on and your being all covered up," Valentino replied, trying to make his excuse for being in the neighborhood sound real. He was unsure just what he wanted to tell her or how much he would reveal of his mission. But he did want the conversation to continue.

"Come sit in the back, Carl. We can visit for a while," Ellen suggested. "The house is a mess. I wasn't expecting any company, you know."

"Sure. Sure."

She led him up the driveway in towards the back of the house. There, in the yard was a picnic table, obviously old, with chairs placed around it. The chairs looked as if they had seen their better days, too.

Once seated, he took a long look at her face. He could see the effect of the passing years in the lines of her face, but she was still pretty. "Ellen, it's so good to see you again. How have you been?"

"Well, Carl, I've been getting along pretty well. At first it was tough, very tough. You know, your husband goes off to work and you never see him alive again. That's tough on people, especially me. Eddie and I had a great thing between us."

"I know, I know," Valentino said earnestly. "I remember you two together very well. Very well…." He trailed off. It seemed as if he was looking into his memory bank and could see the picture before him.

"Yeah, its been hard," Ellen said, bringing him back to reality. "But like everything else you get through it. And I did. The church and God were big things for me and they helped me through it all."

"Have you seen any of the others we used to see regularly, anybody?" Valentino asked looking into her face.

"No. Not really. Eddie's funeral was a big thing out here. It seemed like the streets were overflowing with policemen. They looked great, all in their dress uniforms. They were great that day. After that…" she said looking off into the distance.

"Yeah," Valentino asked, "what then?"

"Well, you know how it is. Once you're out of sight, you seem to get out of mind. After Eddie's funeral, a few of the wives would come around. Then, after a while, they only called. And then, nothing. Silence. I can understand that," she said, tears welling up into her eyes.

"That's too bad," Valentino said sadly. "Too bad. But what have you been doing?"

"Not much of anything," she replied. "Nothing really, just volunteering at the church. You know, it's just around the corner and up the block. I walk up. I do the linens and cook for the gatherings. Just routine stuff."

Valentino nodded in silence. A few moments later, Ellen broke the silence.

"Tell me about yourself."

"Not much to tell. Just regular police work. You know the drill. I never got into anything as exciting as Eddie. I was transferred over to the Brooklyn DA's Office. I do the stuff around there that has to be done. Nothing great but it gives me time and I look forward to getting out. To get my pension and retire to somewhere, probably a warmer climate," he said shivering a little from the cold.

"Yeah, Carl, but what brought you to Flatbush? You weren't just driving around for the DA. What are you working on?"

"Well, to tell you the truth, Ellen, I am working on something. It could be big or it could be a little thing, a dry hole, just nothing." He tried to look as disinterested as he could but she could sense something more.

"What is it, Carl? I haven't heard a good police story in quite a while."

"Ellen," he started, leaning forward as if to guard a big secret. "It's about the Flatbush killings. You probably heard something about that."

"Sure did, Carl. It was a big thing out here, you know. It got everybody excited. But it seemed to clean out the drug dealers from the Junction. It was bad down there, but now it seems to be under control."

"Well, Ellen, somebody tipped the DA off to a suggestion that somebody out here, one of the good citizens, might have been involved. Might even have been the mastermind," he whispered. "What do you think of that?"

"Wow," she exclaimed leaning back off the table. "That's something else." She looked at him and then looked away. Her eyes seemed to look off into the distance. He tried to read her body language but there seemed to be little to go on. He studied her carefully and followed her reaction closely.

"Carl," she said quietly, too, after a slight pause. "Carl, that's big news, big stuff. I don't suppose you can tell me who the likely suspect is, can you?"

"No, I can't," he replied quickly. "I can't and it would probably not do you any good anyway. You know, police work is like that. Just hunches and nothing really as hard evidence to go on. Eddie probably never told you much either. I don't know if it will materialize into anything. Just can't tell yet."

Ellen had stiffened and he could see it in her appearance as she seemed to withdraw. He wasn't sure it meant anything but, if body language was truly readable and he could read it, he would conclude he had struck a note with her. Was it because she knew something, or was it just because she could sense someone she knew might be in trouble? He couldn't tell. She was aware he was studying her, and when he said that, she realized she had reacted more than she would have wanted to and felt uncomfortable.

"It's getting cold here now, Carl. I think I'll go in. It's been very nice seeing you again. Please stop by again, if you're out in this neighborhood. I can always cook up some coffee."

She got up and he did, too. He leaned forward and kissed her politely on the cheek, reaching up to do it. She was taller than he was. He turned and walked quietly down the driveway. He sat in the car for a short while, trying to go over what he had just seen and heard. Then he drove away.

44

The district attorney was working hard, as always. He was sitting back in his chair, sleeves rolled up and green eyeshade that he affected sitting snugly on his head. The overhead light and the light from his desk lamp threw a huge shadow behind him and gave an eerie look to the office.

Valentino strolled in. "Well, what have you got to report?" Skolnick asked.

"Not much, really," Valentino replied. "Unfortunately, not much."

"Carl, I've known you too long. What is it you found out? You know you can't hide anything from me."

"I know the woman, Mr. Skolnick. I once knew her well. I knew her husband, Eddie Coburn. He was a cop with me. When I switched over to here, he switched to the narcotics division. He got killed—blown up—when a narcotics bust went bad, really bad."

"That's a coincidence, isn't it?" Skolnick asked whimsically.

"Sure is, sure is," Valentino repeated himself, as if his mind had wandered from the reality of where he was. "Sure is a helluva coincidence."

"But, Carl—you haven't told me what you found out. Please tell me. I'm right in the middle of another case."

"Well, I really didn't find out anything you can use, I don't think. I didn't tell her about the anonymous letter, but I did visit with her for a while. I did it under the pretext of old friends trying to renew a friendship. I think I carried it off quite well."

"So, what do you think? Is she the culprit? Or was she in on it?"

"I hope not," Valentino almost whispered. "I hope not. For her sake, I hope she isn't in on it. But she did show a deep interest in the fact that we were suspicious that it was a good citizen from her neighborhood who may be our party of interest, to put it carefully, you know."

"Interesting take, Carl. Very interesting take," Skolnick seemed to muse, leaning forward and putting his elbow on the desk. He lowered his chin to his hand and said, "That's really interesting, Carl. We may be able to make something out of that after all."

"Huh?" Valentino asked promptly, seeming disturbed at the suggestion. "What can you make of that? There's nothing solid to go on there."

"But we might be able to get more out of her with a little pressure. You know, Carl, the subtle stuff. A few more visits or something may get her to reveal whatever it is she might know about the killings. How about that?"

"I don't know. She seems as if she would be a mighty tough customer, someone who would be resistant to that kind of stuff."

"Come on, Carl," Skolnick said laughingly. "Don't you think I know how little there is to go on? Of course I do," he said, leaning forward. Then he suddenly brought his fist down on the desk with a thud. "I know that. But there are ways to get her to talk. I have to think about it. She's our only reed to lean on so far, a weak one maybe, but a reed nevertheless. I'll think about it."

45

A clerk in a gray jacket, called a Kaplan Kooler, strolled around the district attorney's large office and distributed mail and interoffice memos to the various members of the staff. A few days after Valentino's meeting with Ellen Coburn, the clerk delivered an envelope to Valentino's desk. It was a white envelope, large in size, but thin. On the front of the envelope, the DA had written, "COME SEE ME BEFORE YOU OPEN THIS."

Valentino knew by instinct it had to be something sensitive. He picked up the envelope and walked directly over to Skolnick's office. The door was closed and Valentino gave a soft rap on the frosted glass panel as he opened the door.

"You wanted to see me about this?" he asked.

The DA looked up, again peering over his half eyeglasses. "Sure, Carl. I sure did. Have you opened it yet?"

"Of course not. I wouldn't open it after seeing the message on the front."

"Sorry, Carl. I forgot what I wrote there."

"What is it?" Valentino asked impatiently.

"It's a subpoena, Carl. I want you to serve it on Ellen Coburn. You know her from before and you just saw her. You're the best one for the job since you can identify her." Skolnick wanted Valentino to swallow that line of thinking. He knew it was disingenuous and did not want Valentino to think he was being used because of an old acquaintanceship.

"A subpoena!" Valentino exclaimed. "What do we have on her that we have a right to examine her?" Valentino asked nervously, sitting down.

"We're gonna squeeze her, Carl. We're gonna squeeze something out of her about those killings. You said yourself she seemed to know something about it."

"Yeah, but it was only my read of her reaction. That's nothing to go on legally. I don't have to tell you that. You wrote the book on that stuff."

"Carl, believe me. I know we're on shallow ground here but we have only one lead. It's her. She has to be the agency through whom we get to the bottom of this. Think of it. We'll be heroes."

"But, Mr. Skolnick, we could also look stupid or awful here. Bothering a nice lady, the widow of an ex-cop, a hero cop. You know her husband was killed in the line of duty. The police won't like it. It's like an accusation, you know."

"Just do it, Carl. I'm willing to take the risk. Everybody will see it as an effort to solve a heretofore unsolvable crime. If we score with it, we'll be big. Just do it, soon, too."

"You know me," Valentino answered halfheartedly. "I'll do it as a loyal soldier but I don't like it. You know that. I don't like it at all."

"That doesn't matter at this point, Carl. Just go do it right away. I'm anxious to get started grilling her. I'll do it personally."

"Can I ask you what does the subpoena tell her to do?"

"Sure, Carl. It mandates that she appear here on a certain date to be examined on the record about those killings. She can ask for a different date than what's in the subpoena--you know that. We're always flexible on that," Skolnick said, with a disinterested attitude and a wry grin. He considered the matter done. Over with.

46

Valentino was reluctant to leave on this mission. He never liked serving subpoenas. He thought they were really clerical jobs, done by people who had little skill and very little knowledge about what they were serving and why. It was even worse when you knew the person you were serving and, worse yet, when she was the widow of a fallen hero cop. Yet Valentino was loyal and dutiful.

Arriving at the house on Farragut Road, he saw no signs of life outside. He rang the bell and Ellen answered it almost immediately. Had she seen him drive up?

Ellen was wearing an old housedress, yet she looked quite fetching in it. It had no real shape but her pretty looks and cheerful smile on greeting Valentino disposed of any thoughts he might have had about her dress.

"Well, hello again. Carl," she said on greeting him. She was very cheerful and seemed really glad to see him. "What brings you out this way so soon?"

"Well, Ellen, to tell you the truth," he replied without setting foot in the house,"to tell the truth, its on business. Lousy business that brings me here."

"What is it, Carl? What makes you so sad looking?"

"I have to serve this subpoena today, that's what it is," Valentino said, shuffling his feet and trying not to let their glances meet.

"Carl,"she exclaimed. "You must have served lots of them in your day. Thousands, probably. What's so tough about this one?"

"Ellen," Valentino said somewhat embarrassed, "Ellen, I have to serve this one on you." He looked at her. She was astonished at what he said. She took a step back into the house.

"Me!!" she blurted out. "Me!! What would you be serving it on me for? What would you want with me?"

There was silence for a short while, the short, aging detective in a rumpled suit standing in the doorway talking in a low voice to a woman in a housedress. It must have made a crazy sight.

Suddenly, she became cheerful again. "It's something about Eddie, isn't it?" She touched his hand at the thought. Had the police department found new evidence or something that would make the circumstances of her late husband's death more explainable? Could it be that?

"No, Ellen. Nothing like that," Valentino said, again shuffling in embarrassment. "I wish it were, but it isn't."

"Then, what is it about, Carl?" she said demandingly. "What is this all about?"

"It's about the Flatbush murders. The DA thinks you might know something about them-- might have an idea of the people who were responsible. Heaven knows, we haven't had any other luck with evidence. So this is his shot in the dark."

"But, Carl,...me?" she questioned, again retreating into the house another step. "What do I know, what could I know?"

"Believe me, Ellen," Valentino said comfortingly. "I have no idea. I have no thought about why he's picking on you." He handed her the envelope he had been turning constantly in his hands. "Here it is. It specifies a date for you to come in and talk about it. You can get that postponed, at least once."

She took the envelope he was handing her. She slid her finger under the envelope seal and extracted the one page that was in there. She studied it carefully. "Well, Carl. This is certainly a shocker. Do I have to go there? Do I need a lawyer?"

"Yes, Ellen. You have to go," he said. "You do have to go. You can get the date changed, as I told you, but you do have to go." He studied her face intently, trying to read any strange body language he would not have expected. There was none, although she was deep in thought.

Suddenly, she became rigid. She backed in the house and said, "Well, thanks, Carl. It's been great seeing you again," and started to close the door.

Valentino recovered quickly. "Ellen, I'm sorry. You have to know that." She cut him off halfway through his speech.

"Thanks again, Carl. Great seeing you." And she closed the door.

After the door was closed, Ellen leaned against it, safely inside. She stroked her chin and began to think the entire episode through. She would need a lawyer. She would get one. What would she do with the Bereavement Committee? How should she get them together? Would it be safe? She would have to avoid panicking at all cost, and avoid scaring the others too much so someone panicked. For a brief second she dwelt on the likelihood of panic among the group. She wondered where the weak reed would be.

Even more, would it be safe to get them together so quickly? Could it wait until after Sunday Mass? That would be better, more natural she thought.

And the police may be watching her moves. They oftentimes did that. They followed a suspect they thought they had shaken to panic proportions. Not her, she thought. Everything orderly. She and the committee could tough this out.

47

It was a relief to Ellen when Sunday rolled around. She was bursting with the need to get this information out to the members of the Bereavement Committee she relied on and who had been "in" on the thing with her. She knew now, if never before in all the years she was married to a policeman, that it is extremely difficult for a person to keep their feelings and worries inside and hide them from the rest of society successfully.

The committee always gathered instinctively after every ten o'clock Mass on Sunday. Most of the members smoked and lighted one cigarette after another, trying to be part of the crowd, and to linger to feel important.

Finally, about a half hour after the gathering had collected, the group began to disperse, until only the main members were there with her. They could sort of sense something was on her mind, but knowing Ellen, they had no idea what it was about. As they stood alone there, now, gathered on the corner just outside the church, Ellen spoke to them. "I have something important to tell you. I don't know why, or how it came about, but a detective I knew for many years, while Eddie was alive, visited my house one day, a few days ago. It was a surprise to me, but he was in the neighborhood for something. I don't know what it was."

Saviano spoke up, "So what? It could be nothing. He may have just seen you or the house and recognized you and stopped. It could be something like that."

"No, Rudy. I don't think so. He was certainly there nosing around for information on the killings. I thought the department had forgotten about them by now, but something must have triggered their thoughts to revive the investigation again. I don't know what it was, but something must have done it."

"You seem so sure of their motives, Ellen. What makes you so sure?" Ira asked.

"Well, I have to tell you but I want you to have no signs of panic. Don't act any different tomorrow from what you did today. We must not change our behavior as the department is known to watch people in circumstances like I am in right now. That detective, the one I told you about a few minutes ago, showed up again on Wednesday and served a subpoena on me. I thought it was something new about Eddie's death but he made it clear it related to the investigation of the Flatbush killings."

"Wow," several of them exclaimed at once. "Wow," Wickham repeated. "What does that mean, Ellen?"

"I can't tell yet. I just know I have to tough it out and we all have to remain calm and not change our behavior in the slightest. We cannot discuss this again until I call you together again. We can't talk about this at all, not even to each other. We have to be absolutely silent from here on in. Absolutely no telephone talk. As they said in World War II, 'Loose lips sink ships.'

"I'm going to go to a lawyer. I don't think they know anything right now and the subpoena is just a fishing expedition. It's an attempt to flush something out that they don't know about in the hope that we'll stumble. I don't even know right now if they consider me a suspect."

"You know these lawyers, Ellen. They always make a big deal, a huge deal, of their clients having to tell them everything. Are you going to do that?"

"Absolutely not," Ellen shot back, squaring her stance toward the committee. "I'm going to tough this out all the way. I don't know what they're after but I won't tell them anything. I hope it blows over."

"So do we, Ellen," Saviano chimed in. "We went into this with our eyes open. What we did was right. We only got rid of the dregs, the crap, of the drug society. Nobody could ever complain about that if they were in their right mind."

"I agree," Ira said. "We knew what we were doing and, if we have to pay a price for it, we did the right thing. It had the right effect. The drug thing at the Junction dried up. The cops wouldn't do it. Somebody had to. It's like the wild west thing, you know."

"I agree wholeheartedly. I'm not ashamed or worried about what we did. We did do the right thing. It saved our kids. That had to be done. It was self defense, or something like that," Ellen murmered, still trying to control the voices at the ad hoc meeting.

Then, after a brief pause, as she studied the faces of the committee, she continued. "I got you people into this and I'll go to my deathbed, if I have to, to get you out. If worse comes to worse, I will protect you at all costs. Just trust me a little more. Behave as I told you and let's see where it goes from here."

Everybody nodded in agreement. There was nothing else to do. They began to drift away, towards their houses, but more so now in deep thought. They must have changed their behavior somewhat as they were much more pensive now. Ellen observed them as they broke up. She worried about their inner thoughts and their inner peace. Something that had seemed dormant had suddenly sprung to life. It all depended on her right now.

48

Lawyer Willie Mitchell's office was really never neat. Since his great gal Friday had passed away, murdered by a boyfriend, the office was never again tidy. The gals who came in to replace her usually were disinterested in the details of the job and the tasks it contained, so the office, her desk and Mitchell's grew disorderly.

Nobody expected a neighborhood lawyer or his office to be an outstanding example of order or neatness. People understood Mitchell, and took to him out of a sort of charm he exuded as he spoke to them about their legal matters. He almost never spoke to them authoritatively like the great lawyers were known to do, but the clients liked his ways. They understood him, at least they thought so.

He gave out advice freely on family and other domestic disputes and was a valuable sounding board on the aspirations and dreams of the people in the neighborhood. They liked him. They trusted him. He kept their secrets. He was one of them. He went faithfully to Mass at St. Vincent's and was a leader in the Holy Name Society and his wife was an outstanding church lady in the Rosary Society.

Mitchell was their go-to guy, the guy you could rely on to be on your side once he understood your problem. He gave off the aura of someone who, together with you, could get almost any legal job done, and he usually did. But they never had very esoteric problems either.

Everybody recognized Mitchell was no 'Harvard Lawyer' as the saying goes. His clients brought to him mainly mundane matters that affect families and family life in the little world of St. Vincent

Ferrer Parish. He usually got them done easily and with no great infringement on their time. He took the cases, handled them with a quiet aplomb and as little client burden as possible. Most clients considered their involvement in even their own case to be a nuisance and so respected the way Willie Mitchell performed. He was a professional, their professional, and he respected their status in life and did not overcharge them at any time. They knew him, his wife and his children closely. He was their guy.

So, it was no surprise that his office would be the first stop for Ellen Coburn. She meant to expose the fact that she had been served with a subpoena but she would tell him nothing of her involvement in, or knowledge about, the Flatbush killings. She knew from experience she could trust him. Talking to your lawyer is like going to confession to a priest. They are pledged to secrecy, to protect your revelations even at the expense of their own hides.

Ellen knew Mitchell well from church activities. She did not have a high opinion of his intellectual prowess but felt he was adequate at this point. She felt she could manage him while he laid out the parameters of the legal process, insofar as the initial subpoena was concerned. She counted on that and her ability to evaluate what he would tell her. She put all things in proper perspective as she decided what to do next. After all, she was now in the protection mode. She had a huge responsibility and didn't doubt for a moment her ability to tough it through, protecting her committee.

"Good morning,Willie," she said as she entered. Knowing him as she did, she felt formality was not required and they could talk level to level, as friends, as well as lawyer to client.

"Ellen!" he exclaimed. "What a surprise. Glad to see you. What brings you down to the Junction and to my office today?"

"Well, to tell you, Willie, it's a legal matter. I have to talk to you as my lawyer and to discuss what has come up. It's a legal thing and who do you go to then, but a lawyer?"

"Great," Mitchell replied, sitting down quietly behind his desk. "I'm glad you came and you know I'll do everything possible to help. What can it be? Please sit down."

Ellen seated herself and leaned forward across his desk, facing him. She began speaking in a low, hushed voice and Mitchell leaned toward her, straining to hear. "First of all, Will, I have to say that what I am going to tell you must be kept in the strictest confidence. Absolute confidence."

Taken aback, he leaned back away from her and studied her curiously. "Of course, Ellen, of course. You know the lawyer-client relationship is strictly confidential. I'll protect whatever you say and keep it between us. I want you to understand and appreciate that and what it means."

"I do," she said matter-of-factly.

Mitchell studied her as she sat silently for a moment, concentrating to formulate her words. He thought it would be on something going on or happening in the rectory or concerning some family in the parish. He could tell it was an item of great consequence to her. He could see the trouble in her expression as she collected herself, preparing to reveal this great secret, whatever it was.

"Well, Willie, I have to tell you I've been served with a subpoena from the district attorney's office." As she spoke, she opened her purse and began to unfold a piece of paper she had. Then she handed it to him across the desk. He leaned forward to receive it and took it in his hands. He studied it as she studied him, his facial expressions, key to his reaction.

"Wow! That's a surprise. What do you make of it? Do you know anything about the subject matter of whatever they're investigating?"

"Absolutely not," she replied with great conviction. "I don't know anything about what they're looking into. When I first got it, a detective I know brought it, and handed it to me. At first I thought it might be something more about Eddie's death. It turned out not to be."

"But what did he say? Did he tell you anything about it, about why they decided to serve you, of all people? Did he tell you whether any others were being served? There *must* have been something he said."

"He did tell me I have to go down to the Supreme Court to be examined orally by the district attorney—under oath. He suggested I retain a lawyer, so that's why I'm here."

"I'm sure glad you came. This could be a very sticky thing. We have to figure out what they're searching for, what it is they think you know and why they would subpoena you, of all people."

Ellen took a deep breath and stared at Mitchell's face. "I guess I do know the subject matter is about the Flatbush killings."

Mitchell reacted in shock and surprise. "What! What would they subpoena you about on that subject? Why you, why now, why?" he asked, still somewhat in shock. "I have to believe you know nothing more about it than you've read in the papers. Same as me. Same as everybody."

"No, of course not," Ellen said rapidly in an almost disinterested manner. "Of course I know nothing about the killings, certainly no more than everybody else." That was her first lie to him. She felt bad about it, knowing that, from here on in throughout the interview, she would have to act properly, guard herself against saying too much. She did not want him to weigh her words and possibly misconstrue some statement that might lead to deeper questioning.

After a slight pause, she continued. "Of course, I don't know anything. I can't understand why they would pick me out to come down for the examination. They must know I'm very active in the parish and might have heard something, or know something that might lead them to an identification of the killer. They're very frustrated. They can't get to first base, it seems. They probably think that, as a widow of a policeman, I might be inclined to pass on gossip I may have heard. This is an act of desperation for them. I just know it."

"Ellen, this is some act of desperation, even for them. There has to be something else. Why would they figure out that you, of all people, are the one to examine? It just doesn't make sense."

"I know it, Will. That's why I'm here. I'd kind of like for you to inquire, let them know I have an attorney. I would hope you could postpone the examination somewhere into the future--far into the future if you can. I have no hesitancy to tell you I'm unnerved about it, at least a little. Then I'm annoyed. Who the hell do they think they are?"

Willie was half taken aback by her aggressiveness, and then a little shocked at her reaction. "Hold on, Ellen. Just hold on for a minute. If this is really an act of desperation, if nothing they discovered triggered it, we'll find that out quickly. As for postponing the examination indefinitely, I don't know if they'll let that happen, even if they have precious little to justify it."

"Well, that's why I've come to you. Let's see what comes out of this. I know it's a preliminary thing for you to get into, but I hope you'll do it. As a favor to me. Of course I'll pay you." She got up to go, confident she had made her point, that she had gotten her first shot as a response to the subpoena. Maybe when the district attorney finds out she's got a lawyer, a trial lawyer at that, he'll relent and just forget the entire thing. Maybe. She hoped. That would be the best. At least she hadn't blurted out anything she would have to retract. She could tell the committee members that they were still safe, very safe.

49

If Ellen Coburn fervently prayed for a perpetual delay of the deposition pursuant to the subpoena, her prayers were misplaced. Both the original notoriety of the Flatbush killings and the political heat derived from their remaining unsolved dictated against it.

District Attorney Skolnick was a political animal. He also had great ambitions for his political future, thinking the mayor's office, or even the governorship were not beyond his reach, if he could find the secret to political popularity. He was determined not to let any stone go by untouched if it could be the magical elixir he sought. The anonymous letter seemed to be the key to his dream world.

When Willie Mitchell called the district attorney's office, the call was switched to Skolnick. Apparently the word was out in the office that the big man himself was going to handle that case, and the staff was alerted as to what to do in the event of a communication involving it. The district attorney himself rarely handled cases in person, instead of his usual practice of assigning them to his large staff. This one was different.

Mitchell asked for a postponement of the date set in the subpoena for the deposition. Skolnick was gracious about it, but insisted any postponement be very brief.

"This is a major case, as you know, Mitchell," Skolnick barked into the telephone. "Everybody is watching and I have to handle the public's trust very carefully."

Mitchell winced when he heard that platitude. "But what made you select Mrs. Coburn?" Mitchell asked timidly.

"We have a lead that put us on to her as a suspect or at least a person with substantial knowledge about the incidents."

"Come on…" Mitchell responded quizzically. "You have a lead that told you she had some knowledge of the crimes, or some involvement in them?"

"Sure do," Skolnick responded arrogantly. "Sure do, and we're gonna pursue it to the very end, as far as we can go."

"I find that hard to believe, Mr. Skolnick," Mitchell replied. "She's a housewife, a widow of a hero policeman. How can anyone have fingered her for anything but going to church too often?"

"I don't know why he or she did. I don't ask about their motivation, at least at this stage. I just take the evidence as it comes," Skolnick said impatiently. Almost immediately, he realized he had let out something he should not have let out. He tried to go on, but Mitchell had alertly picked up on it, too.

"What do you mean 'he or she?'" Mitchell interjected. "What do you mean by that? Don't you know whether your informant was a man or a woman? How can that be?"

Skolnick now knew his secret was out of the bag. Mitchell was smart, he thought, not the timid neighborhood practitioner he liked to call himself. He will bear watching.

"Well, I can't give you much more than that. I have to keep my cards close to my vest. Sorry," he said, trying to shut off the conversation.

"Mr. Skolnick," Mitchell lectured, "you're a man of the people. You serve the people, not only to convict criminals but also to protect the innocent. Mrs. Coburn has a right to know how you came by this informant, and what he or she said. You are duty bound to tell us."

"Don't lecture me," Skolnick raged. "You're in no position to do that and you may hurt your client. Do your duty. You called for a postponement. You can have that. March 26 is the date. Be there with your client at the Supreme Court Building, second floor. No excuses." He slammed down the phone.

Skolnick sat back and reviewed the events that had just transpired. "So Mrs. Coburn was concerned about the deposition," he mused. "She may have good reason to worry about it," he thought, "likely more worry than an innocent person should have."

All in all, Skolnick was happy with the events. The case was moving forward. The anonymous charge now had a physical form, and an attorney to boot. He wasn't sure, but he felt Willie Mitchell was not going to be a formidable opponent, not someone who he would have to be afraid of. He leaned forward and sipped his coffee. He was relishing the thought of the battle now.

Willie Mitchell wasn't. He was terrified that he was in over his head, that he could not serve his client, and friend, to the full extent she deserved. He was a man who knew his limitations. All lawyers seem to know their limitations. It is instinctive. Mitchell knew he was not a great trial lawyer. He certainly knew he was not meant to be lead counsel in major criminal cases. And this was a case of murder--four murders to be exact. That was not his cup of tea.

However, where Willie Mitchell feared he was not up to the battle, and Skolnick perceived that correctly, he misjudged Mitchell completely. Aware of those limitations, Mitchell knew he would have to call in appropriate counsel now. He didn't know the extent of the district attorney's proof, or who or what the 'informant' was, but he knew the scheduled deposition was now more than a formality. He knew he had a tiger by the tail and would have to do something about it. He would call in qualified counsel. He would call in his friend, Steve Donoghue.

50

When the phone rang, Ellen Coburn was already in the kitchen. As soon as the speaker told her it was Willie Mitchell, she became anxious and started to sweat. Her speech became nervous and high pitched. And she spoke quickly.

"Ellen, the district attorney agreed to a new date for the deposition. It'll be on March 26. He is demanding that we accept that date and not seek any further adjournments. That's understandable, but I don't want you to think of it lightly."

"What do you mean? What's the purpose of the deposition?"

"The district attorney has what he considers a lead of sorts that tells him he should look into you, to see what you know about the Flatbush killings. He was mysterious on who or what gave him this lead. But he wants to pursue it, vigorously." His voice trailed off at the end as if he was sorry he had to say it.

"Well, Willie, you say 'vigorously' but what does that mean?"

"It means just that, Ellen. It means he's gonna try to get you to tell him what you know about the Flatbush killings. He'll press hard to get that information from you, whatever it is. The deposition will be under oath, you'll be sworn as a witness."

"Wow," Ellen fairly shouted. "Wow. How important he must think I am! I wonder why? I actually don't know anything more than what was in the papers or on TV. Honest."

"I believe you," Mitchell stammered. "You seem honest to me. I've known you a long time and have been impressed by lots of things about you--your fervor in church and church activities, I've seen you run the Bereavement Committee as it performed important functions for the church and the parishioners. You're the lead of that group and you lead it well. I believe you when you say you had nothing to do with those killings and know nothing special about them. But that's me, coming from a background of knowing you in a religious setting and admiring the things you've done over the years."

"And...?" Ellen questioned.

"Well, the DA,-- he doesn't know you from Adam or anybody else. He knows a little bit about you but he views you as a well-informed lady on what goes on in the area at the very least. He may have an informer who is telling him you had some role in it or know more about it. I wasn't able to find out anything about his informant but he'll have to tell us before the deposition. I don't know exactly what that does for us, but we'll evaluate it then."

"Well, Willie, I guess we'll have to prepare for the deposition," Ellen said, dreading the thought.

"Yes, Ellen, we will. I do want to talk to you about strategy, about how you should go about responding to the DA's questions and probing. We have to talk about it. It's been worrying me sick. This type of case is far beyond my limited abilities. I really want you to have a better, more experienced and better qualified attorney on your side."

"Oh,Willie, why? Why should I leave you now? You've been our attorney forever. You helped us buy this house. You handled Eddie's estate. You handled my mother's estate. You've been our friend, counselor, adviser, confidant and all- around trustworthy guy. Why pick another attorney now?"

"Ellen, listen. Please listen." He was pleading with her to understand the predicament she was in and how important it was for her to have the best possible legal protection. And it wasn't him.

"Ellen, this case is beyond me. I'm a guy who can do those things you just spoke about--closings, estates and even some minor, very minor, criminal things. But nothing beyond that. We need somebody better. I'm overmatched by the DA. He has the full force of the government at his disposal. He has rooms full of associates. They know the criminal law inside and out. I don't. I have to look everything up and even then, I have to study it to hope I understand it. I'm not even sure of your rights at this time. I may bungle it. I beg you to allow me to retain other counsel for you. I'll stay in it. I won't charge you. But I do want you to consent to getting other counsel."

"OK, if you say so," Ellen replied halfheartedly. "Please pick out somebody who's good but won't break me with their charges. I'm not rich, you know. If we're gonna do this, I want to get someone who'll make that DA sit up and listen to him. I hate that arrogant bastard."

"Believe me, Ellen, I want that, too. I've got just the guy to do it, too. Steve Donoghue. He's the best. Is it all right if I call him?"

"What's so good about him, Willie?" she asked contritely, embarrassed at having cursed only a second before.

"Ellen, he's experienced. Everybody knows him. He has a great reputation and all the judges respect what he says. He's a high type guy, a straight shooter and will protect you to the best of his ability, and that will be to the best you can be protected. I don't think you have anything to fear but, with Donoghue on your side, you certainly won't have anything to fear."

"OK, Willie. Let's get him. You've said so many nice things about him, I can't wait to meet him. Bring him on."

51

Steve Donoghue was not the least intimidated by the challenge. He relished the coming battle with District Attorney Skolnick, whose legal skills he hardly appreciated. However, he recognized that, in the scenario of a large, publicly-paid, office, he would have on call a cadre of very competent attorneys--career men, not politicians--who would advise him, if he listened. That could make him much more formidable as an opponent and, therefore, a force to be reckoned with carefully.

Donoghue was one of those old style attorneys who saw it as their obligation to fight for their client every step of the way, on a grand scale if necessary. Every issue would become a battleground and an effort to have the state, represented by the district attorney, capitulate and withdraw or accept dismissal.

If an attorney could be hardened in previous battles, Donoghue was hardened that way. He did have natural endowments such as a great mind, quick wits and high intelligence. He had come through many fights on a far ranging spectrum of cases, from small ones to large corporate ones, mostly in the criminal law area. Adding his deep experience in prior trials to his natural talents, plus a hard-driving, relentless energy, made him a formidable force, too. He was definitely the man of the hour for Ellen Coburn. He was clearly the best choice of an attorney to represent her in this matter, the type of knight she needed to ride to her rescue as soon as possible.

In their first meeting, Donoghue made it clear to Ellen that the best way to win this fight was to go all out on the first issue that presented itself and fight every later issue to the fullest. He didn't think she had any constitutional right to avoid the subpoena or the deposition, but she did have rights in the deposition that he wanted her to assert.

"I think you should take the position that you won't answer questions, any questions, on the grounds of your constitutional rights. If you agree with me, I'll write out something for you and at every question you will just read it back to the stenographer."

"Do you mean I would do that with every question? What if he asks me my name and address?"

"He will. He most certainly will. But, as I said, you will just read him that statement every time he asks you anything. Understand? Please don't make a mistake and just start answering. It could waive your right to remain silent. Probably not, but why complicate things?"

"I understand, it's one of those legal things," Ellen answered with a surprised tone. "What does that do for us?"

"It means he'll be frustrated in getting any answers from you. None at all. His tactic will net him nothing."

"Yes, Mr. Donoghue, but where does that lead us in the entire scheme of things?"

"It could mean the entire thing ends with that frustration on his part. If he's telling the truth that he has a tip from someone, someone he doesn't know, not even their sex, he might have nothing else. That's flimsy grounds for a deposition. He might just give up, but that's not likely. We will just have to continue to frustrate him at every step, if we can. We might convince him to drop the entire thing. It would show him he's in for a knock-down,drag out battle and he might not relish that, especially in the media."

"What's the likelihood of that happening?" Ellen asked. "I don't have to tell you this thing has me very nervous, very scared. I don't

relish being involved in things like this, even if I have nothing to fear. It's just not pleasant to think about."

"I can't predict with any accuracy what would happen. He would know by this strategy he isn't going to be able to glean anything from our side. I'm hoping he would like to let it die rather than risk having his frustration exposed publicly for a long time, with him trying to make something out of nothing. We call that a fishing expedition. The public exposure thing is a mighty element on our side."

"I'll do what you say. You have the experience and the know-how and that's what I had Mr. Mitchell contact you for. I trust you implicitly. I have a feeling it will spark a lot of confrontations, some of them unpleasant, but so what? This subpoena and the deposition are unpleasant to me, so let's give Mr. Skolnick some unpleasantness to chew on, too."

"That's the girl," Donoghue announced happily. "That's the attitude, too. We need to be steadfast in our decision and push it as far as we can. We just might get this thing nipped in the bud."

"You have no idea how wonderful that would be," Ellen gushed. "It would be just wonderful."

"Yes, I do," Donoghue answered. "I know how a client or an accused, and you're not even an accused, feels about these things. Everybody worries about a miscarriage of justice. They worry about being convicted of something they didn't do and, God knows, that does happen. Fortunately, not very often. We like to think that, in all cases, justice is accomplished, as imperfect or long delayed as it is."

"Well," Ellen said, standing up as she said it, "we'll do what you say. Please write out that statement for me and I'll read it as often and as clearly as I have to. Your plan sounds good and we'll go with it. All the way."

Donoghue smiled, looking up at her. "You're a great lady. I hate to see someone like you put through this type of hell but politics sometimes dictate what happens in life. Skolnick is a political animal. He sees the police haven't been able to solve the Flatbush murders, so he wants to take a crack at doing it. He thinks it would make him a hero, a big hero. Who knows where his political ambitions are directed or what a boost they could get from the solution to this case? You might be his only hope to do that. We'll see."

Ellen put on her jacket and walked out after shaking hands with Donoghue. Once outside in the crisp air, she breathed a few deep sighs and headed toward the subway. "If only Donoghue did know," she thought. If only he knew she was trying to hide something deep and dark. She was happy he suggested the strategy he did because, if it played out the way he said, she wouldn't have to answer anything and it might blow over. She was praying it would.

She definitely knew the rest of her committee would be happy to hear the strategy being adopted and its likelihood of success. They would breathe easier and she wanted that. She was deeply concerned about them and their own internal fears and concerns about the entire thing blowing up in their faces. She always tried to calm the waters, and this news would certainly help--a lot.

52

District Attorney Skolnick was primed for his taking of the deposition of Ellen Coburn. He knew it was a fishing expedition but it could be a plentiful one. The field was entirely open to almost any type of question he could propound. He thought long and hard about the questions he would ask, pondering the legal effect of them and the possible answers he would get. It always helped to have at least thought about the probable answer to every question. Every lawyer did it.

His thoughts and his likely dreams about the heroic role he envisioned for himself, though, were dashed by the phone call he received from Steve Donoghue a few days before the scheduled deposition. He hadn't imagined that Ellen Coburn would be as astute as to hire a top-level trial attorney to represent her. He thought all along that Willie Mitchell would be her mouthpiece and he didn't have a very high opinion of Mitchell's legal ability. He had sized Mitchell up correctly as a typical neighborhood single practitioner, better at closings and wills than at depositions, especially one on so serious a subject as serial murders.

Now he had to shift gears, and quickly. He had to revise his thoughts about how the deposition would proceed and just what obstacles to a home run would fall in his path. He was much more uncomfortable now, with the prospect of facing Donoghue as his adversary as opposed to Mitchell. Everyone he spoke to had nothing but high praise for Donoghue and many told of their own personal experiences in going up against him to their regret.

Skolnick was even more ill-at-ease after their initial conversation. Donoghue was a pushy, demanding attorney, who knew his way around. He was totally conversant with an accused's, or suspect's, legal rights and constitutional protections and threw that knowledge around like a football. Skolnick resented that and that led to a deep dislike of Donoghue personally.

After the preliminaries in which Donoghue told him he was now the attorney of record for Ellen Coburn, Skolnick became somewhat nervous. Donoghue then asked him:

"Tell me Mr. Skolnick, what possible evidentiary material do you have that would lead you to seek out this lady?"

"Well, Mr. Donoghue, ..er..can I call you Steve?"

"Sure you can. You can call me almost anything. I don't have a hang-up about names or titles."

"Well," Skolnick started nervously, "to tell you the truth, the information we have is confidential to us and is proprietary."

"Sure it is," Donoghue replied. "But the type of information it is is not either confidential or proprietary. It has to be disclosed to me ahead of the deposition. That's the rule, you know that."

Skolnick was ready for that. He knew to expect that type of exchange from Donoghue from the people he had asked about him and from his general reputation. "Steve", he said quickly, "you're partially right about that. The timing of that disclosure is not as clear as just stated. The jury is still out on the timing, so to speak," Skolnick laughed nervously into the phone.

"Mr. District Attorney," Donoghue shot back quickly, hoping his sudden formality would bring the district attorney around, "I hope you're not going to allow this simple deposition to fall into a round of motions to obtain that disclosure. You're correct. My right to it for my client at this moment in time is not that absolute but, the minute I get before a court or judge, you *know* I'm going to come

out with the answer. You would be risking a long delay, if that's what you want. You know the judges take a long time to decide motions like that. They like to be like oracles, and write for history and the record, especially on individual rights, you know that."

Skolnick digested that as sharply as it was intended. "This guy really does mean business," he thought. Regrouping, he said, "OK, Steve. No reason to start threatening motions and all those things. I'll provide you with that type of information when we meet for the deposition on the 26th."

"Nothing doing," Donoghue answered, appearing angry. "Nothing doing. I want that information well before the deposition. I have a right to decide what to make of it and I'll damn sure not head into the deposition without that opportunity. You're not going to deprive my client of any right she has. You can make book on that."

"Steve, Steve," Skolnick responded, attempting to restore calm and pleasantries. "Let's not paint ourselves into corners we don't want to be in. We don't have to have total adversarial roles here. I didn't mean I was going to push you to the wall on this. We should be friendly adversaries."

"Well, just what did you mean?" Donoghue asked.

"I meant I would give you the answers you want, but in all good time. I have to consult with my staff on the rules and then formulate just what we will give you. You understand that."

"No," Donoghue answered abruptly. "No. I want those answers either now or in the next two days or it's motion practice for the both of us. Maybe we can both use the experience at motion practice. I'm hell-bent to give you that chance if I don't get this minimal cooperation."

"OK, Steve. You asked for it. We got an anonymous tip that Mrs. Coburn was the person we should talk to about information on the

Flatbush killings. It didn't accuse her of being involved. Just that she would have information we could use and should have."

"WHAT!!" Donoghue exclaimed loudly. "An anonymous tip. Was it a phone call, a meeting or a letter? What was it?"

"It was a letter, Steve," Skolnick answered. "An anonymous letter."

"My God, Mr. Skolnick, *an anonymous letter*! Not even someone you could call as a witness! Not a piece of evidence of any kind. And you go and start a big rigamarole about my client, putting her through this torture as a suspicious person. How can you do that? How can you expect to have the right to serve a subpoena on her on the basis of an anonymous letter? That's not a responsible thing to do. You should be censured for something like that."

"Look, I know it's a shot in the dark. When the police are at a loss to solve the killings, I have to do what I can. You have to understand that's my public responsibility."

"No. It is *not* your public responsibility. *It is not your responsibility at all.* Your responsibility is to the public and my client is one of them. She deserves to be treated as an innocent person until you have at least a good cause for suspecting her. You don't have any cause for that. An anonymous letter is nothing at all."

"I know, I know what you're thinking," Skolnick answered quickly. "I don't mean to tell you your business or your client's rights , but.."

Donoghue interrupted angrily. "You sure don't and never think that you can. I know what my client has a right to and what she doesn't. This deposition is not at all justified under anything that may be in your possession or dreams. I'll bring a motion to have that subpoena quashed. I'm going to do it by Order to Show Cause. You're familiar with those, I assume."

"Steve, for God's sake. Let's not get into those things. It's a simple deposition we want. We want to ask her what she knows. What's wrong with that?"

"Everything. Everything's wrong with that. You have no right and I'm not going to let you get away with bullying someone on the basis of a lot less than even a rumor. I'm gonna quash that subpoena. You can bet on that." Donoghue slammed the phone down.

"Steve, don't go..." Skolnick tried. He knew it was over once he heard the dial tone. He had gotten a lot more than he bargained for. Now he could see his heroic thoughts going up in smoke. What to do?

53

Donoghue was on the phone immediately to Ellen Coburn. "The deposition is gonna be held in abeyance for a while. There's a good shot we won't have it at all."

"Wow. That would be terrific," Ellen gushed into the phone excitedly. "Tell me. What's going on? What happened? This is almost the last minute before the scheduled day. What went on?"

"I found out what provoked Skolnick into serving that subpoena on you. They got an anonymous letter in the mail. They don't have any idea who sent it, where it came from or why the person, male or female--they don't even know that, would finger you as the person in the know about those killings."

"My God," Ellen exclaimed. "My God, can they do what they did with so little provocation?"

"Evidence, Ellen, evidence. It's not provocation, it's evidence. They have nothing at all to go on. The deposition was really a deep water fishing expedition. The law doesn't allow those. The DA has to have more than that, much more. He has to have some cause to do something that major in any case."

"Wow, Steve. I'm happy to hear that the deposition is off, I hope for good."

"I don't know that yet, Ellen. I have to prepare an Order to Show Cause and serve it on the district attorney's office and then file it with the court. The court will assign it to a judge and he, or she, will decide the date for argument before the court. I'm gonna ask for a temporary stay of the deposition. I just about know it'll be granted when some judge signs the Order to Show Cause. They sign virtually all of them, no matter how trivial the basis or how important the issue is. The deposition will then be in abeyance. It can be rescheduled, but, if the judge quashes the subpoena, that's the end of it. The end of your troubles with the district attorney--this time anyway."

"God bless you, Steve. And God bless Willie Mitchell for calling you in to help me. I am truly grateful. Really grateful. When does that order get done and served? Will I need to be in court when the judge hears the argument?"

Donoghue sounded truly happy when he replied. Out of breath for an instant, he said, "I'm going to my office now to prepare the order. I expect to get it to the court for signature tomorrow early and serve it on the district attorney about four o'clock. That's when the order will have been signed and ready to serve. This is a great turn of events for us. That also sets the date for the court hearing on the motion—we call it an Order to Show Cause. I know you appreciate the result, and that this is only the first step. I hope you understand all the legal gizmos I just described to you."

" I sure do," Ellen answered happily. "I sure do and I sure appreciate what you've done and are doing. Keep it up. We'll get this thing over with and done. Thank God for that."

"Ellen, let me ask you…" Donoghue paused. "Do you have any idea who might have sent that anonymous letter? Not that it's important, but I'd just like to know, if you think you do. It would be good to know who your enemies are, and maybe why."

Ellen answered quickly. "I certainly have no idea who would do such a thing. I haven't the foggiest thought about any such person doing that to me and I'll never understand why someone did it. I'll think about it, you can bet on that, for a long, long time. I'll tell you if I come to any thoughts of a specific person. I'll let you know immediately."

"OK," Donoghue said. "I will want you at the oral argument. It'd be good for the judge, whoever it is, to see you in court. You'll make a terrific impression. The judge'll see right away that you couldn't be involved in such a thing. He'll love you. I'll call you tomorrow when I know the court date. Good night for now."

"Yes, yes. Good night. I should say good night, sweet prince. I'll certainly get a good night's sleep tonight for a change. Thanks for the great and wonderful news. And God bless you again."

Ellen hung up the phone happily. "An anonymous letter," she thought to herself. "An anonymous letter. Who would do such a thing?" Walking away from the phone, she stopped and thought for a while. Then she stroked her chin and smiled to herself as if she had a pretty good idea who it was. "Hmmm," she thought.

54

Walter Coffin had seen it all. Born into a typical Irish family in the Bronx in 1929, the year the Great Depression hit, growing up was a test of endurance for economic reasons alone. He also had to survive the family problems associated with the "Irish Disease" which were plentiful and not exclusive to his family. The "Disease" hit almost every Irish homestead in the Bronx, and probably most of them everywhere.

From an early age, he was posted to perform various chores in the family home and also to help earn his keep by doing odd jobs in the neighborhood. Those jobs were hard to find because of the competition from other kids in other families in the area. He often would come home empty-handed to his disappointed father and very understanding mother.

His three brothers were no different, although they seemed to be a lot less innovative than Walter, and he stood out among the lot. He was also innately more ambitious than others in the neighborhood and he stacked up very well when compared to them. Parents would often tell their children to be a lot more like Walter.

Being larger than his peers, Walter would often be put into the position of defending his family honor or the honor of his brothers. Fighting came natural to him and he developed a reputation as someone who should not be trifled with. As he grew into his teens, that reputation gave him a great distinction when he was recognized by people, and they seemed to take to him. Fortunately, God made most of the giant creatures gentle, and Walter was cut from that cloth. He had a genuine aspect to his character, a sincerity to him, and, along with his broad Irish smile, he was very likeable. He never asked for and never took more than was coming to him under any circumstance.

Walter was smart but not distinguished in school and he got through without difficulty, but without a lot of studying either. Graduating from high school in 1946, he had earned a Regents diploma that, in those days, was touted as the equivalent of a college degree, or at least minimum required sufficient to make a living. Nobody at this economic level seemed to get or want any further education than that.

World War II had just ended the year before and veterans were coming out of the military service in droves. They were flooding the streets and sucking up just about every type of job available. Veterans even got extra credit on civil service exams, which gave them a leg up above the men who had not gone into the military service during the war, for whatever reason. Many of the veterans got on what became the "52-20" club, a government stipend that every veteran got, if he applied, that was supposed to sustain him through that transition to civilian life again. You got $20 a week for 52 weeks, one solid year.

The veterans had another advantage, too. They had the GI Bill, a government program that performed virtual miracles. The GI Bill was the most advanced single social program of the twentieth century, if not of all history. Veterans had their schooling paid for generously. They got money for college tuition, for books, for living expenses at college, and married veterans got even more because they needed it. Under the GI Bill, a veteran could become a chemist, an engineer, a doctor, a lawyer, and even a priest, a rabbi or a minister. Whatever he chose, no strings attached, and best of all, no payback required. The payback would come through American prosperity from the expansion of industries that now would have a host of educated employees, some of whom would never have been able to reach that high on their own. Most of them.

Recognizing that the returning veterans would need housing, the GI Bill also provided low cost loans for mortgages on houses to motivate new construction. Sensing the economic expansion the law would create, industries and builders were energized. There began the biggest and greatest social advance in the history of mankind, exceeding by far the well-documented advances of the industrial revolution. Actually, the GI Bill is responsible for virtually all the global growth and prosperity that has taken place from the middle of the twentieth century to this day.

The number of returning veterans caused a colossal work force to be available in the industrial market. The military force that toppled the Axis was being dismantled with a fury. There didn't seem to be anything for any new graduates from high school to do to earn a living.

However, the military, just having disgorged its draftees after the needs of the war ended, was beginning to restock with younger people to keep the military in somewhat respectable shape. The draft was still going on, but much lighter numbers were required. If you were eighteen years old, you had to register with the draft. If you got drafted, you went into the Army. To avoid that, you could enlist in the Marines, the Navy or the (then) Army Air Corps. In those services, the terms were three or four years as opposed to the draftee Army term of two years. Walter chose the Marine Corps.

Actually, he was persuaded to enlist at one of those kiosks the Marines would set up outside the local movie houses, where patriotic movies were playing. Walter had just exited with his friends after seeing a John Wayne heroic movie titled Guadalcanal Diary, or something like that. In that mood, he and a couple of his friends were easily persuaded to enlist, and enlist they did.

Paris Island, where newly enlisted Marines were sent for their basic training, was a hot and steamy place in the summer. The humidity was overwhelming and the recruits suffered on the long marches across the landscape, toting rifles and heavy weapons. Recruits who were not in shape would often pass out from the heat and exhaustion on the marches. The other training, through obstacle courses, exposure to live ammunition being fired over their heads as they crawled though mud and slime, and the constant drilling, made life difficult. When you added the almost inhuman drill sergeants to that picture, life became virtually unbearable.

Bear it they did, though. The recruits were always chided and ridden about being babies, guys who could not take it, and cowards. That made them fight even more to qualify. The drill sergeants always held punishments over their heads and they often had to take forced marches at night after a full, hot, day of training, because of some small infraction by someone, or for no reason at all. What seemed unfair to those young and enthusiastic boys, was hardening them into good soldiers, real marines.

Walter fit in well with the military. He was in fairly good shape, kept up with the crowd and seemed to outshine the others in his platoon. He didn't escape all the hazing by his drill sergeant, but he bore up with it well and easily made graduation from basic training. The group was now a platoon of qualified soldiers, fit to take up the cudgels for the United States from the Halls of Montezuma to the shores of Tripoli, and anywhere else on the globe. They were scheduled to ship out now, for what would become permanent duty.

About a week before shipping-out orders came through, a call went out for volunteers for the Paris Island boxing team. Faced with a posting to Korea, Walter volunteered for the Camp boxing team instead, and was accepted. He played out his entire Marine career stationed at Paris Island although he traveled for competitions to various bases around the country and a few abroad. He got what he had expected, a chance to see the world. He also got the GI Bill.

Nearing the end of his enlistment, he applied for and was accepted in the undergraduate program at Georgetown, near Washington D.C. Things were going his way now and, while at Georgetown, he volunteered to work at the Capitol, as a congressional aide. In that capacity, he met and became fast friends with another young aide on the Hill, this one an aide to a new congressman, soon-to-be senator from Texas, then Senate Majority Leader, and, ultimately, president. That was Lyndon B. Johnson and the aide was Bill McKenna, a young Irishman from New York City.

McKenna's star was on the rise and Walter hitched his wagon to it. McKenna persuaded Walter to go to law school when he graduated from Georgetown. By that time, Walter was completely infatuated with a tiny blonde he had spotted from a distance walking across the campus. She was to become his joy of life. He fell deeply in love with that beautiful classmate, a girl named Ann, and they married in their senior year. With the GI Bill in his pocket, Walter had it good.

Ann came from Amityville, New York, about midway east on the south shore of Long Island. After graduation, they moved to her home town. Walter, through his connection with McKenna, who was now the Assistant Health Commissioner in New York State, received one political job after another. Meanwhile, he enrolled in St. John's Law School at night and graduated and became a lawyer. Still with the help of his good friend, Bill McKenna, he kept getting better and better political rewards. A short time after admission to the Bar, with McKenna's help, Walter was appointed as an Assistant Special Prosecutor in a nursing home scandal that rocked the State.

Years passed and Walter and McKenna kept up their close friendship. Finally, Walter had had enough of the strains of public, but not elective, office and suggested to McKenna that he would prefer to be home more, and desired a seat on the Supreme Court bench in Brooklyn. McKenna pulled the political strings and Walter was nominated and elected to a fourteen year term on the bench.

Walter served the judiciary very well. He became a jurist with a tough reputation, hard on criminals, hard on lawyers, a no-nonsense judge with little patience for perjuring witnesses and attorneys who designed their cases that way. He was also a good 'law man', meaning he understood and applied the law, but with a great sense of equity, and very fairly. He had a super sense of what should be done to make things come out right and he did them fearlessly. His reputation made him one of the most sought after judges for tough cases, both criminal and civil.

Near the end of his second term, Walter hinted at retirement from the bench. He was addicted to golf, as was McKenna, and they never let anything interfere with their weekly Wednesday afternoon golf date. McKenna was a very good golfer and Walter—well Walter was great company. By now, McKenna had his 'dream job'. He was Police Commissioner of New York City. What Irishman could dream of any more?

Walter, in his last two years on the bench as his second term came to a close, started to take things more easily. He kept his Wednesday golf dates with Bill McKenna religiously. They met that day almost every week at Nassau Country Club out in Oyster Bay. It was a club for the elite, those new elite who were just not old-elite enough to get into the swanky Piping Rock Country Club. For that, you had to be born in Glen Cove or Oyster Bay or Locust Valley. It was good enough for Walter and McKenna.

55

August 1969 was the last of three very hot and steamy summer months on Long Island. The humidity made the island a place to be endured, not enjoyed, that summer. Although the Supreme Court in Brooklyn was now air-conditioned, the judges and the clerks and others who worked in the building continued to close up at four o'clock each working day. That was the continuation of an old system before air-conditioning. The Supreme Court building was hot during the summer and the workers convinced the city they needed that little respite each day. Actually, all government offices in the city enjoyed the same respite and it continued forever, even after air-conditioning arrived to make life more bearable. A benefit once given is forever. It can never be retracted even when the purpose for the benefit no longer exists.

1969 was also a year in which the New York Mets were coming of age. With pitchers like Tom Seaver and Jerry Koosman, the Mets were making their presence known in the National League and were outside possibilities for winning the pennant. Possible, but not probable, even though they were being called the Miracle Mets and their creed, created by relief pitcher Tug McGraw, "you gotta believe," was making everyone notice them.

That day was no different in Oyster Bay, New York. It was hot and steamy and the ground seemed to reject the sun's heat and send it streaming back into the faces of strollers, runners and pedestrians of all types, including golfers. Walter Coffin arrived at the Nassau Country Club earlier than his partner, Bill McKenna. He went out onto the driving range to hit some practice balls. Practice was important, especially for a journeyman golfer like the judge.

Besides, not being the member there, he liked to wait for McKenna to arrive before approaching the starter. Starters in most golf clubs are men of immense importance in their little corner of the world. They had limited power but exercised it to the fullest, imposing their will on many golfers, even members. Coffin didn't like the starter there and always had some difficulty of some sort with him when McKenna hadn't arrived yet. Today was no different, so the judge avoided him.

After about a half an hour, McKenna did arrive and approached Coffin on the practice tee. "Are you ready to go yet, Judge?" McKenna said, hailing him from a distance. Coffin nodded. He had been ready for a while and tried to be patient as he waited. The wait was over.

The starter would immediately tell them they were late for their tee-off time. He would try to fit them in after about ten or so minutes as the other golfers were on time. Nothing like small men with a little power. Their status in political life availed them nothing; in fact, it probably made the starter a little happier to be able to make men of such stature wait.

As they waited, sitting on the brick wall near the starter's desk, with their drivers in hand, they began to chat. "Look, Walter," McKenna started. "We have a little problem that I'm going to ask you to solve for us, if you can. As always, I'm not asking you to do anything improper, not in the slightest. This problem needs your fine hand to tune it properly."

"Well, lay it on me. What's the problem, as you call it?"

"Walter, it involves those killings out in Flatbush. Somehow, the DA, that little prick Skolnick, has gotten a bug up his ass that some woman out in Flatbush was involved or has vital information that could lead to the solution of the crimes. And crimes they were, Walt, you and I know it, make no mistake about it."

Coffin looked puzzled. "What's my role in this supposed to be?"

"As you know, the crimes have the black population screaming murder and for the head or heads of somebody. The mayor is scared shitless they're after his head. He now burps every other second instead of every two minutes or so in less stressful times. I can't stand that bastard or his dyspepsia. He's afraid of his own shadow."

"Yeah, we all know that," Coffin said in agreement, looking down as he plowed the surface of the ground with his driver. "But you haven't told me what you want me to do."

"I'm getting to that, Walter. Give me time to catch my breath. The murders have gone unsolved for several years now, as I said. This is Skolnick's only possible route to a solution of the crimes. It's all political. He sees his star rising with the reverends and the black community if he gets to the bottom of this--gives them what they call 'justice'. We, the mayor and I, think he has very little to go on."

"Ábout a month or so ago, I got an anonymous letter in the mail. It was short, very terse. It simply said that this woman out in Flatbush could provide some insight into the killings. You know anonymous letters. They get checked out but usually lead to nothing. I checked this one out personally. I went out and watched this lady. She lives on Farragut Road. I watched her leave her house, walk to the church, St.Vincent Ferrer, and enter to go to Mass."

"So what?" Coffin asked. "So what? Thousands of people go to Mass daily, and thousands more go frequently. What can you make of that?"

"Nothing, Walter. You're exactly right. You can't make anything out of that. If you saw this woman, you couldn't believe anybody could accuse her of anything. She is so plain, about fifty or so, nice build, and kind of pretty. A very nice person."

"Yeah, Bill, you're taking a long time to get to the nub of this one. What else is on your mind?"

The Commissioner continued. "It turns out she's the widow of a hero cop, one who was killed some years back in a botched up drug raid. His name was Eddie Coburn. I didn't know him personally, but everybody that did know him and is still around the headquarters, say he was a great guy, a great cop. They seem to imply that he was killed by some turncoat cop, a bad actor who was connected to the mafia. I don't know anything about that but I just throw it in in case you remember the incident."

"Yeah," the judge replied. "I think I do remember something about that. I think it happened up in the Bronx or Harlem."

"Yeah," McKenna went on. "It did happen in Harlem, but that's not important here. What is important is I personally sized up this lady. We have no idea where or from who the anonymous letter came, or why anyone would send it. But both the mayor and I think Skolnick got one of those letters, too. Whoever sends them usually sends several, one to different people. It turns out Skolnick has subpoenaed this lady to a deposition. If that's Skolnick's only tangible link of her to those crimes, it is stupid."

"Yeah, I agree," the judge sighed. "But you know Skolnick. He's entirely a political animal. His motivation is usually only for his own political star. Nothing more and nothing less. All political opportunity. So what if he subpoenaed her. What does that have to do with me?"

"Well, Walter, it doesn't have anything to do with you right now or just yet. I think Skolnick is fishing, hoping to open this Pandora's box to a wider inquiry. It would keep the damned thing in the papers and on the TV forever. Once the reverends get wind of it, the whole thing is likely to burst open. You know how they do it--marches, boycotts and other types of disruptions that create havoc. We don't think Skolnick has anything here beyond that anonymous letter we think he got, and we want it stopped if we can get that accomplished. The case is being assigned to you. We're hoping you can find a proper judicial way to get it to end without dramatics, without hysterics and without riots. Understand? Do you see my point?"

"I sure do," the judge said, emitting a sigh and sitting back a little. "I would have to think about it, see the evidence, see where the DA is going with it, what he wants to do. I can't give you any assurances right now. As you know, right is right and wrong is wrong. There have been a few murders here and it's dangerous to let even one murderer, no matter how nice, get away with it."

"Sure thing, Judge. But I want you to remember the types of people that got murdered. As they said in the operetta the Mikado, 'there's none of them will be missed.' Look at what they were—petty criminals, drug dealers, and users. They beat up their women, some of them had children with various women they weren't supporting and weren't married to. They all had criminal records. They were not useful citizens, they were the dregs of society, which is far better off without them. They created liabilities for society with their illegitimate kids and never supported them. They were a disease that we're better off without, believe you me."

"Listen, Bill," the judge pontificated. "I can't promise anything right now. I hear you and believe society is better off without those guys. Nevertheless, we can't let people get the idea that they can go around and select other members of society they think don't contribute to the commonweal and kill them off. That's anarchy. I'm sure you know that. I'll look into the problem you raise but I do have to uphold the law, for the sake of that same society, as you understand. In the eyes of the law, even a prostitute has to be paid or she has a justiciable complaint." He stared at McKenna while he said those words. He wanted McKenna to understand his feelings and to take that message back to the mayor. After all, he surmised, that's where the entire idea came from.

Just then, the starter motioned to them. "You two are up next. Please have your clubs ready within the next five minutes." They got up as if obedient to that summons, but they were happy to have the conversation end. Both of them.

56

"Call the calendar, Mr. Short," Judge Coffin said to his court clerk as he mounted the bench and pulled his chair closer to himself for easier seating. "Call the calendar," he repeated.

The clerk, resplendent in his blue shirt and gray pants, the uniform of the civil service court clerks, stood up for the occasion. "All rise! The Supreme Court of the State of New York, in and for the County of Kings, is now in session. Judge Walter Coffin presiding. Please be seated."

After a brief pause, the clerk shouted, "Case number one on the calendar, People of the State of New York versus Ellen Coburn, Respondent." It didn't matter to him that the Coburn case was the only one on the court's docket in that courtroom that morning.

There were only about five or six people seated on the spectator benches in the room. "Ready for argument," one voice shouted. Then another shouted "Ready". Judge Coffin looked up. "Then issue is joined. Approach the bench."

Two men rose and started up towards the bench. Within seconds they were perched in front of Judge Coffin. "Who represents who?" the judge asked, although he already knew. The taller of the two men leaned forward, "I represent the Respondent, judge, Ellen Coburn. It's her Order to Show Cause that is before the Court today. My name is Steven Donoghue, attorney."

"OK," the judge said. "I can assume then that you're representing the People of the State," peering over his half glasses at the shorter man.

"Yes, your Honor, I am. I'm the District Attorney of Kings County, Jared Skolnick."

"OK, then. Suppose, Mr. Donoghue, since it's your client's Order To Show Cause, that you tell me what this is all about."

"Your Honor," Donoghue began, "this is the most atrocious case of governmental misconduct and overreaching that I have ever seen or heard about."

"Now, now," the judge interrupted, reacting by leaning back and extending his arms outward with his palms up as if to surrender. "You're both here before me. There's no jury here, nobody to impress. Just tell me the facts plainly and without any of the trial lawyer histrionics. I can hear the case and make up my mind. I don't pay attention to that Hollywood stuff anyway." A tiny smirk worked its way across Skolnick's face. The judge noticed it. "That goes for you, too, Mr. District Attorney, when it's your turn to speak. OK?" The judge slowly shifted his gaze back to Donoghue.

"Your Honor, Mrs. Coburn is a widow of a hero police officer who died in the line of duty..."

"Mr. Donoghue," the judge broke in, "I'll say it before Mr. Skolnick objects to what you're saying. What does that have to do with the gravamen of this Order to Show Cause? I told you, we don't need the extra embellishments. Just give me the facts of the case. Nothing more. I don't need it and it will never persuade me. Please go ahead."

"OK, sir. Your statement is noted. I'll try to keep my remarks to the plain facts, as you want them." Donoghue was clearly embarrassed by the judge's admonition. He was not used to being scolded like that. He knew that Judge Coffin knew who he was and had not expected that tone of voice.

"Your Honor, " Donoghue continued, "Mrs Coburn, listed in the caption of the action as the respondent, is a person who resides alone in her house in Flatbush. Mr. Skolnick is seeking to depose her because he feels she has some inside information about the Flatbush killings that could or might be helpful in solving the crime. Despite the fact that Mrs. Coburn denies she has any such information, and I believe her, Mr. Skolnick insists any information may help and is pushing for this deposition. I am given to understand he has no tangible evidence to base this on, actual eyewitness, or any other type of evidence to go on. He is fishing, a pure fishing expedition and without any possible link between her and the killings or anyone connected with them. He should not be allowed to abuse the powers of his elective office or the process of this Court to hold a fishing expedition with no basis at all. If he is allowed to depose her with no grounds for his suspicion, he could theoretically examine every person living in Flatbush under the same guise."

It was clear Skolnick wanted to speak and defend himself. Instead, the judge cut him off. Staring at Donoghue, he asked, "What is this type of evidence you say he has? That's up to me to decide whether it's sufficient in law to warrant granting him this deposition. What to you might be flimsy or not even rising to the level of 'evidence,' might in the law be sufficient to warrant his proceeding. After all, the Flatbush killings were heinous crimes. Anti-social behavior like that cannot ever be condoned or overlooked."

"I understand that, Judge," Donoghue rushed to answer. "That's my position on it, too. However, Mrs. Coburn has certain rights as do all members of the public in this democracy and she has the right to be free of invasive action like this without any basis."

"Mr. Donoghue," the judge said impatiently, slapping his palms on the desk. " I hope we're not gonna get into a big entanglement here about the Constitution and the rights of man. This is a simple motion for a deposition. That's what I see, and it will be decided on the basis of the rules relating to discovery of evidence and depositions, and nothing more. Understand?"

District Attorney Skolnick was glowing. The judge was carrying the ball for him and getting along just fine doing it. He didn't want it to stop.

"Now, tell me, Mr. Donoghue," the judge continued, "what do you think is the basis for the district attorney attempting to depose Mrs. Coburn? Surely he knows the law. He is the highest criminal prosecution person in this county. He is elected to serve the People and must know the outlines of his job and the limitations on it, don't you think?"

"I sure do think he knows his job and his limitations," Donoghue said. " I have the highest respect for Mr. Skolnick's legal knowledge and for that of his office."

The judge sat back in his chair, leaned back and peered at Donoghue over his half glasses. It was a skeptical look, as if he believed that last statement wasn't true. Skolnick noticed that.

Donoghue went on as if not noticing the reaction of the judge. "I just think that his anxiety to do his job for the People to the fullest sometimes dims his view of those limitations. As you know, most limitations on governmental officers, and attorneys too, are self-governing. We have to be able to recognize those limitations, those flaws, in ourselves. Sometimes we just can't see a flaw in our own actions, even when the flaws are glaring."

"Nicely put, Mr. Donoghue," Judge Coffin said with a smile. "But let's get away from these philosophical theories and go back to the so called 'evidence' in this case."

"Now, Mr. Skolnick," the judge started, facing Skolnick now. "Suppose you tell me on what you base your supposed right to examine Mrs. Coburn, if you please."

"Right, your Honor," Skolnick said quickly, almost nervously. He hadn't expected the judge to turn to him so suddenly, especially after the judge's talk with Donoghue was going so well for him---Skolnick. "We all know how heinous the Flatbush killings were. I'm not gonna bore you with a recitation of those facts. Suffice it to say that four innocent human beings were suddenly murdered and hung up as public exhibitions. The persons who committed these crimes must be brought to justice. That's my job."

The judge looked flabbergasted. He sat back in his chair, stared at the district attorney with an incredulous look for a while, and said, "Mr. Skolnick. You're not gonna pretend for a minute here in court that those four persons were innocent victims. They had horrible records. They were not good citizens. In fact, they were public detriments. They were drug addicts and dealers. They wove a path through every center of incarceration in this state. They left behind a trail of illegitimate children and their abused mothers who will probably be wards of society for eons. Innocent victims? Rubbish!!"

The district attorney was taken aback by the judge's words and attitude. He hadn't expected such a point of view from a member of the bench, sworn to uphold the law. He stared at the judge, contemplating his next move. After a while, he spoke again. "Well, Your Honor, regardless of the stature of the victims, murder is murder and the public interest in stopping such criminal acts must be upheld. That's my job and I take the charge seriously."

"I know you do, Mr. Skolnick. And I understand your position. I just want you to know and realize that everyone present here is aware of the deceased, and their stature, as you call it, and their records. We all know that. You can make book on that."

"Well, Your Honor, I want to get to my position here on this requested deposition. I received an anonymous letter telling me that Mrs. Coburn would be the one who could tell about who committed these crimes. That's what I'm after—that information."

"Wow," the judge emitted. "That must have been some letter to have the district attorney personally be interested in following up on it, himself. Please tell us what the letter said—or even better, offer it into evidence and I would like to look at it." The judge was leaning forward, boring into the situation like a suddenly awakened giant.

"Your Honor," Skolnick said sheepishly, "I don't have it here. It's back at the office being subjected to examination to see if we can find any worthwhile fingerprints on it."

"Wait a minute," Judge Coffin said somewhat angrily. "You- mean- to- tell- me-you- the- District Attorney- of Kings- County- Brooklyn, came into this court to oppose an Order to Show Cause to quash your subpoena, that your basis for issuing the subpoena was an anonymous letter, and you didn't bring it with you? That's insulting to this court."

"If Your Honor please," Skolnick interjected defensively, "it is being subjected to lab tests for fingerprints. I didn't think you'd be interested in seeing the actual anonymous letter. I thought it best to not interrupt the investigation process."

Leaning forward across his desk, placing his clenched fists down on the desk to support himself, the judge said angrily," Well look here, Mr. District Attorney, we're gonna take a brief recess. Your office is just across the plaza. You go out there in the hall and call your office. Have one of your associates get that letter and bring it over here, pronto. Do you understand?"

57

Skolnick knew the judge was highly incensed. He was upset himself at not having thought to bring the letter. That stupid letter. He raced out into the hall and into one of the phone booths. He dialed his office, got the appropriate and responsible person, and had them comply with the judge's demand. The office was close to the court, just across the plaza as the judge had said. Within about fifteen minutes, someone from his office brought the letter to him.

He was out in the hall, waiting for it. As he waited, he ran through the circumstances in his mind. How could he have done such a thing? How could he have placed the entire thing in jeopardy by doing such a stupid thing? *Of course*, the judge would want to see the letter, or at least know its contents. Now he thought the entire deposition might have been blown, and with it his grand dreams of advancement to loftier positions. But he also knew that all was not actually lost just yet.

Taking the letter, the district attorney moved swiftly into the courtroom again. He found the judge still on his bench, talking with the attendant and Steve Donoghue about baseball, of all things. He wondered how the judge could go from firebreathing anger one minute to a quiet conversation about baseball the next.

"I have the letter, Judge," Skolnick called to him as he entered.

"OK, OK," the judge answered. He motioned to Skolnick to bring the letter forward. "Please hand it to the bailiff to be entered into evidence. I don't suppose you have any objection, do you, Mr. Donoghue?"

"No objection right now, Your Honor, but I do want to reserve my rights to object to it being entered at any later date if I need to do it."

"I assume that's all right with you, isn't it Mr. Skolnick?" the judge asked. Skolnick just mumbled his agreement.

After the clerk had entered the letter into evidence, he handed it to the judge. "Please show it first to Mr. Donoghue."

Donoghue took the letter, read it and handed it to the bailiff to give back to the judge. "I want to say that it is a very skimpy letter, one or two lines only. And I do want to point out that it is without any cover at all. Anybody handling it will have his or her fingerprints on it. So much for that aspect of evidence."

The judge glared at Donoghue. "Now, now, let's have no more of this petty criticism. It has no place here. I want to read this letter. That's the entire essence of this case, isn't it?"

Again Skolnick mumbled his agreement. He was clearly uncomfortable now. In fact, he was sweating a little and acting a little nervously. He watched carefully as the judge took the letter from the bailiff. The judge waved the letter in the air with a flourish and brought it up before him so he could read it.

In a second, he looked up angrily. "This is it? This is your 'evidence'?" the judge asked disgustedly. "This is what you are basing your right to a deposition on? This little thing, this two line letter. It doesn't say anything. It could be from anyone --even you . It could be from a deranged person. You wouldn't want anyone in your family to surrender their legal rights on such a flimsy basis as this, would you? I would never allow the badgering of this person on whom you have absolutely no evidence, no 'probable cause', as we say in the law, as you well know, to examine. This letter is worthless!" He slammed the letter down on his desk and it got away and popped over the desk toward Skolnick. "You're trying to make political

hay out of thin air, or worse,--smog. I will never allow it in my courtroom. That would be the total absence of justice. The total twisting of our Constitution. Do you hear that?"

Skolnick could sense the matter was lost. He tried to think of ways to save it. "But, Judge, we don't know who it's from. It even could be from one of the murderers himself. It could be from a citizen who saw something, who saw Mrs. Coburn learning about it. It could be…" but the judge cut him off.

"It could be a lot of things but we don't know. You can't just ask to depose someone on the basis of something you know nothing about. This is no evidence at all, no basis for the deposition of this fine lady."

"But, your Honor…" Skolnick wasn't about to give up that easily. "We just can't treat that letter as trash, as if it doesn't concern us. A little time from now, if the media found out we had that letter and did nothing, they would crucify us. You know that."

"Well, Mr. District Attorney, you're protected." The judge lectured pointing at Skolnick and thrusting his index finger forward. "You did something. You tried as best you could. If the media wants to crucify someone for no deposition being held, let them crucify me. Order to Show Cause granted! The subpoena is quashed, invalidated, rendered null and void!. Do you understand that? This matter is ended! Finished! You should be ashamed of yourself for what you're trying to do. If the public learns of this, you will be finished in political circles. Too hot to take a chance on. Do you understand that? There will be no deposition, do you hear? Court stands adjourned." The judge turned and walked away, waving his hands in disgust.

58

Ellen could not restrain herself. Joyously, she leaped forward toward the counsel table and embraced Donoghue. "Does that mean we've won?" she gushed nervously.

"It sure does," Donoghue replied with a huge smile across his face. "We've won. Justice won."

Just then Donoghue noticed Skolnick trying to look invisible as he shuffled papers into a pile and stuffed them into his briefcase. He was obviously angry. Going over to him, Donoghue held out his hand to shake hands with the district attorney. "No hard feelings, I hope, Jared. It's just another case."

"That's right," Skolnick said in reply. He was still acting angrily. "It's just another case, or another step in that other case. Whichever...,"

Donoghue put his hand on Skolnick's arm. "You're not planning to appeal this, are you?"

"Appeal? Appeal? What appeal? Didn't you see that? There was no notetaking by the stenographer. There's no record of what happened here. How can I appeal on that? That old fox of a judge faked me out," and he shrugged his shoulders. He shook Donoghue's hand, nodded and smiled faintly at Ellen, and walked out the courtroom door.

"What did he mean by that?" Ellen asked.

"I'll explain it to you," Donoghue said, taking her by the arm and starting to walk toward the door. "This thing today was not a total victory. It doesn't stop Skolnick or some other prosecutor from trying the same thing again at some future time. They'll have to make that try on at least a little better evidence. They'll have to do better than an anonymous letter that says nothing. If the anonymous letter had been more direct, more accusative, he might've gotten his deposition. This is a safe landing so far, but other things could happen."

"How likely is that to happen?" Ellen inquired, showing her alarm.

"Not very likely. However, Skolnick was bruised by this event today. He's not saying it, but he's mad as hell. He's probably the one we have to worry about. He's personally involved now. He's a loose cannon."

"Well, I'm gonna celebrate today's victory and this win as a great event. I'll have to worry about the future some other time," Ellen said stoically.

Outside, in the fresh air, the day was splendid. It was warm and sunny, the type of day that makes one's spirits soar. Donoghue breathed in the fresh air deeply. "I'll tell Mitchell of the results. You should make sure he keeps this event today and the results very, very confidential. The less talk about it anywhere, especially in the parish, the better we'll all be," Donoghue warned.

"I understand. Completely," Ellen replied.

"I'll leave you here, now," Donoghue said. "Please be careful and enjoy your life. Call me if you hear anything and know of anything that might involve this subject. I never asked you if you had anything to do with those killings and I don't want to know. I don't even want to know if you knew anything special about them. It's over as far as I'm concerned, and it should be over for you, too."

" I can't thank you enough for what you did for me. I'll be eternally grateful." Then, after a pause, she asked, "What about your bill? When will you send it?"

"Forget about a bill. Chalk it up to a chance to do something for someone special and at the same time do something for justice, too. You know, the only thing that stands between oppressive, overzealous or ambitious government officials is the law. The major instruments of the law are the lawyers. Please always remember that. Without lawyers to represent people all rights are almost nothing. Property or anything. Lawyers protect that for everybody. You can see that in your case. That ambitious district attorney could have run roughshod over you except for the courts and your lawyer. Not all lawyers are great, not all are smart, some are mediocre, some are downright stupid and some are awful cheats. But they're lawyers. And lawyers are the only thing that stand between us and the government and all other things."

He smiled at her, almost embarrassed by his tone and his outburst. Then he smiled and said, "Just remember—justice is justice, not always what one thinks it is, or what one expects. That's enough of a lecture for today. Goodbye." Standing on the steps of the Supreme Court building, they said their goodbyes and hugged one another.

Ellen watched as Donoghue briskly walked away, toward the subway station that would take him out of her life. "There goes a great guy, and a great lawyer," she thought to herself.

59

The new decade had just been ushered in, without any fanfare, just a few months ago. It was a sunny late July day in 1974, and the party fishing boat, the Adventurer, was making its way back into it's Sheepshead Bay dock, with about thirty party fishermen aboard. People gathered on the dock to see the catch. Many came to buy several of the fish that the fishermen would sell, since they didn't want to take them home.

The catch was primarily bluefish, a somewhat large fish that was a prize for fishermen. They loved the chance to hook one and do battle with it as the fish fought for its life. They were an itinerant species, and traveled to this area once a year in great schools. When someone aboard the boat got one hooked, it was usually followed by several calls of "fish on" from the other anglers on board. Those fish traveled in large numbers and were caught in large numbers, until the school moved on.

Bluefish was an oily species, and was not a particularly delicious fish to eat, unless specially prepared. It was usually only tasty on the day it was caught, as frozen blues tended to deteriorate as time passed. As a result, the fishermen would only take one or two home, at the most, and try to sell the others to the waiting spectators.

Among the fishermen on the party boat that day was Carl Valentino, now a retired detective from the New York City Police Department. As he stepped up over the gunwale of the boat and onto the dock, he spied someone he thought he knew among the crowd. He walked through the crowd up to that person. "Ellen. Ellen Coburn. Is that you?"

Ellen recognized him immediately. "Carl. It's great to see you. How is your retirement going?"

"Great," Valentino answered. "Just great. How are you doing?"

"I'm doing great, too, Carl. I've come a long way since that nasty business. I've remarried and my life is really going great."

"Congratulations!" Valentino said, smiling broadly. "Who's the lucky guy, anybody I know?"

"Yes. As a matter of fact, I think you do know him. It's Walter Coffin. You probably remember him as the judge on that case the district attorney brought against me. You know, the one with the subpoena you served."

"Yeah," Valentino, surprised, answered quickly. "I sure do remember him. He's a great guy. You married *him*? You two should be happy together. I wish the best for you. Please forget that subpoena stuff. I didn't want to serve it, as you well know."

"I know, Carl. Take care of yourself. Enjoy life to the fullest. That's what I'm doing."

Ellen then turned and walked back from the dock onto Emmons Avenue. She crossed and went over to Lundy's, a famous seafood restaurant for over a century on Sheepshead Bay. He could see her meet up with someone who he then recognized as the judge. Valentino watched as they hugged each other. He shrugged, clapped his hands, and turned to go back to selling his fish. There was a big smile on his face. "Justice was done," he thought.

History - 747

Printed in the United States
206946BV00001B/1-117/P

9 781438 903675